Avenged

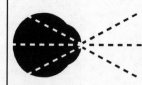

This Large Print Book carries the
Seal of Approval of N.A.V.H.

AVENGED

JANICE CANTORE

THORNDIKE PRESS
A part of Gale, Cengage Learning

Detroit • New York • San Francisco • New Haven, Conn • Waterville, Maine • London

Copyright © 2013 by Janice Cantore.

Scripture quotations are taken from the *Holy Bible,* New Living Translation, copyright © 1996, 2004, 2007 by Tyndale House Foundation. Used by permission of Tyndale House Publishers, Inc., Carol Stream, Illinois 60188. All rights reserved.

Thorndike Press, a part of Gale, Cengage Learning.

Thorndike Press® Large Print Christian Mystery.

The text of this Large Print edition is unabridged.

Other aspects of the book may vary from the original edition.

Set in 16 pt. Plantin.

LIBRARY OF CONGRESS CATALOGING-IN-PUBLICATION DATA

Cantore, Janice.
   Avenged / by Janice Cantore. — Large print edition.
     pages ; cm. — (Pacific coast justice series ; #3) (Thorndike Press large print Christian mystery)
     ISBN 978-1-4104-6034-9 (hardcover) — ISBN 1-4104-6034-7 (hardcover)
   1. Policewomen—Fiction. 2. Large type books. I. Title.
PS3603.A588A93 2013b
813'.6—dc23
                                             2013014801

Published in 2013 by arrangement with Tyndale House Publishers, Inc.

Printed in Mexico
1 2 3 4 5 6 7 17 16 15 14 13

*I'd like to dedicate this book and
all my writing to my father and mother,
Rocco James Cantore and
Doris Adeline Cantore.*

*They were truly wonderful parents, and
both will be sorely missed until that sweet
day I see them again in heaven.*

*Thanks, Mom. Thanks, Dad. Love you
both a lot.*

ACKNOWLEDGMENTS

There are so many people in my life who deserve a big thanks for their help in the writing of this book, people who prayed, people who answered questions to help with the technical aspects of the story, and people who supported me with encouragement. I don't want to leave anyone out, so I just want to say, *"Thank you!"* You know who you are.

Dear friends, never take revenge. Leave that to the righteous anger of God. For the Scriptures say, "I will take revenge; I will pay them back," says the Lord.

ROMANS 12:19

PROLOGUE

Bam! The door to the van slammed shut.

Diondre struggled to sit up, spitting out blood. He'd bitten his tongue when the Ugly Dude shoved him in the van. *He never even said what it was he wanted.*

Next to him, Rojo cursed. On the other side, Crusher sobbed, and Diondre could tell by the smell that he'd wet his pants. The Ugly Dude was Crusher's friend, his new supplier, so this was his fault, and Rojo swore at him.

"Crush," Diondre said when Rojo finished. The van moved, jerking Diondre into his friend. "Come on, man. We got to get out of this. What does this guy want?"

"Us dead," Rojo hissed with heat.

Diondre ignored him. "Crush, talk to me." As he spoke, he tried to loosen his hands and felt the plastic cuffs cut into his wrists.

Crusher sniffled. "I don't know, man. He

told me he had stuff for us to move — lots of stuff. He gave me the money for the TV. I swear I thought he was on the level. I don't know why he's trippin'."

"What did Trey say?" Diondre asked about their boss, the OG of the gang. Tough and smart, Trey would be outraged that three of his homeboys were being treated this way.

"Didn't tell him."

This brought more curses from Rojo, and fear erupted anew in Diondre. If Trey didn't know where they were, they were as good as dead. He pushed himself up a bit so he could lean against the side of the van, fighting for control as panic threatened. He thought about what his friend Londy had said to him earlier in the day.

"Man, the gang life ain't no life. It's just gonna get you sent to jail — or worse, dead."

Londy used to roll with the Ninjas, but no more. He'd been trying to get Diondre out of the gang. Diondre wanted out when he was with Londy, but when Rojo and Crusher came calling, he wanted to be with them. And now he was going to die.

"God is there if you call." Londy's words rang in Diondre's thoughts as loud as if Londy were in the van with him. Diondre squeezed his eyes shut and focused on

everything Londy had told him about God. He prayed all the words he remembered, trying hard not to cry.

"You praying, D.?"

Opening his eyes, he saw Crusher looking at him, face dirty with smeared tears.

"Yeah, as best I can, man. As best I can."

"Pray for me, too, will you?"

Diondre nodded as Rojo cursed them both in Spanish. The van came to a stop, and the side door whipped open. Moist, foggy air that smelled like the ocean assaulted Diondre's nostrils. He hoped they weren't at the ocean. Diondre hated the ocean because he couldn't swim.

But there wasn't time to consider where they were because the Ugly Dude and his two friends were at the door and they all had guns. Diondre hoped Londy was as right about God as he had been about the gang life.

1

"Direct evidence?"

Carly Edwards recognized the tone; District Attorney Martin had switched to his court voice.

"No," she answered clearly, no sign of hedging or apologizing.

"DNA?"

"No."

He took off his glasses and held her gaze. "You will be on trial here, Officer Edwards. Do you realize that? Galen Burke may be in jail charged with two counts of murder, but in a few weeks his lawyers will make you the focus of the trial."

"I'm ready."

"Are you up to having your entire eleven-year career dissected and second-guessed to the nth degree? Are you ready to have every arrest you ever made placed under a microscope and torn apart without context by people who have no idea what it's like to be a uniformed cop?"

"I have to be because I'm not letting a murderer walk."

DA Martin sighed and pinched the bridge of his nose. "He won't walk. We have him on the fraud and —"

"Galen Burke murdered Jeff Hanks, a good cop. He'll get off with a slap on the wrist over my dead body."

"Be prepared for what we're facing. Burke's lawyers want the jury to doubt you, to mistrust you. The game is deflect and obfuscate."

Carly willed her thoughts to the present, yanked her .45 automatic from its holster, and released the clip onto the bed. She pulled the slide back to eject the last round from the chamber, and it bounced down next to the clip. She moved the slide back and forth on the empty gun. This was a pre-shift ritual. Always make certain the slide is operating correctly and then reload the weapon before reholstering and going to work. Tonight her movements were abrupt, jerky.

The word *game* echoed in her mind and stung like being slapped with a whip of a thousand razor blades. DA Martin and the special Sunday afternoon trial-prep session had left a sour taste in her mouth.

I don't put my life on the line every night to play a game.

"Maybe you need a change, babe." Nick leaned in the doorway, arms folded, watching as Carly put her things together for work.

Her brows scrunched as she looked at him and frowned. After a few seconds she turned away and reloaded the weapon. "Do you consider what we do a game?"

"The DA really got to you."

She shoved the gun into its holster. "Our job is to put bad people — guilty people — in jail and keep innocent people safe. That shouldn't be a *game.*" She spit out the last word and turned to face him, dragging her kit off the bed, suddenly feeling downright grumpy.

"The court system is what it is. We have to build the strongest case possible so it's a game where we're the favorites."

"I hate that. Burke killed Jeff. He's up to his neck in his wife's murder. He can't get off."

Nick stepped toward her and put his hands on her shoulders. Carly let out a huffy breath and then held his gaze. Grumpiness fled when she lost herself in the deep blue of those eyes.

"You'll do fine on the stand. The DA just

doesn't want you blindsided. It's a circumstantial case, and Burke's lawyers will do just about anything to save his skin. But I have faith in you."

She dropped her kit, and he pulled her into his arms. "Why do you always know the right thing to say?" she said as she snuggled into his shoulder and felt his lips on her brow.

"Don't let the pressure get to you." His strong hands rubbed her back and Carly could have purred.

"Sometimes I'm just tired of it, you know?" She spoke into his shoulder. "I feel like I work hard to do the right thing and all my effort means nothing."

"It's not for nothing, but I know sometimes it feels that way. Like I said, maybe you need a change. Consider a detective slot so you're playing a different position in the game."

She pushed back to glare at him and saw his grin.

"Ha." Sighing, she stood on her tiptoes and gave him a kiss. "When I'm not so tired and cranky, I'll think about it. Deal?"

"Deal. I'll walk you out."

All the way to the Las Playas police station, Carly brooded about Galen Burke's upcoming trial. Testifying in court was, for her, the worst part of the job. It did seem to be a game — one of gotcha. Lawyers were able to seize upon a misplaced comma in a police report and make it look as if that meant everything else was wrong or misleading. Even though she went to court confident in her work and conclusions, she found the mental gymnastics involved in testifying more exhausting than a five-mile swim. The Burke trial would be the biggest one of her career, and she dreaded it.

As she stepped into her uniform, buckled her gun belt, and stood in front of the mirror to check her appearance, she pushed the trial out of her mind. *I have to put my game face on,* she thought, a mirthless smile on her face as she took the stairs to the squad room, arriving just in time for the 10 p.m. squad meeting.

"Okay, listen up." Sergeant Barrett brought the graveyard squad meeting to order at a minute after ten. "Captain Jacobs is here to address the watch."

Carly cast a tired, raised eyebrow toward her partner, Joe King, at the next desk. The captain rarely addressed the night watch unless it was important. Joe gave a slight shrug as friendly banter in the room quieted.

"Good evening, gentlemen and ladies."

Jacobs smiled, his tone authoritative but genial. "I'm here this late because I wanted to personally address every watch. The last couple of weeks have been trying, but all you guys in uniform have been doing an exemplary job. Keep up the good work. We expect more protests, and we know these people want a confrontation. I'm proud that none of my officers have let themselves be baited."

Carly felt somberness grip the room. For the past month they'd been dealing with loud, messy, and sometimes-violent protests over a revamping of the old marina and the addition of a new marina and shopping area on the water. A radical fringe environmental group calling itself Oceans First wanted the marina and oceanfront returned to a pristine state and had been trying to halt the renovation. They wanted the shoreline free of all commercial development. They'd been successful in stopping the removal of part of the old marina and pier, pending an environmental impact report, but they hadn't been able to stop the new construction.

"We've been in the process of appealing the protestors' camping permit," Jacobs continued. "I'm optimistic we'll win and be evicting them from Sandy Park soon." Applause broke out in the room. Sandy Park was a large grassy area between the marina complex and the mouth of the commercial harbor. It had been a peaceful picnic spot, but was now turned into a trash heap/tent city by the protestors.

When the applause petered out, Jacobs continued. "I know the protestors are more active in the daytime when cameras are present, but there's been an uptick in vandalism during your hours that private security can't seem to stop. I want extra patrols around the construction site. If you contact any protestors, be the professional officers I know you are. And most of all, be safe."

Murmuring began as Jacobs left. Barrett didn't try to quiet everyone; he talked over them and sounded irritated, Carly thought. He added some housekeeping items about keeping patrol cars clean and paying closer attention to radio traffic, then dismissed the watch.

"I can't wait for the construction to be over and all these troublemakers to be gone," Joe said as he and Carly grabbed their kits and headed for the elevator.

Carly grunted in agreement. The demonstrations had started out as annoying, with mindless chants and marches and outrageous lawsuits. The protestors had lost all lawsuits but two. Two days ago a mini riot had erupted for no apparent reason, ending in multiple arrests and two cops going to the hospital.

Carly's watch had been held over to day shift too many times in the last two weeks, and sleep deprivation contributed to her cranky mood. She found herself wistfully hoping that all she and Joe had to deal with tonight was vandalism and they'd hit EOW on time.

They stepped out of the station into the rear parking lot. It was a mild June night with the kind of haze that developed into thick fog as the night wore on.

"I'll get us a sled," Joe said.

Carly nodded and stood on the top step to wait for him. She let her mind wander over the past eleven years. She'd always only wanted to be a police officer, a *patrol* officer. Had the dream run its course? Was it time for detectives?

"Edwards."

"Yes." Carly turned to face Sergeant Barrett.

"You and Joe have a DCC down in the construction area. Walk around the yard for a bit first thing."

Carly nodded and was about to ask if they were to look for anything in particular, but

Barrett had already gone back inside the station.

"Why do they call it a district car check anyway?" Joe asked as he turned left out of the lot and headed for the construction area.

"I think it comes from the old days. Beat cars were district cars, and they were given special assignments — DCCs, or district car checks. You know cops hate change, so it stays the same."

"Hmph. I guess BCC just wouldn't have the same ring to it."

They reached the construction yard quickly. Since the marina was part of their beat, Carly and Joe had walked the area many times. The yard was also patrolled by private security 24-7, but Carly never thought they were as vigilant as they were paid to be.

Joe stopped at the gate, and Carly got out to unlock it and pull the gate open so he could drive through. Once she was back in the car, Joe drove to the far end and parked at the old marina, where the pier with a boarded-up Walt's restaurant would stay until an environmental impact study could be prepared, outlining the ramifications of its removal. From Walt's north, a beautiful new seaside shopping plaza was taking shape. It would be connected to the inland

Apex shopping complex by a pedestrian bridge over Seaside Avenue.

As they got out to walk around the yard, Carly told Joe about the DA, her frustration about the upcoming trial, and Nick thinking she needed a change. "I know I'm not tired of my partner, but . . ."

He didn't say anything for a minute.

"It's not a bad thing to think about change," he said finally. "Sometimes I think about doing something different."

"Detectives? What detail?"

"Narcotics would be my first choice, but I think it would take too much time away from my family. Violent crimes would be interesting. Don't feel guilty about wanting a change; you've been in a pressure cooker over Burke. And the closer the trial, the higher the heat."

Carly rubbed her face. "Don't remind me."

She stopped as they reached the stairway leading up to the new pedestrian bridge. "I, uh . . . I had no idea they were almost finished." Her stomach fluttered.

Joe chuckled. "I hear they're on track to finish in less than three weeks."

A dedication ceremony was scheduled for when the pedestrian bridge was complete. The bridge would be called the Teresa

Burke Memorial Pedestrian Bridge in honor of the late Las Playas mayor.

Carly shivered as they continued past the bridge toward partially finished restaurants and shops, not afraid to admit that yeah, she was nervous. Her nerves jumped and tingled when she thought about it, much different from the trial anxiety.

"The thought of the trial is frustrating and irritating, but the thought of being singled out in a huge public ceremony is downright scary," she said.

"Hey, without you, Burke would have gotten away with murder and Londy would be in prison right now. Have Burke's lawyers given any hints as to their defense strategy?"

"So far I think they're just trying to make me look wrong. They also reiterate every time they can that Burke is a victim; his wife was murdered. He may have been a poor bookkeeper, but he's not a murderer." Carly imitated Burke's lawyer with the last sentence and drew a smile from Joe.

Bang. A sharp, distinct gunshot close by cut off her next comment. Her hand flew to her gun.

Bang. Another sounded, and before she could speak, a third.

She looked at Joe, intently peering into the darkness. Carly pulled out her radio to

25

advise dispatch. "Can you tell where they came from?" she asked him before she keyed her mike. "Flanagan said the protestors wanted to go out with a wallop. You think some nut in there has a gun?"

Joe shook his head. "Sound echoes here, but I think that came from farther out, near the Catalina dock."

Carly keyed the radio. "1-Adam-7, we heard what sounded like three gunshots, possibly from the Catalina dock area. We'll be investigating. Please advise if you get any calls regarding possible gunshots."

"10-4, Adam-7. Be advised, we're getting a call now. Stand by."

They hurried back to the black-and-white. Joe started the unit and turned for the gate. By the time Carly pushed the gate open, dispatch said they had one call about possible shots, a complaining party who lived in the old marina. The CP also thought the shots came from Catalina Shores.

They weren't that far away. The new Catalina Shores terminal was attached to the north end of the marina complex but on the other side of Sandy Park. There was also a large hotel, the Bluestone, between them and the park. It was encircled by construction fencing and was dark and unoccupied at the moment.

"The CP called from a cell phone." Carly read more information sent from dispatch on the computer screen as Joe turned north on Seaside. "From a marina employee. It's Jarvis; he lives aboard a boat. Says he heard three distinct gunshots."

"I know Jarvis," Joe said, making a face. He slowed as they rolled past the park. Now calm, none of the protestors seemed concerned about anything. "He sleeps at work during the day. Why doesn't it surprise me that he's up now?"

A longtime marina patrol officer, Jarvis had a well-earned reputation as a slug.

"He doesn't want contact; just called to make sure the beat car checks it out," she read.

Joe sighed. "I doubt we can blame Oceans First; they've mellowed out."

Carly's gaze roamed and her ears strained for any noise out of the ordinary. But other than the hum of the black-and-white and the sound of the water in the distance, the night was quiet. When Joe turned left onto the ramp to Catalina Shores, Carly unsnapped her holster.

Marina Access Way ended at the Catalina Shores parking structure and dock, a business that ferried people back and forth to Catalina, twenty-four miles across the channel. This was the only part of the renovation that had finished early.

Carly picked up the radio to announce that she and Joe were 10-97, on scene. Carly had seen no traffic or headlights anywhere. They reached the parking structure attached to the Catalina Shores pier, and again Joe slowed so they could listen. During business hours a parking arm would be down and drivers would have to pull a ticket to get in. At this time of night, the arm was up, and from what Carly could see, the lot empty. She knew that a section of the lot on top was marked off for long-term parking, for those people leaving their cars to spend more than a day on Catalina and for Catalina residents who wanted to keep a car on the mainland. She couldn't see up there at the moment.

Yellow fog lights illuminated a good deal of the area in spite of a lingering haze. Joe cruised slowly. Both he and Carly had their windows down, and heavy, foggy salt air swirled in. Joe brought the unit to a stop at the drop-off area as Carly advised dispatch they would be out of the car.

After sliding her nightstick into its ring, Carly waited for Joe to meet her on the passenger side of the car. They both carried flashlights but didn't need to turn them on as they walked up the steps to the ticket offices. Then Carly saw the foot.

Hand out, she stopped Joe. "Here." Sliding the flashlight into her sap pocket, she drew her weapon. The foot stuck out from behind a stone bench.

"Hello?" Carly called as she and Joe separated slightly to come at the person from different angles.

There was no response to her hails.

And as she made her way around the bench, she saw that there wouldn't be.

Three bodies lay partially hidden behind the bench, facedown, hands secured behind their backs. They'd been shot execution style.

2

"Joe, this one isn't dead." Carly knelt beside the first body, which was twisted a bit sideways. The rise and fall of his chest, though shallow, was unmistakable. She'd seen a lot of death in her career. A dead body always took on a deflated, waxy appearance. Carly understood why the Bible called the earthly body a tent. When life vacated a body, it looked like something as void and empty as a flattened tent.

"What?" Joe knelt next to her. "That has to be reflex." Even as he spoke, he had his radio out, telling dispatch they had three shooting victims and requesting an ambulance.

Carly shone her light on the victim's head wound, emergency-aid training flooding her mind. He was definitely breathing, so no CPR was needed, but she wanted to be sure he kept breathing. She found a weak pulse, and before she could ask, Joe leaped up to retrieve their first aid kit.

Pulling on disposable gloves, she did what she could to stop the victim's bleeding and make certain his airway was not obstructed. She cut the plastic ties around the man's wrists, knowing the medics would need access to his arms.

Man. As she studied the face, she realized that the victim was barely a man . . . and she knew him. Hector Macias was just eighteen. She looked at the other two victims, and her breath caught in her throat as she realized she knew them all. Fighting emotion that would hinder her ability to think clearly, Carly bit her bottom lip and looked away from the faces. The hole in Hector's head was obvious, and the amount of blood spreading on the ground beneath him made Carly flinch. She might be patching up the already dead. Still, she kept at it.

Assisting units arrived and began helping where Joe assigned them. The scene and Catalina launch were completely searched and secured. Carly knew that if the person or persons responsible were still here, they would have seen them. Marina Access Way was one lane in and one lane out. Yet only a few minutes had passed since they heard the shots. *We probably missed them by seconds,* she thought.

Fire Station 1 was close, and medics showed up quickly to relieve Carly. She stepped back to remove the gloves and collect her thoughts. By now, the assisting units were scouring inside the perimeter for any evidence or clues. Sergeant Barrett pulled up just after the medics.

"Your buddy is outside the tape, raising a ruckus because I won't let him come closer," Barrett told Carly as he walked up to survey the scene.

Carly shook her head and said nothing. Her "buddy" was Duncan Potter, the younger brother of a corrupt police officer Carly had been forced to shoot and kill in self-defense. A photographer by trade, Duncan carried a mobile scanner tuned to the local police frequency and had taken to following Carly and Joe to big calls, snapping photos. She'd confronted him once, and he'd told her that his sole mission in life was to document for the world that she was dishonest.

Since Potter was a stringer and had legitimate press credentials, he had a right to access as long as he didn't interfere. Barrett justified keeping him away from this one because homicide wasn't yet on scene.

"This is the first time I've seen such a blatant gang killing," the sergeant said as he lit a cigarette.

Carly and Joe had made that same observation. Spray-painted all around the bodies was *9SN* crossed out with the numbers 187, the California Penal Code section for homicide. Above every crossed-out *9SN* were the letters *PAPZ*. The paint was still wet. Goose bumps rippled down Carly's arms as she recalled the conversation she'd had with Londy Akins just last week. A former member of the Ninth Street Ninjas who'd turned his life around, Londy had landed his first job as a barista at Carly's favorite coffee shop.

She and Joe responded to a vandalism call at Half Baked and Almost Grounded. Someone had thrown a metal newspaper stand right through the front door. The shop had also been marked with graffiti, much like what she and Joe saw sprayed around the three shooting victims. Except there the Ninth Street Ninjas marked it up, and their markings were not crossed out.

"You have any idea why 9SN would tag this shop?" Carly had asked Londy.

"They say they didn't," he said. "I asked. But someone wanted us to think it was the Ninjas."

Just like here, now, someone wanted to be certain the Playboyz were blamed for the shooting. Why?

Las Playas had two main downtown gangs: the Ninth Street Ninjas and the Pine Avenue Playboyz. The downtown commuter line neatly divided the two rival neighborhoods. When Carly first came on, before the rail line went in, there were two other gangs who claimed to control Las Playas — sects of the big LA gangs — and they were in the middle of a bloody gang war. But arrests and the rail line had calmed things down, and the violent LA influence had disappeared. The Ninjas and the Playboyz filled the void. Carly knew both gangs were heavy into drugs and auto theft. But with the exception of an occasional tagging war, things were quiet.

"It's overkill," Carly said almost to herself, pushing the interaction with Londy to the back of her mind and stepping a bit away to take in the grisly scene.

"Since when are gangsters subtle?" Barrett said with a puff of smoke. "Your beat takes in Ninth Street; did you recognize the victims?"

Carly nodded, the sting of knowing the kid she'd patched up returning. He'd just turned eighteen, and the last time she'd arrested him, she'd warned him that adult crimes would cost him a lot more time than juvenile crimes. He was a smart kid with an easy wit. The waste of it all weighed on Carly like a heavy load. What was he involved in that brought him here to be executed?

"We've arrested them all at one time or another." She looked at Joe, who hiked a shoulder.

"It's either auto theft or tagging with these guys," he said. "They're all Ninjas."

"Hector, the one breathing, goes by the name Crusher," Carly continued. "Martin Cruz uses the moniker Rojo, and the third is Diondre Baker, or D."

The third one also gave Carly pause. She'd seen him two weeks ago away from work. He'd been at church. D. had attended an outreach put on by her church's youth ministry. Londy helped organize many youth outreach events for the church, working tirelessly to get kids from his neighborhood out of gangs and into church. He had brought Diondre to the event. But what dug into Carly like a sharp spur was the impression she'd had that it hadn't taken much to get Diondre to church. He'd wanted to change, to get away from the gangs.

So why was he here, two weeks later, with a bullet in his head?

"Why would they be here?" Joe asked,

crossing his arms. "This is far from both gangs' turf."

"Who knows why these morons do anything," Barrett hissed.

He'd been in a bad mood all night. Carly had noticed that during the squad meeting. She wasn't going to ask what was wrong. Things had been frigid between them since Carly's former roommate and best friend, Andrea, had broken up with Barrett. Carly was happy about the breakup; besides being married, Barrett was old enough to be Andrea's father.

The medics rolled by with Hector, headed for their rig.

"You guys have anything to tell us?" Carly asked.

The senior medic shook her head. "Sorry; it's a miracle he's still breathing. That bullet went through and through." She dragged her finger across the side of her head, from the back to the front. "I doubt he'll wake up, but —" she shrugged as they pushed Hector to the rig — "who knows?"

"I made the necessary notifications," Barrett said as the medics pulled away. To Carly that meant homicide was on the way. Barrett threw his cigarette butt to the ground and crushed it with the toe of his shoe. Abruptly he turned. "You guys sit tight. Corley is solo tonight; I'll have him go to the hospital to get an update on the kid. Three units are assisting you down here; cut loose whoever you don't think you'll need. And I'll tell that idiot Potter he has to sit tight until homicide gets here." He strode to his car. "I'll be at the station if you need anything."

"He'll be in a snit for a while, I bet," Joe said as they watched the sergeant's car drive away.

"Why? What's he all bent about?"

Joe turned to her and said, "You haven't heard?" When Carly shook her head, Joe continued. "His wife filed for divorce and suitcased him. I think he's renting a room at some dive hotel on Seaside."

Carly's first thought was that Barrett had gotten what he deserved. Wincing at the mean-spirited idea, she mumbled, "Sorry, Lord," under her breath and walked to where she could lean on the fender of their patrol car. She blew out a breath and pulled a roll of breath mints from her pocket. She really wanted coffee but knew that wouldn't be possible for a while.

Joe stood next to her. She handed him the mints after she took one. For a minute they munched in silence.

"This will bring Nick out, won't it?"

Joe's voice shook Carly out of her brooding and she had to focus. He was talking about this triple shooting.

She nodded, thankful for the subject change. Nick had just been named the gang detail supervisor. It was an assignment he relished and for a time had thought he'd never get. He'd been shot in the hip in the line of duty a little over a year ago, during the mayor's murder investigation. His rehabilitation had been long and hard, but finally, three months ago, he'd been cleared for full duty. Captain Jacobs had asked him to interview for the slot in gangs. The gang sergeant planned to retire and Jacobs said he wanted a squared-away sergeant to replace him. Flattered, Nick put his card in and got the job. He'd just spent a week at a gang school in San Luis Obispo and was as excited as Carly had ever seen him about his new assignment.

Folding her arms, Carly forced her thoughts back to the scene now encircled by yellow tape. "I just hope his first assignment as gang sergeant doesn't put him right in the middle of a gang war."

3

Carly and Joe were released from the crime scene an hour after their EOW. While they'd waited through the early morning hours, Carly had realized that more often than not lately, the job itself did leave her feeling aggravated, not challenged. Like standing around a crime scene while everyone else worked, patrol work had become tedious. Was that just spillover from her worry about the trial or was it because thinking about the trial made her feel like working hard at this job didn't guarantee success?

Detectives Peter Harris and Jorge Romo were the on-call homicide guys assigned to investigate the triple shooting. They'd called the gang detail out to assist at 4:30 a.m. Carly had grinned at the sight of her sleepy-eyed but focused husband arriving on scene, moving with the fluid grace of the athlete he was.

The look on his face still brought a smile

to her lips — the excitement she was certain only she could see. For so long he'd been afraid that his injury would keep him from being a cop. Carly knew how much it had meant to him when the doctor cleared him for full duty. Passing the physical agility test and landing a job like gang supervisor was icing on the cake. Now his first big case was a double — most likely triple — homicide. Seeing Nick was the highlight of a shift spent mostly securing a scene.

Carly pulled into the driveway bathed in brilliant early-morning sunshine. It was a day made for a swim, and she felt as though she had enough energy for a crossing to Catalina. Turning off the motor, Carly gazed at the house she and Nick had purchased six years ago. She twirled her new wedding band with her thumb. It had been nine months since they'd remarried, and still Carly felt like she had on the honeymoon. In awe, amazed that things could be so fresh and new with a man she'd been married to, on and off, for nearly ten years, all she could do was thank the Lord.

She climbed out of the car, dragging her equipment kit across the seat as she did. Nick would likely be out all day. Even with his afternoon gang assignment, they usually made a point to have devotions together before she went to sleep. They wouldn't be able to do that today, and the fact that he and his people would be turning over stones in a gang neighborhood to find a killer was a worry she tried to dismiss. Nick was a good and careful cop.

Once she opened the front door, an injection of dog love chased away fatigue and anxiety. Maddie, their black Lab, was all wagging tail and happiness. As the dog weaved around her legs, Carly smiled, set her kit down, and knelt to scratch her. Hugging the warm, happy dog did a beautiful job of chasing the ugly images of murder from her mind.

"Okay, sweetheart, walk first and then bed." Carly paused to set her handheld police radio in its charger and then grabbed a bottle of water before hooking Maddie to the leash. They were off.

They lived only two blocks from the Huntington Beach dog park. In the warm sunshine the walk relaxed Carly. She released Maddie to play as soon as they were inside the gate at the park, then found a place to sit in the sunshine.

The pleasant warmth acted like a sedative. She had almost dozed off in a sitting position when the chime of her phone jolted her awake. She pulled it out of her pocket and read the caller ID.

"Good morning, Mom."

"Oh, I expected to leave a message. Glad you're not asleep."

Carly yawned. "I will be in a few. What's up?"

"Londy called me, very upset. I turned on the news and saw what happened at Catalina Shores. Three shot. Are they all dead?"

Carly closed her eyes and brought a hand to her brow. She doubted that the coroner had notified the families this quickly, but it didn't surprise her that Londy had already heard about the victims of the shooting. Word traveled fast on the streets, especially if it was bad word. Odds were that the remaining Ninja gang members were already juicing up to retaliate.

"No, one of them is still alive — or was, when I logged out. But Londy's friend Diondre didn't make it."

"Oh." A moan of sorrow came through loud and clear. "Londy was afraid of that. Diondre was supposed to meet him this morning and didn't show up. But one young man is still alive? Who?"

Carly thought a moment and then said, "Tell Londy it was Crusher. He went to Memorial Hospital."

"I will. This is just so sad. Londy arranged

for Diondre to get a job at Half Baked."

Carly heard the distress in her mother's voice. Her heart for troubled youth was breaking. Carly had told her more than once that she set herself up for disappointment with these kids. With Londy she'd been lucky. She stifled another yawn as Maddie bounded over, exhausted, tongue hanging out.

She hadn't known that Erika and Ned Barton, the couple who owned and operated Half Baked and Almost Grounded, were going to hire Diondre, but she wasn't surprised. They were good people. They'd given Londy a chance with a job and had not been disappointed. It made sense they'd trust Diondre.

You just can't save them all, she thought. "Tell Londy I'm sorry about D."

Carly woke with a headache around six, but Nick still wasn't home. For a time she lay in bed and tried to force herself back to sleep, successful only with dozing for a few minutes. What brought her fully to consciousness with a smile was her husband's lips on her brow. She should have known he was in the house when she felt Maddie jump off the bed.

"Oh, hey," she murmured, reaching up to

hug him but pulling away as his scratchy face rubbed her cheek and the smell of cigarettes assaulted her nostrils. He'd been hanging around Mickey Tumanyan, a long-time gang officer who was also a chain smoker. She opened her eyes to Nick's bloodshot blue ones. "And you look really tired."

He smiled as she lay down again. "I'm whacked. I'd love to fall into bed and sleep for a week, but I'm starved. Came home for dinner." He stifled a yawn. "And since I got called out, I didn't get to do the shopping."

"Shirking your responsibility because of work?" Carly teased. They'd divided house-hold chores; Nick did the grocery shopping and yard work while Carly took care of house-cleaning and bill paying. He'd teased her the other day about shirking her duties because Maddie had found a toy behind the couch with a huge dust bunny attached to it.

"Guilty as charged," he said. "But I come bearing a peace offering. I brought home pizza."

"Pizzamania?" She sat up, already salivating at the thought of their favorite local pizzeria.

He grinned. "Sausage and pineapple. Put together a salad while I shower?"

"You bet," she said, throwing her arms around his neck, ignoring the beard and tobacco odor this time.

As Carly made her way to the kitchen, Maddie popped in through the dog door and shadowed her. Carly was wide-awake, and her headache faded as she fed the dog and inhaled the wonderful aroma of pizza. Her idea of heaven was a deep-dish pizza, a pitcher of Diet Coke, and a quiet corner with her husband. And knowing there was pizza kept her smiling even when she opened the nearly empty refrigerator. Salad wasn't that important, she thought. Which was good, since they had no lettuce. All she found were two tomatoes and some Italian dressing. And no Diet Coke. They'd have to settle for iced tea.

By the time Nick joined her, she had the table set with sliced tomatoes, pizza, and tropical iced tea.

His hair was still wet, but when he hugged her from behind and rubbed his smooth cheek against hers, she could only smile and lean into his arms.

"Okay, I guess now *you* smell better than the pizza."

"Hummph." He kissed her, then sat, reaching out to grab a piece of sausage and pop it in his mouth.

"So how did it go? Tell me what's happening with the shooting," she said, sitting across from him.

Nick ran a hand down his face. "I'll tell you everything after at least a few bites." He said a quick blessing and they dug in.

"Crusher is still alive, and he might just stay that way."

Carly swallowed and arched an eyebrow in surprise. "I didn't think he really had a chance with a head wound like that."

Nick reached for a second slice of pizza. "He was even conscious and talking in the ER."

"Talking? Did he say who shot him?"

"No. According to Kyle, he was awake but confused. Kept asking for Rojo and D."

"His dead friends." Carly rubbed at gooseflesh on her arm.

Nick nodded. "He couldn't answer direct questions. Doc told Kyle while the wound is serious, the bullet entered and exited without doing a lot of damage. Victims of head trauma have a better chance if only one side of the head is injured." He bit into another slice of pizza and spoke with his mouth full. " 'Course, only time will tell. His mom was there."

"That must have been hard."

"Yeah, but she's a strong lady. You know

Crusher had five brothers and sisters?"

"I knew he had a big family. He's a fence kid, I think — not all bad. I arrested him a lot as a juvenile and always came away feeling like he didn't have a hard-core attitude."

Nick took another piece of pizza. "He just wants to belong to something. His mom said as much. She's praying for Hector and asking the same thing of their priest, but she couldn't stay at the hospital; she had other kids to care for. And she was praying they don't end up like Hector."

Carly sighed, understanding where the woman was coming from but still amazed.

"She told the doctor to let the police talk to Hector if he was able to and she also said she'd pray for us, that we'd find out who shot him."

Carly smiled. "You will."

Nick reached for his tea. "We served some search warrants on the Garnets, made some arrests, and confiscated some guns. But everyone denies shooting up the Ninjas."

Carly cocked her head as she chewed. The Garnets were the known leaders of the Playboyz. Three brothers — Marcus, Harley, and German — alternated control, depending on who was in jail at any given time.

"Marcus Garnet is still in jail, isn't he?"

"He'll be out by the end of the summer,"

Nick said. "German's on parole, and he was minding his p's and q's. Claims he's not feuding with anyone. Harley is the big gang boss right now and we couldn't find him." He frowned. "The thing is, this really doesn't feel like their kind of gig. I mean, they are thugs and crooks, no doubt, but their MO has always been for cowardly drive-bys and intimidation. I can't see any of the Playboyz having the guts to execute three guys point-blank like that. Besides that, this is so out of the blue. I haven't been in gangs that long, but there was not the ghost of an inkling that something like this was brewing."

"I agree. I thought the whole thing looked staged."

"Staged to start a gang war?"

"Yep, for whatever reason."

Nick tilted his head. "Mickey thinks that too. But who would gain from such a war? We've been through this before. Nobody wins."

Carly could only shrug. She knew what he meant, and as the memory came alive in her mind, fear sliced through her like a sharp claw. But the last thing she wanted was Nick worried or second-guessing himself because of her fear.

He closed the pizza box. "Want some coffee?"

"I'm meeting Andi at Half Baked before work."

"Then I'll just make a cup."

She didn't want to tell him she was afraid for him. Telling him that seemed so weak, so faithless. So clingy.

When she'd first been hired over ten years ago, there'd been a bloody gang war going on in Las Playas. Back then, crack cocaine was the product of choice for both gangs, and two main groups fought over turf. Carly remembered all too well the bloody toll the war extracted. Thankfully, no officers lost their lives, but over the course of the five-year war, four innocent people were killed. One family lost a three-year-old, caught in the cross fire during a family barbecue where five other people were wounded. She'd been in training when she'd been dispatched to the crime scene that resembled a war zone.

The carnage broke the backs of both gangs, and now neither existed in the city. The Ninjas and the Playboyz had formed to fill the vacuum and began as tagging crews. Were Carly and Nick seeing the start of something vicious and bloody?

Carly prayed with all her might that they weren't.

4

As Carly drove to work that night, she battled an icy fear creeping through her — that she would lose Nick in the line of duty.

But God was in control, right?

That's what her mother reminded her of frequently. It was also a recurring message at church. However, one of the hardest things for Carly to face in her relatively new faith was the fact that bad things often happened to good people. When Jeff had run interference for her on Correa's yacht before sacrificing his life, she'd found herself in this odd conundrum: his death left Elaine, a wonderful woman, a widow and single mother to three children. It should have been Carly who died that night. Yet Jeff never could have made the swim she made. If she hadn't jumped when she did, she would have died along with him and the killers most likely would have gotten away with several murders and major theft. Jeff's sacrifice was the only way.

But why? They were both fighting bad guys.

God is in control.

"Ugh." Carly slapped the steering wheel. Nick had been sleeping when she'd left home. He planned to be back to work at midnight. When she'd kissed his forehead before leaving, the memory of the night with Jeff had grabbed her by the throat. She thought she'd put the demons from that incident away, but now, as she worried about Nick, they came roaring back. Just because Nick was a good and honest Christian man didn't mean he couldn't be snatched from her in an instant. That thought scorched her mind and made her physically sick to her stomach.

When they'd been married the first time, neither one of them had been Christians. *And,* she thought with some bewilderment, *I never worried about him then as much as I do now.*

Working to defuse the fear, she turned up the radio. It was a few minutes before she reached her destination. A light fog drifted about, and she wondered if it would get thicker throughout the night.

Andrea had asked to meet Carly before work for coffee at Half Baked and Almost

Grounded. Even though she knew Andi just wanted gory details about the shooting, Carly was glad for the diversion. It was eight thirty and the shop closed at nine thirty. Carly had to be to work by ten, and she never minded being early.

Carly smiled at Erika, who stood behind the counter. "Hey, glad to see you got the door fixed." The door had been completely smashed with the vandalism from the other night.

"Ned and Londy were able to fix it. That's why Jinx and I have the night shift."

Just then, Jinx, Erika's cousin, poked her head out from the kitchen. "Hi, Carly."

"Hey, Jinx."

Ned and Erika owned the shop, but it was truly a family effort. Erika was the queen of the kitchen, baking a lot herself but also employing great cooks for all aspects of the bakery/ restaurant. Ned, her husband, did the least in terms of physical work, but he was by far the most inspiring man Carly had ever met. He'd been a Marine deployed in Iraq when a rocket-propelled grenade hit the vehicle he was driving. Ned lost his left hand and suffered a traumatic brain injury in the explosion. He'd been in a coma for three months and doctors said he'd never come out of it when all of a sudden he woke up.

Carly connected immediately with Erika when the woman shared the story of her husband's struggle back from the catastrophic injury. He was far from 100 percent — there were issues with memory, concentration, and migraine headaches — but he was alive and working as hard as he could to get his life back. He never complained, instead doing as much as he could to help with the business.

"What will you have?" Erika asked.

"Just a large house blend."

Erika handed her the coffee. She wouldn't take Carly's money; in fact, the shop was a well-known pop, a place any cop would get coffee for free. The policy also applied to servicemen in uniform. Carly put a five in the jar on the counter designated "Donations for the Wounded Warrior Project." Nodding thanks, she took the coffee and joined Andrea.

Her friend, as usual, looked immaculate, even though Carly knew she'd just gotten off work. Her nurse's scrubs were perfectly creased, looking as though she'd just put them on rather than worn them for an entire shift. Every shiny blonde hair was in place.

Carly self-consciously ran a hand through

her unruly, thick hair as she sat. She had given up trying to figure out how Andrea did it. They'd been friends since they were kids. When Carly went through her divorce, Andi was there for her, and together they'd rented an apartment by the beach. Andi's friendship had been a haven for Carly during the year she and Nick were apart.

"Hey, Andi, what's up?"

"What's up with you? Will the city be embroiled in a gang war, and will ace reporter Alex Trejo miss all the action?"

"Ah, you look a little too gleeful at the mention of a gang war."

"Just channeling my sweetie, Alex. You know he'd love covering a story like this." Alex, Andi's current love interest, was the local police beat reporter and Carly's former nemesis turned friend. He'd also been a part of the investigation into the mayor's murder and had helped Carly when Joe's infant son had been kidnapped.

"Yeah, I do," Carly said. "And to tell you the truth, I missed him this morning. How is he doing?"

"Chomping at the bit to get back to his newspaper crime beat. He's gotten over the shock of his mom dying suddenly, but he hurts. And his dad is a basket case." Andrea shrugged one shoulder and ran a finger around the rim of her cup. "The short answer is, he's having a tough time. He was never close to his dad; there's a lot of bad history there. But the man is so lost since his wife died that Alex can't believe he's the same father he grew up with."

"Does he know when he'll be back?"

"Maybe in a week."

Carly told her about the shooting and how everyone thought it looked staged. "The thing is, two gangsters are dead. You know there's going to be payback."

Andi nodded. "And you're worried about Nick."

"Don't remind me. Tell me about your day; get my mind off things."

Her friend rolled her eyes but complied, filling Carly in on all the latest hospital happenings.

Carly sipped her coffee and listened while Andi talked. She sat facing the door, a habit from her rookie days when training officers drummed into her head the need to be aware of her surroundings and the people in them. It was Monday night, and the shop was virtually empty. There had been a group of four college students at a table in the back when she walked in, but they left about the same time she settled in with Andi. She figured she and Andi would be the last people Erika kicked out.

The front door opened, and Carly looked that way from reflex. When she saw the man entering, Andrea's voice faded into the background and every alarm bell in Carly's head went off. His stride, the way he carried himself, said trouble, and Carly feared she was about to witness a robbery. She groped for her backpack and the security of the weapon inside.

Andrea stopped midsentence. "What is it? You look like you've seen a ghost." Andi started to turn but Carly stopped her.

"Don't turn," Carly hissed. Her backpack was in her lap, gun within reach, but she didn't want to overreact by yanking it out. Without taking her eyes off the man, she told her friend, "Keep talking but get out your phone and call dispatch. Tell them to send a car here for a suspicious person."

"Suspicious person? You look as though you see Freddy." But Andrea did as Carly asked.

Carly kept her eyes on the man, calming a bit when he placed both hands flat on the counter. No gun. Eyes narrow, she studied him, feeling more relieved when she saw nothing to convince her he had a concealed weapon.

He wasn't Freddy, but he was fresh out of

prison — of that Carly was certain. Ex-cons had an air about them, and it was strongest right when they got out. Their posture, how they wore their hair, even how they dressed gave them away. It was a by-product of the institutional lifestyle, where they were monitored and directed by someone else 24-7.

He wore a long-sleeved black shirt, buttoned up all the way, and black chinos with a sharp crease in them. His head was shaved, and dark, prison-style tattoos snaked up his neck from beneath the shirt collar toward an ear that looked half–chewed off. He'd given the dining area a once-over, so he knew Carly and Andrea were the only patrons inside.

Carly's tension returned to full as she noticed Erika's reaction to the man. Her expression and body language told Carly she was not happy to have him on the other side of the counter.

"They're coming," Andrea said. "Now will you tell me what is going on?"

Carly shook her head, straining to hear what was being said at the counter. But classical music was playing and Erika and the man were speaking in low tones. Then Erika stepped back, folded her arms, and waved a hand toward the door.

"You should go," she said clearly and sharply.

The man stomped his foot and with a sweep of his hand knocked the donation can toward Erika, who had to step aside to keep from being struck. The clang of metal and coins hitting the floor brought Carly to her feet.

"That's enough," she said, sliding her backpack to Andrea, making a split-second gamble that the man was not armed and wanting her hands free.

Erika and the man both turned her way. In three quick steps, Carly was at the counter. "She asked you to leave."

He looked at Carly with two of the darkest and coldest eyes she had ever seen. And now, close, with a full-on view, she could see that his face was a mess of divots and scars. Either he'd been in a car accident or he'd been in a lot of fights.

"This doesn't concern you, sweet cheeks," he said in a harsh, raspy voice, indicative of damaged vocal cords. He took a half step her way — to intimidate, she was sure. They were even in height, but he was a good forty pounds heavier than she was and solid, not fat. *Prison weight training.*

Carly took the balanced stance that years of weaponless defense had taught her and refused to be intimidated. "It concerns me because I'm a police officer and you just committed vandalism bordering on assault." Without taking her eyes from the man's, she addressed Erika and sensed, rather than saw, that Jinx was watching from behind the kitchen door. "Do you want to file a complaint, Erika?"

"No, no," she answered in a clipped, tight tone. "I just want him to leave."

Carly wished she'd said yes but wasn't going to argue with Erika. She shrugged and kept her own tone light. "Hear that? She said it again." Carly pointed to the door. "Time to go."

His whole body tensed, and a muscle jumped in his jaw. She knew he wasn't going to comply, and because of that she was ready for his next move.

The man rocked back like he planned to leave, then pivoted to his left and swung his right hand toward Carly as if to sweep her away as he'd swept the can off the counter.

The hours she and Nick and Joe had practiced weaponless defense paid off. Carly simultaneously stepped back and reached up, catching his open hand and using his forward momentum to jerk him off-balance. With a quick twist of his wrist and hand, she spun him, turning him so she was behind him, bending his elbow and pushing up and in on the palm, increasing the tension in her hold until the muscles in his forearm were taut and he was on his tiptoes.

The guy was a knot of muscles, which only made it easier to control him because he had no flexibility. Pressure in a control hold applied the right way was all it took to successfully restrain someone.

The man cursed and struggled, but once Carly set the hold, he wasn't going to get free without breaking his wrist. She planned to hold him until the on-duty unit arrived.

"I gave you a chance, pal. Now you're under arrest for assaulting an officer."

"Carly, please, no." Erika leaned over the counter. "You don't understand. This is a family matter. Just let him go."

Carly frowned, tightened her grip, and looked at Erika. "You know this guy?"

She nodded. "Yes. He's my brother-in-law. He's Ned's brother."

5

"He was in prison in Arizona. I didn't know he'd been released." Erika held her hand to her temple as she explained once the patrol unit arrived. "What a nasty surprise to see him here."

The uniformed unit who'd responded to Andi's call had taken Dean Barton, as Carly had learned his name was, outside to complete a field interview card. Carly wanted to ascertain the situation with Erika. Barton was quiet and compliant with the officers, but both Erika and Jinx were visibly upset. *And frightened,* Carly thought.

"I guess he expected something different from me and that made him angry," Erika continued. "The last time I saw him, Ned was still in the hospital." She shuddered as if that was an unpleasant memory.

"Why was he in prison?"

Erika gave a long-suffering sigh. "He's a drug addict, and he was falsifying prescriptions. He beat up a druggist who didn't believe his prescription, fled, stole a car, and led the entire Yuma police department on a chase."

Jinx stepped forward. "His original sentence was ten years, so I'm surprised he's out. It's only been six. I know Ned hoped we'd be notified before he was released."

"Yes." Erika bit her bottom lip. "I have to call Ned. He needs to know his brother is free." Something in her voice told Carly this news would not be the precursor to a happy family reunion.

"You're afraid of him. Why don't you press charges? I can arrest him for trying to hit me."

Jinx and Erika exchanged looks. "It's a long story," Erika said after a minute. "Dean has always been the troublemaker in Ned's family. When he was sent to prison, we thought we were free of him. I'm sorry he found us. We certainly didn't leave him a forwarding address."

"If you arrest him, he'll blame us," Jinx said.

"Yes, he will. And that will create more problems. If you can let that go —" Erika held Carly's gaze — "Ned and I would both consider it a favor."

Carly checked her watch. "Erika, I have to

get to work. If Dean has any warrants, I'm going to arrest him. If not, I'm going to tell him he's not welcome here and you need to look into a restraining order, okay?"

Erika's face flooded with relief. "Thank you, Carly. Sorry this had to come up."

Carly cocked her head toward Andi, who'd been listening to the conversation. She motioned that she was leaving the coffee shop, and Andi fell into step with her.

"That's what I like about hanging out with you," Andi said as they walked out the front door. "Never a dull moment."

Carly just shook her head as Andi continued to her car. Dean Barton stood between Lopez and Flanagan, the afternoon unit who'd responded to the call.

Lopez stepped over to Carly and handed her a field interview card. "He's clear. Says he got out of prison a month ago and just got to Las Playas today."

Carly took the card. "No parole?"

"Apparently not," Lopez said. "He says he was released without conditions, and there's nothing on the computer to contradict."

"Did you ask him what he was doing here?"

"Claims Erika and Ned are family. He was looking them up. Guy is covered with prison tats and muscled up. I'd sure hate it if he were part of my family."

Nodding, Carly walked to the police car parked on Pine, where Barton stood, stiff with thinly disguised anger. "Mr. Barton?"

He turned his cold eyes her way but said nothing.

"You're not welcome here — I think that's obvious — so it's a good idea if you stay away."

"It's a free country. I'm a free man."

Carly fought the anger she felt, knowing it would get her nowhere if she let this guy provoke her. Voice level, tone light, she said, "Yeah, and I'm the cop you tried to punch. The only reason I'm not taking you to jail right now is because Erika asked me not to."

She paused to see if he'd react in any way, but he didn't. "A word to the wise: unless you want to find yourself back in jail, stay away from here."

She held his gaze. After a minute, he looked away.

"Can I go now?" he asked Flanagan.

Flanagan nodded and tossed him his wallet. Barton shoved the wallet into his front pants pocket and walked away. Carly's gaze followed him as he crossed the street to where another man stood, leaning against a white van. She realized then that the second man had probably been watching the activity in front of the coffee shop. He was taller than Barton but not as thickly built. His face was covered in a dark beard. When Barton reached the van, they exchanged a few words; then Barton walked to the driver's side and climbed in while the bearded man took the passenger's seat.

The van was new, and as it pulled away, Carly saw the pale green of an out-of-state plate. She was able to read three letters, but the van disappeared around a corner before she saw the rest. In any event, she was too preoccupied with the men inside to dwell on the van. There was something familiar about the bearded man; but still disturbed by Dean Barton, she couldn't remember if or where she'd seen him before.

She looked at the FI card in her hand and caught Flanagan as he was getting into the squad car. "He didn't say where he was staying, did he?"

Flanagan shook his head. "Said he'd find a hotel since his family didn't seem happy to see him."

"Thanks." Carly checked her watch. She needed to get going.

She tried to stop herself from obsessing about Barton. But he was evil — of that she was certain — and a wave of gooseflesh rippled down her arm as she hurried for her car.

Joe was already there when Carly slid into the squad meeting a few minutes early. Taking a seat next to him, she exchanged hellos with him.

"I hear Crusher is hanging on," he said.

"Yeah, Nick told me the good news when he got home," she said, quickly filling Joe in on the fact that Crusher had been awake and talking in the ER. But her mind replayed only one thing: the confrontation with Dean Barton. The parolee had really gotten under her skin. He was trouble with a capital *T*. Would it be trouble for her or more trouble for Erika and Ned?

The meeting came to order, and Barrett read off the watch report.

"For starters, gangs will be in at midnight," he said.

Carly partially tuned him out. She knew this from Nick. He was splitting the team: half would cruise the Ninja neighborhood and the other half the Playboyz. They wanted patrol officers to stop and interview any gang members they came across and to pay attention to any new graffiti.

Carly refocused when Peter Harris took Barrett's spot and briefed everyone about the shooting.

"All three gang members were shot with a 9mm," he said. This was new information for Carly. "As for Macias's condition, he's holding his own." There were murmurs in the room with this information. Pete looked Carly's way. "Good job with the quick first aid."

Joe hooted in agreement and Carly felt her face get hot. Applause broke out, and she punched Joe in the shoulder.

When things calmed down, Pete continued. "Macias was talking initially, but not now. He's still alive and in a drug-induced coma. We're not posting an officer on his room because he's in intensive care and monitored closely by hospital staff. Right now this looks like a gang hit, so that's how we're treating it. Everyone be safe out there."

As the meeting broke up, Carly filled Joe's ear with the tale of her confrontation with Dean Barton. "He really gave me the creeps. It was as if he had a neon sign over his head with *Danger* flashing in bright-red letters."

"Maybe you should call Arizona and ask about him. If he made as big a splash with the PD as Erika said, a cop back there will remember and maybe give you some insight."

"I plan on doing that at EOW."

Carly was first up to drive. While Joe completed the vehicle inspection, Carly logged on to the computer to check out everything going on in the field. Barrett had bumped them up from beat duty to wild car status, which meant they were not tied down to a beat and could handle calls anywhere. She figured he did that in case something went down with the gangs. She and Joe wouldn't be assigned to anything that involved Nick if it could be helped. Department policy did not allow married officers to work together, especially if one outranked the other. While some officers thought the policy stupid, Carly reserved judgment. She loved Nick dearly but wondered whether she'd be distracted by worry for him if they were involved in a high-stress situation together. It was a question she was not ready to answer, so being a wild car suited her just fine.

Her musing was rudely interrupted and she had to shift gears quickly when their police radio screamed with emergency traffic.

"All available units, respond to One Marina Plaza for a 415 crowd, growing violent."

There was trouble in the marina.

"Let's go," Joe said as he pulled his door

closed. Carly hit the accelerator and burned rubber out of the lot after another black-and-white.

An afternoon sergeant keyed his mike to give specific instructions to responding units. Carly could hear yelling, glass breaking, and air horns blaring in the background. She braced herself for what they were rushing into.

When she and Joe screeched to a stop at what officers called the DMZ, a two-hundred-foot-wide buffer zone between the construction area and the protestors, a mini riot was boiling over. According to the judge's ruling, the protestors weren't supposed to encroach into the zone, but apparently something had happened. It looked as though all of afternoon watch was facing off in the zone with about a hundred chanting protestors. Carly could hear them repeat a profanity over and over in remarkable unity. Basically they implied that the police were hassling them for no reason.

She and Joe immediately ran to a couple of officers who were struggling to arrest two troublemakers. Carly sneezed when the acrid smell of pepper spray hit her nose, and her eyes burned. She could hear an afternoon sergeant on his PA giving an order to disperse. By law, the order had to be given three times and audible to all in the area before the police could wade in and clear the area. She braced herself, wondering if this would be the night they'd don riot gear and clear the place out. Violence would provide the cause to act before the court case finished.

Once the two cursing, spitting protestors were cuffed and secured in a squad car, Joe grabbed his and Carly's riot helmets from the trunk, and they joined a skirmish line with the other cops.

"Natives are restless," Flanagan told them. "They know they're likely to be evicted, and I think they want to go out with a bang."

But even as Carly pulled the protective face shield down, the chanting was fading. The two who were going to jail had probably been the spark plugs, and now they were gone. There was debris on the ground, but as Carly dodged a bottle, she concluded that there was less flying through the air. And the sergeant didn't give the audible, official order again.

A stubborn group of chanting, taunting protestors occupied their time and attention. Shoulder to shoulder, Carly and the other officers stepped forward in unison, moving the mass of people in front of them back across the DMZ. It was as delicate as

71

it was forceful. Carly and the others held riot batons and worked to be as menacing as possible without being the aggressors. The objectors slowly complied and Carly could tell from their faces there was no fight left in them, but for form's sake they moved slowly. After about forty minutes they were back in the park. Carly learned from Flanagan that the protestors and a private security officer had gotten into a screaming match that ended with the security guard being pelted with trash and debris. Security had responded with pepper spray.

Once the situation returned to an uneasy truce, the skirmish line held position for about twenty minutes before Sergeant Barrett released the afternoon guys from the scene and almost all of the graveyard units to their normal beats.

Relieved they hadn't had to go into full riot mode, Carly took her helmet off and ran a hand through her damp hair. Her feet hurt and her back was plastered with sweat. Musing that riot control was just about the most unpleasant physical task patrol officers were called on to perform, Carly chalked a plus in the detective column. In the event she did decide to change, a detective assignment would mean she'd never have to face a riotous crowd again.

She and Joe stashed their riot gear in the trunk, and Carly was happy to return to the normalcy of patrol. But once they were out of the marina and rolling through city streets, the atmosphere was heavier than it had been facing the mini riot.

"Things are tense," Carly said when they pulled up to a loud music call on Ninth Street, the fringe of Ninja turf. Guys were out in yards, on porches, glaring.

The music was lowered as they made their way up the walk.

A hostile man met them at the door. "Where were you all when my homeys were smoked?"

This was the kind of contact that would never be positive, so both Joe and Carly said as little as possible and thanked him for turning the music down. He cursed them and slammed the door.

"This neighborhood is a powder keg," Carly observed as they got back into the car.

When Joe just grunted, she cast a glance his way. "You're awfully quiet tonight."

He yawned. "I didn't get much sleep. A.J. has a cold."

"I thought you seemed distracted." She pulled away from the curb as Joe punched in the call disposition on the computer.

Settling into patrol mode, eyes roaming, she acknowledged how comfortable she felt with Joe. Did she really want a change in this relationship even if the work itself had become tedious?

Trying not to think about the job in those terms, Carly concentrated on the world outside the patrol car. Traffic was moderate, and she watched each car passing the other way.

A priority-one call went out in another beat, and suddenly fear for Nick bubbled up again. She worked hard to steady her thoughts and focused in on a green sedan, catching the driver's eyes as they came even, then passed. She saw him clearly enough to see his lips register "Oh no" and a curse.

"Joe!" She stomped on the brake and waited for traffic to clear so she could make a U-turn. "That's Trey Porter; I know it. In the green sedan, and he's splitting."

Joe didn't question her observation. He grabbed the radio and informed dispatch that they were in pursuit as Carly clicked on lights and sirens, executing a U-turn with tires squealing. Trey Porter was the leader of the Ninth Street Ninjas. Carly and Joe both knew that not only was his license suspended, but he did not own a car.

As Carly completed the turn, the green

car disappeared around a corner. She punched it and rounded the corner as Joe calmly kept dispatch informed of their location. He relayed the car's license plate and was quickly informed that it was 10-29 Victor, a stolen vehicle.

After a couple more turns, they pulled to within a block of the car. Carly thanked God traffic was light here because Trey barely had control of the sedan. The taillights swerved and the rear end whipped across lanes of traffic.

By now, two units were behind them, and the scream of sirens pumped up Carly's adrenaline. Every cop she knew loved to chase stolen cars.

"He's gonna try to cross the rail tracks," Joe said, raising his voice over the siren.

Carly had figured that, but when Trey jerked left across the tracks where there was no crossing, she nearly lost her grip on the wheel. She followed, banging over the low curb, across the tracks, and over the next low curb.

Sparks flashed from the green car as it bottomed out but continued speeding away. Then the passenger door flew open. Carly jerked the wheel when the passenger lunged out of the car, which had to be traveling at least forty miles per hour.

He didn't get completely clear of the vehicle and hit the pavement right in the path of the rear tires.

6

Carly winced as she saw the rear tires of the fleeing vehicle roll over the passenger's legs. She called out, "Joe!" then steered the patrol car away from the rolling figure.

"The passenger jumped out! Passenger in the street!" Joe radioed to the assisting units.

Carly stayed after the green car, and an assisting unit answered that they would take care of the passenger.

Carly's knuckles were white on the wheel as she strained against a taut seat belt.

Then Trey lost it. He clipped a parked car, and the green sedan spun out of control. Carly slammed on the brakes, screeching to a stop as the car they were chasing slammed into another parked car and finally came to rest. Unbelievably, Trey hurtled from the driver's side immediately and hit the pavement running.

Joe leaped from the patrol car while Carly took a second to jam it into park. Then she was out, legs pumping, after her partner.

Joe was half a block ahead of her by the time she hit her stride. Then everything went sideways. Carly watched in horror as Joe tripped on something and went down hard, skidding across the sidewalk and smashing into a fence. His flashlight shattered on the pavement and bits flew everywhere.

"Are you okay?" She reached him quickly, but Trey had vanished.

"Ah, I twisted my knee," Joe moaned, grabbing his leg and rocking back and forth.

The sound of feet running up behind them caused Carly to turn. She saw Nick and Mickey. Nick started to slow, but she waved him on.

"I've got this! He went right toward the alley." She pointed.

Nick nodded, and he and his partner disappeared into the night after Trey.

Flanagan and Lopez came running up next, and Carly also waved them on in the direction Porter had gone.

She keyed her mike to set up a perimeter, concentrating, wanting to be certain she made it the right size so Porter would be caught inside. She also requested that K-9 start their way in the event Porter hunkered down somewhere. Everybody knew Trey

Porter; he was one of those frequent fliers many officers had contacted or arrested for one reason or another over the years. Someone even came on the air and offered to go by Porter's house.

Carly knelt next to Joe and listened as the intersections she called out were covered. Then she turned her full attention back to Joe. His pants were torn and so was the elbow of his shirt. Spots of blood were noticeable in those places and on his scraped palm.

"You want medics?" she asked Joe.

He shook his head. "No, I'll make it back to the car. Once K-9 gets here, you can take me to Memorial."

"We got a perimeter up quick," she said as she helped him up. "They'll catch him."

Joe leaned on Carly, wincing when he had to put weight on his left leg. Together they made their way back to the car, Joe obviously in pain. On the way, she saw an uneven spot where the asphalt met the concrete and realized that was probably what Joe had tripped over.

Joe saw it too. "Man, why did I have to trip? Why couldn't Porter have hit that?" he muttered with disgust.

Carly heard fire department sirens and from the radio traffic knew that they'd been summoned to look after the passenger who'd bailed out of the stolen car.

Joe settled into the police car and turned up the radio. Carly heard Nick's voice, and her heart raced.

"He's headed out toward Chestnut." Nick's breath came hard from the chase.

Carly hooked her thumbs in her gun belt and tensed.

"We got nothing on the southwest corner of Chestnut and Ninth," Flanagan said.

"He doubled back!" Mickey added.

"He's —" Nick started to say something, then stopped.

"Gang 1, 10-9 your last." The dispatcher asked him to repeat.

Carly held her breath.

"Can anyone with Gang 1 relay his status?" dispatch asked.

An eternity ticked by in slow seconds before there was a response.

"Gang 1, we're in the alley west of Chestnut, north of Sixth, code 4, code 4. Suspect in custody." Nick was still breathing hard but in control.

Carly expelled a breath and wiped sweat from her brow. Code 4 — suspect in custody — were wonderful words.

She looked at Joe, who smiled. "That gang sergeant is on it," he said.

Carly nodded, flushed with relief and pride. "I'm going to check out the car, start the inventory. Do you mind a few more minutes?"

"I'm fine. Don't worry about me. Besides, I want to find out what Porter was doing running from the poh-lice."

"Yeah, I guess I'd like to know why the punk cost me one good partner."

Carly opened the trunk to grab her report forms. The property in the stolen car needed to be inventoried and then the car itself recovered and sent to the tow yard. She was walking toward the green sedan when dispatch called their unit designator.

"I'll take it," Joe said.

The dispatcher had a request from the unit who was with the passenger, the guy who'd jumped out of the car while Trey kept going. They asked Joe to go to a clear channel. Carly listened as she filled out the information asked for on the tow sheet. Omar Garcia, the unfortunate gang member, had a broken leg. The unit needed to know if they were going to charge him with anything or if he was going to be an RNB — released not booked. Carly could hear him howling about his innocence in the background.

"I just got in the car," the gangster cried

in a plaintive whine. "He just picked me up. I didn't know it was stolen."

Joe told the unit to release him, and Carly agreed. Unless they could prove Omar helped steal the car, there was nothing to charge him with. A juvenile might be charged with joyriding in such a case, but Omar was an adult. The medics were transporting him to the hospital anyway, so he wouldn't be disappearing into the woodwork or stealing more cars anytime soon.

She stuck her head in the 10-29 car and saw a collection of fast-food wrapper trash. Pressing the trunk release, she straightened up in time to see Nick and Mickey walking her way with Trey Porter between them. Flanagan and Lopez were also with them, and everyone but Trey was smiling. Running someone down in a foot pursuit was almost as gratifying as catching someone in a car pursuit. This was a twofer.

"Hey, Joe, what happened?" Nick asked.

"Didn't pick my feet up, I guess." He stood, supporting himself on the open patrol car door. "Why'd you run, Trey?"

The gangster didn't answer and wouldn't even look at Joe.

"We'll inventory the car and wait for the tow if you want," Nick said, leaving Trey to Mickey and walking to where Carly stood.

82

Suddenly a camera flash went off. Duncan Potter had found them.

Carly gave Nick a look and ignored the camera. "I'm almost done with the vehicle form. I just have to check the trunk." Together they moved to the trunk. "You can wait for the tow, though. I want to get Joe to the hospital."

"No problem. You did us a favor. Trey was on our list of guys we wanted to talk to tonight. Thanks for finding him." Nick glared at Potter. "Back off. You contaminate anything, I'll be happy to book you."

Potter said nothing — he rarely did — just kept snapping photos.

Carly concentrated only on Nick. "My pleasure. How's it going tonight?" she asked. "Things seem tense."

Nick nodded. "Tense and angry. We're sitting on gasoline waiting for a match to drop."

Carly had an overwhelming urge to grab Nick in a hug and implore him to be careful, maybe even whine a little bit. But she realized he needed to focus on the bad guys right now, not on her personal crisis of faith.

"Any indications that the shooting really was a gang hit?"

Nick sighed. "No one is talking. The Ninjas are angry three of their own were hit, and the Playboyz are on the defensive, waiting for the retaliation drive-bys. We've confiscated a few weapons though, so . . ." His voice trailed off as his gaze went to the trunk.

Stepping forward, she pushed the lid all the way up. "What in the world?" she said as Nick reached in and pulled a tarp away.

There, illuminated by the bright head-lights and the flashing emergency lights of her patrol car, she saw at least two shotguns and several handguns, plus boxes and boxes of all types of ammunition. Plenty of stuff to start a full-scale war and keep it going for some time.

Finally Potter said something. "Did they rip off a gun store?"

7

Carly and Joe returned to the station after the hospital trip — and the piles of IOD paperwork — with only an hour left to their shift. The doctor had wrapped Joe's leg in a splint, then told him to keep it elevated and iced and to visit occupational health as soon as possible, but he was off work for at least a month. Carly offered to drive him home, but since it was his left leg, he told her he'd be fine to drive himself.

Because of the guns they found in the trunk, there was more interest in Omar, Trey's passenger. While at the hospital, Carly had a predictable conversation with the gangster. He was still coherent in spite of painkillers and was adamant that he knew nothing about the car being stolen.

"He just picked me up, I swear! I work at Burger King on the boulevard until midnight. You can call my boss."

"We will; we will. Did you and Trey pick

anything up after you got in the car?"

"I just barely got in the car."

Carly folded her arms. "Yes or no."

"No, no, no."

"I'll send a unit out to talk to your boss right now."

"Good. He'll tell you. Man, I didn't steal no car."

"How about guns?"

"Huh?" Omar truly looked confused, but Carly wondered if the painkillers were kicking in. Doctors told her they were going to have to put a pin in his leg.

She conferred with Barrett about him. After verifying his work story, they continued with the RNB. If they needed Omar, he wasn't going anywhere for the time being.

When Carly said good night to Joe, she was angry. Trey Porter had cost her a good partner. The triple shooting and this moronic gang war had put her husband in jeopardy. She bought some bad coffee from the vending machine and tried to swallow the sour lump of resentment in her throat with a gulp. They hadn't had a chance to take a lunch break, but even though her stomach growled, she didn't feel like eating.

Taking the coffee, she settled into the file room to review their log before heading to the locker room to change. Patrol logs were kept electronically, but officers printed out a copy at EOW to review and write notes if needed. The logs were then initialed and turned in to records. She also planned to call authorities in Arizona about Dean Barton.

A familiar voice sounded from her left. "Officer Edwards."

Carly looked up. "Hey, G-man, Agent Wiley. How are you?" She started to stand to shake his hand.

He waved her down and pulled up a chair, straddling it so he could rest his elbows on the back while he faced her. Wiley looked crisp and formal in a dark suit, the stereotypical picture of an FBI agent, a man who had helped with the kidnapping investigation and rescue of Joe's son.

"Good observation of that stolen car tonight. I paid a visit to Nick and his partner."

"Trying to stay busy?"

"I hear Joe got hurt."

Carly nodded and told him what had happened.

"That's tough, but maybe it's only a sprain and not as serious as they think right now."

"Hope you're right. What brings you here this time of the morning? Are you checking up on Oceans First?"

He shook his head. "From what I've seen, LPPD has been handling the protestors just fine. I actually came to talk to you. I knew I'd find you working these godforsaken hours."

Carly smiled and spread out her arms. "Well, I should've known you'd catch me sooner or later . . . and I hid the bodies so well."

Wiley cracked a hint of a smile, which was about the most he ever did. "I'm heading up a federal task force. We're pulling in good officers from agencies all over Southern California."

"Mission?"

"Homeland security. Under that umbrella we'll work on a lot of different things. There will be travel involved; it'll be exciting, always changing, and infinitely challenging."

"That's great. But why are you telling me?"

"Because I want you to join us. It's been cleared with your chief, should you decide to hop on board."

Her anger forgotten, shock caused Carly's jaw to go slack. "Talk about out of proverbial left field. I don't know what to say."

What would Nick say? shot through her mind as she tried to predict her husband's reaction. He thought she needed a change. A federal task force would certainly be a change. It would afford her investigative opportunities she'd never see in small Las Playas, and that made her sit up straighter. But knowing it would also take her away from home a lot kept her interest muted.

"I didn't expect you to answer right now." He reached into his pocket and pulled out a flash drive. "Here, take this; study it. It has all the pertinent information about the job. I'll be in town for a while. We're monitoring Oceans First, but we're not involved at the moment."

Carly took the flash drive and closed her fist around it even as the gravity of what Wiley had just offered her sank in and excitement started to swell. This was a huge honor.

"This will take some thought," she said, working to keep her tone noncommittal.

Wiley stood. "You've got two weeks. I'm hoping you'll decide soon, but don't rush," he said. "You know where to find me when you've made a decision." He shook her hand once, then turned and left her sitting in the report room.

Carly's mind raced with all she imagined such a job would entail. Homeland Security — protecting the nation, not just Las Playas.

Settling back in front of her log, she couldn't suppress the smile. She'd bet a federal task force wouldn't be tedious.

"Edwards."

Carly glanced up this time to see Sergeant Barrett regarding her.

"Yeah?"

He appeared as though he hadn't slept in ages. Stale cigarette smoke hung around him like a shroud. She remembered what Joe had said about his marriage breaking up.

"Great job with Porter. I told Nick it was a good catch."

She shrugged. "I'm glad we caught him but bummed it cost me my partner. I'd sure like to know where he got that arsenal. Did Nick get anything out of him?"

Nick and Mickey had taken on the responsibility of cataloging and entering into evidence all the weapons and ammo recovered from the stolen car. They were in the evidence section now. Carly was resigned to the fact that she probably wouldn't see her husband again until much later in the day.

"No, Porter isn't talking. But that's not why I came to talk to you. I got called in to take a citizen's complaint on you."

"What?"

Flash drive forgotten, she felt her face

flush hot when she saw that he wasn't joking. The anger she'd felt earlier ramped up to fury. No one had ever filed a complaint against her specifically. She'd been named in a couple of complaints as part of a group in an altercation after a rock concert and once after a riot in downtown Las Playas, something officers regarded as a type of carpet bombing by lawyers on police departments, where they would name in a lawsuit every officer whose ID number showed up on a call.

Barrett stepped into the room and pulled a chair close to Carly. "Look, I know it's nonsense, but you know the rules — someone makes a complaint, I have to take it."

"Who complained? I haven't had contact with any —" Her mind latched on to a name.

"I guess it happened right before you got to work."

"Dean Barton."

Barrett nodded. "I knew you'd remember; the guy has an unforgettable face. Tell me what happened."

Carly sighed deeply and struggled to keep her indignation from surfacing. She told him everything about the confrontation and Erika's desire not to prosecute her brother-in-law. While Carly could have arrested Barton for taking a swing at her, Barrett would understand why she didn't. The contact with Barton was precipitated by what he did to Erika. Carly taking him to jail would have dragged Erika into the mix whether she wanted to be there or not. Since Carly had defused the situation with a simple control hold, in her mind it was a no harm, no foul situation.

"I get the picture," Barrett said when she finished. "The guy is basically whining that you stuck your nose in where it didn't belong and put your hands on him for no reason."

Carly kept her mouth shut, fearing she'd say something she'd regret.

"I'll have to talk to the coffee shop people, but as far as I'm concerned, this is a service complaint that doesn't bear further investigation." He stood to leave. "That guy is just playing the system, trying to get to you because he knows he can. Don't worry about this." He waved the paper. "But file a brief follow-up about the contact, just in case."

Carly sat back in her chair, watching the sergeant walk away and fighting frustration. Her ten-year streak of no complaints was now over. Biting her lip, and mortified that the situation made tears threaten, she turned to a terminal and typed a quick follow-up, explaining the circumstances of the contact with Barton. After printing a copy, she ground out her initials on the bottom. Tossing it on the in-tray, she grabbed her kit and hurried to the elevator.

She changed clothes with fitful, irritated energy, snatched her wedding ring from the top shelf, and slammed her locker closed. Holding the ring, she took a deep breath as she slid it back on her finger. The action calmed her as much as picturing her blue-eyed husband in her mind did. Carly hadn't changed to her married name at work. Even when she and Nick were married the first time, she had remained Carly Edwards at the PD. It was never a women's lib thing but rather a practical move meant to keep mistakes from being made when it came to subpoenas or commendations or any paperwork issues.

Now, when she slid the ring on and prepared to go home, she was Carly Anderson, happy to leave the work persona in the locker room. When her phone chimed with a text, the emotion boiling inside about Dean Barton had eased. Blowing out a breath, she sat down and opened the message, thanking God that it was from Nick.

MAKING FOOD RUN. HAVE TIME TO MEET

AT HBAAG?

"Oh yeah," she said out loud as she replied to the text, grateful she wouldn't have to wait all day to see Nick and relieved she didn't have to stew for hours before telling him about the avalanche of bad news that had hit her this morning.

8

Half Baked and Almost Grounded looked crowded with morning traffic when Carly arrived. Part of her wanted to talk to Erika and Ned, get more information on Dean. But she didn't want to drag them into the drama. The complaint would be resolved at intake — she believed Barrett — but it still pricked her that Barton had filed it in the first place.

She pulled into the lot behind the shop and saw Nick's plain car. He was still in the driver's seat, talking on his phone. Her heart raced a bit. He still did that to her. Eight years of marriage, a year of separation, and nine months of a second marriage, and he still percolated her pulse. Even the scar on his forehead, the result of a smack to the head by a bad guy, did nothing to diminish his handsomeness in her eyes. He was her *GQ* hubby.

Walking to his car, she leaned against the

front fender. He held up one finger and quickly finished the call before getting out of the car.

"Hey, how's Joe?" he asked as he closed the door, shoved his phone in his pocket, and faced her.

She folded her arms and shrugged. "Doctor said his knee is sprained and that he's likely to be off work for a month. But he has to go to occupational health and get an MRI. Did you get anything from Trey?"

Nick shook his head. "Trey lawyered up." He stepped forward and ran his index finger across her forearm. "Losing your partner for a month is tough, but it's not the end of the world. What else is wrong?"

Cognizant of the fact they were in a busy parking lot, Carly swallowed, fighting frustrated tears. She told Nick about the complaint by Dean Barton. Nick leaned next to her, his hip touching hers, and listened.

"When it rains, it pours." He took her hand and pulled her toward the shop. "Let's go in and get something to eat. We'll both probably think clearer about all this with some food in us."

He smiled and she squeezed his hand, feeling slightly better and all of a sudden hungry. Now that she'd told him the bad news, excitement from the good news of the task force offer bubbled up. She'd tell him about that over breakfast.

Inside, the coffee shop was bustling. Nick took a number and placed their order while Carly found a table for two near the counter. The food would be delivered to them when ready. She could see Londy working busily in the coffee and baked goods area and Erika doing likewise in the kitchen. Carly also saw Mary Ellen following Jinx around, apparently learning to deliver food and bus tables. Carly knew Mary Ellen had applied, but she hadn't realized that the girl would be working so soon. Like Londy, Mary Ellen had a checkered past. She'd run away from a foster home and even committed a kidnap, snatching Joe's son, A.J., from the hospital about a year ago. But she'd brought the baby back unharmed and later saved Carly's life. When Carly, Joe, and his wife, Christy, went to bat for her, the justice system was lenient. She ended up staying in the juvenile justice system and not moving to adult court.

Mary Ellen had also done a lot for her own cause by buckling down and catching up on missed schoolwork. She completed her high school diploma while in state custody, completing one year's work in four months. Now, while still on probation —

the juvenile system would have jurisdiction over her until she turned twenty-five — she was a ward of her uncle, Jonah Rawlings, who also happened to be Carly and Nick's pastor.

In spite of the crowd, their food was delivered quickly. Nick had ordered veggie omelets and large coffees for them both, plus a huge cinnamon roll to share. It was the type of meal they'd share together on a day off. Carly felt her aggravation fade with each bite.

"Why are you always right?" she asked Nick after half of her meal had disappeared.

"Hmm?" he mumbled with his mouth full.

"I do feel better, at least about the bogus complaint. But I'm so bummed about losing Joe. You know how tough it is to find someone you can work with for ten hours in a black-and-white."

Nick swallowed and nodded. "I do. I'm sorry he got hurt. You were safe with him; he has a good head on his shoulders."

Carly knew he meant physically safe. More than anything, a cop wanted a partner who would always have their back. Joe was that type of partner; she could trust him and they meshed. She took a few more bites of her omelet and then cut into the cinnamon roll.

"Is anyone on your watch looking for a partner?" Nick asked.

Carly shook her head, enjoying the taste of cinnamon and gooey icing. "I would have asked Kyle, but he's retiring soon and has been taking a lot of time off." An old-timer and a good friend, Kyle Corley wouldn't be inclined to be a hard charger, but he wasn't lazy, and he would back her up.

"But I did get an interesting offer."

Nick's eyebrows arched with curiosity as he sipped his coffee. "Yeah, what?"

She told him about Wiley's visit. When she finished, Nick sat back in his chair, and Carly studied his face for some hint about what he was thinking.

"Hmm, that's an awesome career opportunity. Have you looked at the information yet?"

"No, right after Wiley gave it to me, Barrett came in to tell me about the complaint. The bad news makes me think the task force is the ticket. I got so angry after hearing about Barton's complaint — maybe working with the feds is the change I need."

Nick took a minute to respond, chewing thoughtfully. "You need to look over the details and be certain about everything the job requires."

"I agree, but it almost seems like an

answer to prayer." She hated the fact that he had such a great cop face. "I know we both need to look at it. But it was you who said I need a change."

He hiked a shoulder, but she still couldn't read his expression. "While I agree you need a change, I don't think you should make such a big decision just to avoid a situation in patrol you don't want. It will be a commitment in time and energy, babe, and you need to ask yourself where you want your career to go."

She sipped her coffee, knowing he was right but feeling irritated just the same. "You haven't read it, and it already sounds like you don't want me to take it."

A hint of a frown marred his features for an instant and then was gone. "I don't have to read it to know that this is a job that will put you on a path you've never said you wanted to be on. It's a stepping stone to either move up in rank or out to a federal agency permanently. Do you want that?"

Carly sighed and pressed her fingers to her forehead, not wanting anger to rule her response. "I don't know what I want right now. I thought I wanted to work with Joe in patrol forever, but I know nothing lasts forever. In fact, Joe said that just the other night."

"We'll pray about it, then. I'm sure Agent Wiley would want you to be 100 percent certain before you decide." He drank his coffee. "Don't think you don't have any options or that you have to decide too soon without considering all the variables."

"Lately I've just felt like I'm spinning my wheels, working hard to put people in jail and then seeing them slither out on technicalities."

"That's Burke frustration. You know that's not true with every case."

Carly huffed. "Well, I thought I'd be in a patrol car for thirty years. It surprises me that the task force sounds so inviting."

"It's an honor." His elbows were on the table, and he held his coffee in both hands. "Maybe this is a broader career nudge for you. If not in the direction of the task force, maybe it's time to think about detectives here at home." His thoughtful gaze held hers.

"Hmm, you might be right."

"It's just a thought. I know you hated juvenile, but that was an involuntary transfer. This would be your choice. If you do need a change, several details have openings. I'd think you'd want to look at all your options before making a huge leap."

She sat back and looked toward the coffee

bar, where Londy worked the espresso machine. Mary Ellen was busing tables on her own, and the crowd had thinned. "I guess I like the idea of being challenged. A federal task force makes working in Las Playas look like working in Mayberry."

"We're not LA, but we're not Mayberry. You never know — you might love working a detail like violent crimes or even homicide." He reached across the table and gripped her hand, rubbing her palm with his thumb. "Or maybe the change you're looking for is in a different area. Maybe we can think about starting a family."

Carly jerked her hand away. "What?"

Nick chuckled. "Babe, you look like I just asked you to cut off your leg."

"Maybe you did. You're the one who always says that kids end the parents' life."

"It's been a long time since I said that. And maybe one kind of life does end so a new one can start." His eyes were warm, and Carly struggled to stir up righteous anger to flush out the fear.

She couldn't do it. The thought of being a mother scared her to death.

Just then Mary Ellen stepped up with a bag of to-go food. "Here you go, Sergeant Anderson," she said with a smile. "I waited until you were just about finished before putting the order in."

"Perfect." Nick took the bag and handed Mary Ellen some money. "I don't need any change back from this."

Mary Ellen blushed, thanked Nick, nodded hello to Carly, and was gone.

"Looks like she's doing well," Carly said, happy for the subject change.

"Yep." Nick finished his coffee in one gulp. "I've got to get back. Mickey is probably cursing me in all five of the languages he speaks. Those guns opened a can of worms. The serial numbers have all been filed off. We have to call in ATF on this. They have the resources to try to raise them."

He reached across the table and laid his hand down, palm up. After a second, Carly put her hand in his. He closed his hand around hers. "I'm not sure what time I'll be home. Try to get some sleep."

She nodded and squeezed, fighting the unsettled feeling in her gut. "I will. You be safe."

He winked and left the restaurant. Carly watched him leave as she nursed her coffee. She would have left shortly after him if Dean Barton hadn't walked in a few minutes later.

9

He saw her at once and smirked. There was a tall blonde at his side. Carly thought the woman looked familiar but didn't waste time trying to figure it out. She focused like a laser beam on Barton and was on her feet without stopping to think.

"What are you doing here?"

"What's it look like? Getting something to eat. What are you doing? Waiting to harass me again?" His gravelly tone was singsongy and taunting. He winked at the blonde.

Carly felt her face redden with anger, and she was conscious of several people turning their way to watch the confrontation. "You were told to stay away from here."

"I'm here and I'm staying. What are you going to do about it?" He stared at her with cold, empty eyes, the challenge there naked and obvious.

What could she do? She was off duty and there was no sign of Erika anywhere. Barton's threat hung in the air. Carly stiffened and struggled to avoid what she knew the man wanted: a physical confrontation. The trouble was, she wanted one as well. She wanted to smash him in the face and wipe that smirk off.

"You —"

"Carly."

She turned and saw Ned emerge from the kitchen. Taller than his brother, Ned was thinner, and he walked with a bit of a limp. Carly caught Dean's glance at his brother and saw in it undisguised animosity, so Ned's next words surprised her.

"It's okay. He's my brother; he can stay." Ned held up his good hand and continued toward them. He never wore a prosthetic, so the handless arm hung at his beltline. His brow creased in a frown as he cast a glance at Dean, who now grinned broadly, animosity gone. "We're working some things out," Ned continued.

"What about what happened last night?"

Ned sighed. "Like I said, we're working on things."

She studied him and read a lot of things in his face but saw no level of comfort with his brother.

"Me and my lady need some food, little brother." Dean grabbed the blonde's hand

and continued smirking at Carly.

She turned back to Ned. "All right, all right. My mistake." Inside, she seethed all the more, knowing that Dean Barton was trying to set her off.

"You're a stupid cop," Dean said, his scarred face twisted with glee. The woman laughed. "We expect stupid mistakes." He waved a hand dismissively and turned away. "Come on, Bro, buy me breakfast."

Ned gave Carly an apologetic nod. She knew he wasn't happy with the situation. Something else was going on, but she wasn't going to find out what this morning. She said good-bye and left for her car, knowing that it would be a miracle if she got any sleep today.

That night, Carly slid into the squad meeting expecting she'd draw a solo car. Kyle Corley was off, and everyone else was partnered up. She figured it was just as well because she was tired and cranky. Dean Barton had gotten under her skin, and she knew she needed to rise above his taunts. To be on the safe side, she filed a short memo to Sergeant Barrett about the morning incident with the parolee.

And there was a conversation she'd had with Joe before leaving for work that nagged at her. She called to check up on him and mentioned the task force offer.

"I have to have surgery," he said. "Pretty soon too. I'm likely to be off work at least six weeks. You just thinking about the task force, or did you accept already?"

"I'd like to go over the job description with Nick, and we haven't had the time," Carly said, anxiety rising because she feared the more she read, the more she'd want the job badly and Nick would advise against.

Joe's advice was the opposite. "Maybe you should take it," he said. "Christy wants me to look into a detective position. She worries about me in the car. And, well, I've been in one for over five years. Maybe this injury is telling me I need a change. I guess I might be deserting you. But she worries about me, and she has a point — if I work days, I'll be home with her and A.J. every night. And you have options. I'd hate to think of you turning down a plum job offer because of me."

The conversation had left her with an uncomfortable feeling in the pit of her stomach that she'd worked her last night in a patrol car with Joe. Though taking the task force offer would have meant the same thing, somehow it hit harder when it was Joe leaving first.

Was this a sign that she should accept Wiley's offer? Or maybe it was time to move to detectives like Nick suggested. What he and Joe both said was true — she had options. She'd hated juvenile because it had been a forced transfer. If she were able to go to a detail she chose, maybe it would be different.

The idea of detectives, while not as attractive as the task force, didn't tweak her so much now. She wouldn't have to deal with pukes like Dean Barton in a detective detail. Or stand in skirmish lines. But then, she wouldn't have to do that on a task force either. And the task force would be more challenging in a good way. But with a detective slot, she'd still be here in Las Playas.

Her mind was a jumble, filled with pros, cons, and all the changes available to her and the adjustments she would have to make. A new wardrobe. A new daytime schedule. A new partner. But maybe it was time. Time to think about a new career direction, maybe starting a family . . .

"Ah." She gave an involuntary shudder and sat up straight. The officer next to her raised an eyebrow, but she just shook her head.

I cannot wrap my mind around having a kid.

"Okay, everyone listen up." Sergeant

Barrett brought the squad meeting to order and Carly's thoughts shifted.

"The Oceans First people have been quiet today, which is good because things are tense in the field right now over the shooting. There was a no-hit drive-by on Ninth Street earlier with the suspects still outstanding. We've had an upsurge in fight calls with one beating of a Playboy that resulted in a broken arm. There's also been a boatload of tagging going on. Marshall from gangs is here to update everyone on the situation."

Fernando Marshall traded places with Barrett. He was a slim black man who'd been on the gang detail almost as long as Mickey T. Nick had told Carly that Nando, as he was called, had a lot of street smarts and a great rapport with most of the known gang members in the city.

The gang detail normally worked afternoon shift, 4 p.m. to 2 a.m. Gangs were creatures of the darkness. But in order to have coverage twenty-four hours a day, Nick had flexed everyone into three shifts. While Nick was home sleeping, Nando was in charge. Only one sergeant and six officers staffed the gang squad, so Nick's new schedule ensured there were at least two officers on at all times.

"Okay, here's the update," Nando said. Carly knew the update because her husband had told her, but she gave Nick's colleague her undivided attention.

"We contacted ATF about the guns recovered in the Victor last night. They are more than happy to try to raise the serial numbers. If they can, we'll be one step closer to getting to the bottom of this gang war."

"At least all that firepower is off the streets," someone chimed in from the back of the room, and there was a lot of murmured agreement.

Nando agreed and continued. "We need to get these kids off the street if possible, give passions a chance to cool off. If you find bangers with warrants, pick 'em up. If the banger is a minor and curfew applies, go for it. And they keep trying to set up a memorial. The crime scene has been cleared, but they can't get through the gate to set up there. They've picked the Marina Access Way bridge into the Catalina Shores for the flowers and candles. We want to nip that in the bud. Stop them and send them home. If stuff is left, dispose of it. All we need is a spot where people can gather and become targets."

Muffled conversations sprouted when Nando finished and the meeting ended.

Everyone was on edge.

Carly found a car and began the preshift inspection. Working alone meant she wouldn't be too aggressive unless she was working in conjunction with another unit. Graveyard shift typically fielded eight to ten officers in a mixture of one- and two-officer cars for the whole city. Tonight, because of the situation, there were five two-officer cars, Carly, and the gang unit. She decided she didn't mind being alone on this particular night. There was a lot on her mind and she wanted to think. She planned to listen to the radio and pick a pair of officers to follow around.

Right out of the gate, she heard Flanagan and Lopez on the radio requesting a female officer to assist with a search. This was the overlap time, and the afternoon units were still busy. Flanagan and Lopez were stopped on the Marina Access Way ramp, so Carly figured they had interrupted a memorial builder. She answered and made her way to the access ramp to help.

She pulled in behind the flashing ambers and activated her lights as she got out of the car. They'd stopped a beat-up Chevy, currently illuminated with their spotlights. Lopez was talking to an adult male with his hands on the hood of the black-and-white while Flanagan stood watching three individuals seated on the curb behind the unit. He nodded as Carly approached.

She looked over the threesome — two girls, probably late teens, and a boy Carly doubted was a teen yet. She almost laughed when she saw the scowl on his face. He was trying so hard to look mean, it was comical. All the individuals were dressed in Ninja gang attire, which was black everything.

"Officer Edwards, do you mind checking these young ladies for weapons?" Flanagan asked.

"Not at all." As she stepped onto the curb, she saw the flowers, candles, and makeshift memorials on the sidewalk.

She motioned for the first girl to stand.

"I don't got nothing," she said in a petulant, irritated tone.

"I'd like to check that for myself. Turn around and put your hands on your head and interlace your fingers."

The girl complied reluctantly, and Carly reached out to grip the interlaced fingers with her right hand. "Do you have anything on you that's sharp, that might poke me?" she asked as she began the pat down.

"No."

"No guns, knives, or hand grenades?"

That got a derisive snort, but the girl

relaxed and Carly completed the pat down, finding nothing. She repeated the process with the second girl, who was a little less angry.

By the time she finished, Lopez was cuffing the adult male. After he put him in the backseat, he stepped back to confer with Flanagan and Carly. "The driver is unlicensed, and he has a couple of warrants. The rest are all curfew violations."

Duncan Potter appeared on the other side of the bridge, snapping photos. Carly did her best to keep her back to him. He lived on a boat in the marina, and anytime she was anywhere near the marina, he appeared quickly.

Flanagan cocked his eyebrow and looked at her.

"Just ignore him," she said.

He grinned. "We can't mix adult bookings with juvies."

Carly chuckled. "I don't feel like booking all three of them. I'll just take them home unless you think they need to be booked."

Both officers shook their heads. "That's fine with us," Lopez said. "All they were doing was making themselves targets."

"Okay. I'll need to borrow a set of cuffs."

Policy said handcuffs were needed for anyone transported in the black-and-white.

Most officers, like Carly, carried two sets. Flanagan offered one of his sets. She probably could have justified not handcuffing the three juveniles, but since there was only one of her and they were all wannabe gangsters, handcuffs it would be. She would file RNB paperwork on them and release them to the custody of their parents.

Flanagan gave Carly the field interview cards he'd written on the trio. The girls were sisters, so that was easy enough. But the name on the card for the boy gave her a start.

Victor Macias. He was Crusher's little brother.

After releasing the girls to a mother who couldn't care less, Carly headed for Victor's house. "Sorry about your brother Hector."

Victor mumbled something she didn't quite hear.

"What?"

"Where were the cops when he got capped? You don't care."

She clicked her teeth. "I know your brother, Victor, and I care. He's a good kid caught up with bad people. We'll catch who did this."

The boy cursed. "Ain't counting on you. Only his homeys care, and I'm gonna help

114

with payback."

"Payback won't help your brother."

He cursed again, this time more colorfully. "Sure it will. When he wakes up, the first thing I'll tell him is the dudes who shot him are dead. Make him smile."

Carly bit her tongue, surprised at the venom in the ten-year-old's voice but not really knowing why she was surprised. He was a kid of the streets, living in the middle of a gang neighborhood. For the remainder of the ride to his house, she prayed for Victor and his brother.

10

Carly had barely pulled away from the curb at Victor's house when she got a call.

"1-Adam-2, copy a 925 auto, observed out on Seaside Point. CP was a passerby."

Carly acknowledged the call and turned her vehicle toward the coast. A suspicious vehicle on Seaside Point was not all that unusual. Seaside Avenue ran along a jetty and ended at a turnaround on the point that jutted out between the mouth of the marina and the beach. There was a bathroom out there, spots for people to fish, and three boat slips for visiting boats. This time of night on the weekends it often became a parking spot for couples.

Marina patrol officers used to patrol the point and the marina 24-7. But the most recent city budget had slashed the marina patrol in half. As a result, they policed the marina only until dusk and then the area became the responsibility of the police department. With the imminent opening of the new marina and increased commerce and crowds, the city council wanted a reinforced police presence in the marina.

The drive down to the point was pleasant, especially since there was no fog tonight. And she chose to ignore the protestors. While she passed the camp at Sandy Park, it sounded as if they were having a concert of drums. The sound followed her the entire drive.

Off to her left were the lights of the Hacienda, and to the right, the harbor lights. Far in the distance, buoy lights blinked at the mouth of the harbor. It was no surprise to Carly that couples liked to park out here. It was dark, beautiful, and quiet, and the sound of surf breaking on the rocks gave the illusion of being out in the middle of the ocean.

When she reached the turnaround, her headlights illuminated the taillights of a boxy Land Rover. Stopping behind the SUV, she put her car in park, turned on her spotlight, and pointed it to shine directly into the other vehicle. For a minute she waited to see if someone climbed out. The bright spot would definitely destroy any romantic interlude.

She couldn't see any movement or reaction to the light, so she punched the license plate number into the computer to find out who owned the vehicle and whether or not it was stolen. DMV records told her the car belonged to Keith Sailor. There were no reports that it had been stolen. Carly frowned as she pondered the name. If she remembered correctly, he owned a catering company that was catering the bridge dedication. Picking up the mike, she told dispatch she'd be out of the car to check on the vehicle.

Carly grabbed her flashlight and stood for a minute behind her open car door to survey the rest of the point. There were no other vehicles, no boats in the visitor slips, and she didn't hear any voices. Sometimes people rode bikes along the jetty road, so there could be someone fishing, but she didn't hear anything except the rhythmic drumming coming from Oceans First. She glanced behind her and noted that not even Duncan Potter was stalking her out here.

Clicking on her flashlight, she illuminated the parking area and what she could see of the bathrooms. Satisfied she was alone, she closed the car door and approached the Land Rover.

Habit had her unsnapping her gun as a precaution. With the beam of her flashlight adding to the bright light of the spot, Carly slowly moved toward the vehicle. The rear windows were tinted and the light simply reflected back at her.

The front driver's window was cracked open about two inches. Carly shone her light directly in.

Between the bright spotlight reflecting in the rearview mirror and the powerful beam of the Streamlight flashlight, Carly saw the body slumped over from the driver's seat across the center console and onto the passenger seat. She called out but knew the person couldn't hear her.

Stepping close on her tiptoes, she also saw that there was no rise and fall of the chest. The waxy cast to the skin and the dried blood told her the person was dead and had been for at least a few hours.

"The ID here says that this is Keith Sailor," Georgia, the coroner's investigator, said as she looked through the victim's wallet. "But the damage to his face from the gunshot means you'll have to wait for a positive ID through prints."

"That's the caterer, right?" Carly asked with a yawn. She was standing a safe distance away from the SUV. She'd had to wait three hours for Georgia's arrival and was groggy after sitting in her car with only the police radio for company during that time.

Unlike the triple shooting of a couple nights ago, it was obvious this one was self-inflicted. As to the second shooting this week, it never ceased to amaze Carly how things seemed to run in packs — shootings, stolen cars, domestic disputes, drunk drivers . . . It seemed like when they got one, several more of the same would follow.

"Yep, he owned Sailor's Catering. You know, where everything is smooth sailing? They were in the news last month because he beat out the Hacienda for the contract to cater the bridge dedication." Georgia was the only county coroner's investigator that Carly knew who lived in Las Playas.

"That's what I thought." She'd read the newspaper article, not because she cared about the catering, but because the pedestrian bridge dedication ceremony seemed to be getting bigger all the time and all the hoopla made her more nervous about the award presentation. And it reminded her how close the Burke trial was.

Georgia slid the wallet into a possessions envelope. "Strange that after the biggest coup of his catering career he'd commit suicide."

"I ran the scenario by Sergeant Barrett

and he called homicide. They declined to respond. Do I need to call them back?"

Georgia shrugged. "No, this is self-inflicted. Gun still in his hand — that happens sometimes — and the car was locked, keys in the ignition. Once we remove the body, we may find a note." She rubbed her nose with the back of her wrist. "There might have been other stuff going on in his life. I don't see anything here that would make me think this was staged or anything other than a suicide."

Carly agreed. She'd had to use a slim jim to open the door, and she'd looked carefully for any indication that the man had had help ending his life. She found nothing. The absence of a note was not in and of itself suspicious. He might have left a note at his home.

She left Georgia and her assistant to remove the body from the vehicle. This single call would consume Carly's entire shift by the time she filed all the needed paperwork. After Georgia left with the body, she would have to wait again for a tow truck to remove the SUV.

On her way back to the station, the radio began to get busy. Nick had sent her a text at five thirty saying he was on his way to work and would not be able to meet her that morning. Now, it was seven thirty and she heard his voice asking for the watch commander.

In the station parking lot she used the computer to pull up his designator, Gang-Sam-1, and find out what was going on. He and Mickey were following a tip about more guns, and they wanted a search warrant deep in Ninja territory.

Carly said a prayer that they'd be careful and move closer to learning what was behind the shooting and to arresting a suspect.

11

Carly slept fitfully, waking up several times, hoping to find Nick next to her. But he didn't come home, and when she woke up to get ready for work, she was still in an empty house except for Maddie. After a lot of scratching and a hug, she fed the dog and wondered about Nick. Since he hadn't been home all day, she guessed that meant he'd found some leads to follow.

She grabbed her police radio from the charger and took it into the kitchen to listen to what was going on in the city while she munched. There was a fresh loaf of bread on the counter and apples in the fruit bowl. Carly took an apple and then smiled when she opened the refrigerator. She didn't know when he'd found the time, but Nick had obviously been to the market. Deciding on a ham and cheese sandwich, she bit into the apple and began to pull out the necessary items and put them on the counter.

When her phone rang, she saw it was Andrea and punched the speakerphone.

"Hey, Andi, what's up?" she asked, mouth full of apple.

"Glad you are. I talked to Alex earlier, and he told me something disturbing."

"So you called to disturb me with it?" She set the apple down and started putting her sandwich together.

"Well, it concerns you, so I thought you should know. It seems the reporter who is covering for him doesn't like you."

Carly finished making the sandwich and sat at the table. "I don't even know him." She bit into the sandwich.

"It's not a him; it's a her. Does the name Ginny Masters ring a bell?"

Carly frowned and swallowed. "Sort of . . . Wait, isn't that the woman Alex calls the 'dragon lady'?"

"The same. Only he calls her worse things than that. Anyway, apparently you've offended her in some way. It's all over her blog. She claims that you're biased and you profile people unfairly. She's asking for people to contact her if they've dealt with you and had their rights violated. She doesn't think your testimony can be trusted in court."

"What?" The sandwich stopped halfway

to Carly's mouth as her appetite fled and her stomach turned with an unpleasant feeling.

"She was laid off from the *Times* — that's why she's just a fill-in at the *Messenger* — and she wants to get a bigger and better job by breaking a big story. Alex was afraid if he turned his back on her, he'd find a knife in it, so he's been keeping track of her, following the blog. Anyway, you know how big stories about police corruption or misconduct are."

Carly set the sandwich down and wiped her hands on a napkin. "I don't know what to say. I don't even know her. Why is she picking on me?"

"Alex thinks it's because of all the awards he got for his stories about the mayor's murder and your role in uncovering the corruption. Face it — you're the star witness in what is going to probably be the biggest trial ever in Las Playas. Alex has been subpoenaed to testify as well, and he thinks she wants to blow the both of you out of the water, make him look incompetent and you dirty."

"But why? She wants to weaken the case against one of the most corrupt men ever arrested in Las Playas?"

"She wants a national news organization

to take notice of her investigative reporting and thinks this will do it. Look, check out the blog." She gave Carly the URL. "I know she can say just about anything, and there's nothing you can do unless you can prove damages, but maybe something is over the line and the department will make her stop."

Andrea's words brought to mind the warning Alex had given her a few months ago, when Masters first began to work for the *Messenger.*

"She's got designs on my job, but she only wants to use it as a stepping stone," he'd said. "She wants to break a sensational story that will get her some national attention and give her a ticket to some national gig. She thinks she has an angle. Instead of America's most wanted criminals, she wants a national show devoted to exposing America's most corrupt cops. And she's not above stirring the pot, setting things up. Watch your back."

At the time Carly had been basking in a honeymoon glow, and she laughed. The idea sounded so absurd, she hadn't really taken the warning seriously. She and Nick were perfect, so the world must be too. What a jarring fall back to earth.

"I'll check it out; thanks."

"Sure thing."

Carly said good-bye and hung up, then

took a deep breath before she went into the living room and pulled out her Mac. She remembered when Alex Trejo used to write horrible things about the police in general and her specifically. But they'd been through some scrapes together and had gotten to know one another, and now she considered him a good friend. What was the problem with this Masters woman?

Carly didn't spend much time on the computer or Internet unless she was searching for something work-related. She heard people talk about blogs and social networking and knew Andrea and Alex both loved chatting online. She even read Alex's blog from time to time. But recreation for both her and Nick was something active, something outside in the sun or the water. Being stuck in front of a screen was not where she liked to spend her free time. Alex often teased that she and Nick were stuck in the past and that the technical age was whizzing by them, but Carly never felt like she was missing anything, so the computer only came out to serve a purpose.

When the Mac fired up, she punched in the URL Andrea had given her. As soon as the page loaded, she saw what the problem was and felt like she'd been kicked in the gut.

Ginny Masters was the blonde who'd been with Dean Barton.

"But there must be something we can do to stop her! She's trying to make people believe that I'm a rogue, out-of-control cop! It's as if she wants to poison the jury pool or something."

Sergeant Barrett seemed too quiet and read a little too slowly as he sipped his coffee.

Carly had read through the blog posts three times and gotten angrier each time. Masters brought up every major incident in Carly's career and twisted them to make her look shady. In Carly's first officer-involved shooting, her partner that night, Derek Potter, killed an unarmed man. Carly had been cleared of any wrongdoing. But months later she shot and killed Derek Potter after he tried to bash her head in with a bat. Masters made that sequence of incidents look as though Potter was going to spill the beans about something and Carly killed him to shut him up.

In Carly's next big case, she arrested real estate mogul Conrad Sperry and Thomas Caswell, a prominent defense attorney. Again Masters twisted the incident, asking with a snarky tone, *Just why would a cop want to get rid of an effective defense attorney?*

By the time Carly reached the entries about her "cold-blooded persecution" of Dean Barton, a man trying to turn his unlucky life around, she had nearly thrown up. There was even an unflattering photo in the latest blog entry of Carly handcuffing Victor Macias, making her look like a big blue meanie. Carly knew it was one Duncan Potter had snapped. That was the last straw. Masters's poison pen was one thing, but hooking up with Potter took this to a whole different level.

"I don't know what we can do," Barrett said finally. "It's just a blog. Who knows how many people even read this stuff."

"But it's obvious she's trying to make me look bad, stopping just short of saying I framed Drake and Tucker when I was the guilty one. Look at how she twists everything."

"I see it, but we both know it's nonsense. So will anyone else who knows you. She'll just come off as a crank."

"But can't we stop her?" Carly hated to hear herself whine, but the stuff in the blog was much worse than anything Alex Trejo had ever written about her.

"I don't know how. Maybe in the morning you can go to the DA and ask if he thinks there's a legal step he can take. You're his star witness." He shrugged. "Why do you think she's picking on you?"

Carly crossed her arms. "Remember the memo I filed? She was with Dean Barton at Half Baked. I think that may have something to do with it."

"The parolee?" Barrett made a face. "What in the world would a good-looking woman like this see in that guy?"

Shaking her head, Carly picked up her kit and turned for the squad room, wanting to snipe that the woman was not that good-looking and probably wasn't even a real blonde. What she said instead was, "I have no idea."

Carly fumed during the squad meeting, barely hearing the watch report. She'd missed connecting with Nick; he'd been asked to confer with some ATF agents in Los Angeles, which could mean there was news about the guns. Even in her bad mood she had to admit that to get something back this soon was great news. She wasn't going to call and interrupt a meeting like that. When the squad meeting ended, she picked up her kit and stood, only to find herself facing FBI agent Wiley.

"G-man, we've got to stop meeting like this."

"Officer Edwards, while it's good to see you again, I'm actually here about the guns you found. Can you chat with me for a minute?"

Carly looked at the clock and shrugged. "Sure."

Today they sat in the break room.

"How's Joe?"

"He'll need surgery."

"Ooh, sorry to hear that. I was hoping it wouldn't be so serious." Wiley made a sympathetic face. "So you're solo tonight."

"Yeah, so what about the guns?"

"Las Playas requested ATF help with the guns. I just wanted to know if there is anything else, maybe not in the report, that you can tell me about Trey Porter."

"Not really. He's a local thug. Just about everyone in patrol knows him. Usually he's the passenger in a stolen car or he's in possession of a car stereo that doesn't belong to him. Why?"

"The weapons were military grade. How does a local thug get ahold of military-grade weapons?"

"Good question." Her heart raced a bit as she realized Nick was front and center trying to answer that question.

"If there's nothing more you can tell me, I'll let you get to work. And again, you did a great job. Have you given any more thought to the task force offer?"

Carly leaned back and sighed. "I scanned the information, but I haven't made up my mind."

"You're without a partner. Might that make the decision easier?"

"I'm just not sure what I want to do. Do you need an answer right now?"

Wiley shook his head. "I wanted to lobby. Car stops like the one that uncovered stolen guns show that you're competent and aggressive. The task force can use you." He stood. "Remember that this is a unique career opportunity — maybe once in a lifetime — and I'd love to see you on board."

The unique career opportunity did occupy her thoughts, and she found herself thankful for the distraction. But Wiley's visit also made the blog posts rankle her more. Would the feds want her if they saw all that horrible stuff on the reporter's blog?

Every time she looked at the passenger seat, she missed Joe. He would have been a good sounding board and might have even offered some good advice. Being without a partner made Carly doubly glad it was her

Friday. This set of four ten-hour shifts in her workweek had been horrible, and she needed the weekend to regroup.

The night crawled by. She received a text from Nick about 2 a.m. He was home to sleep but on call in case anything went down. Knowing there was nothing worse than a whiny text, Carly told him she loved him, missed him, and wished him sweet dreams.

When her shift ended, after she'd changed, Carly picked up two flyers for detective details looking for new personnel to see what competed with the task force offer. She'd decided on vice and narcotics and then grabbed a flyer for violent crimes as well. The first two details would have erratic schedules; they wouldn't be straight day shifts. Carly wanted to talk over all her options with Nick.

The task force is by far the most attractive job for a lot of reasons, but am I prepared to see less of Nick? That thought almost made her want to toss the task force information in the trash. She wanted a job that would allow her to see more of him. But the thought of the excitement and challenge the task force promised would not let her throw it out. Instead, she considered her other choices. If she decided on detectives, she could talk to Joe. Maybe they could be assigned to the same detail.

As she climbed into her car, she sighed, glad the process of thinking about a new job had kept her mind off Ginny Masters for at least two minutes. With a huff, Carly closed her eyes and prayed, a little ashamed it had taken her this long. Her knee-jerk response to the woman was to get in her face, to square off with angry accusations. But didn't that make the blog posts ring true? Didn't that make Carly a rogue, out-of-control cop?

She knew the Bible spoke of a soft answer turning away wrath. And she knew that the woman's posts were untrue. What she didn't know was how to calm down and let Masters's vendetta roll off her back. She didn't know how to find her soft answer. But Barrett was right — Carly and everyone who knew her would know the accusations were untrue. *So, God, can you help me here?*

After a few minutes she felt better. Then her phone buzzed.

YOU COMING HOME?

Carly texted back she was on her way and didn't even wait for an answer before she started the car. She wanted a hug and she wanted Nick.

12

Carly could tell by Nick's face that he had news. "What?" she asked after she dropped her kit and stepped into his arms for a hug that lasted a fraction of the time she wanted.

"ATF was able to raise a couple of serial numbers." His eyes were bright with anticipation. Finding information about the guns was huge, bringing them a step closer to finding the supplier.

"This soon?" Carly sat on the couch. She noticed Nick's kit by the door; it was the one he used when serving warrants and kicking in doors.

He sat on the coffee table facing her, fidgeting with excitement. "The amount and type of guns we found set off an alert. They've been looking for a batch of guns stolen from an Army reserve base in Arizona about six months ago. A guard was killed."

Carly's brow creased. She was tired and this news was difficult to process. "A theft like that from the Army? How?"

"One of the agents here told me it was well planned and executed. They thought a Mexican drug cartel was behind it, at least with financing. The crooks had night-vision goggles and everything. But it wasn't just guns that disappeared. A quantity of plastic explosive went missing as well."

"Plastic explosive?" Carly sat back, her eyes wide.

Nick nodded. "Enough plastic explosive to take down a large building. The feds now fear that the thieves were domestic terrorists. Since the guns have turned up here, they think the explosives are here as well."

"But why Las Playas? What high-value target would there be for domestic terrorists . . . ?" She stopped when she remembered Oceans First.

Nick read her mind. "Yeah, they think Oceans First might be involved."

"But they aren't big enough — or bright enough, for that matter — to rip off an Army base. And what would they blow up? What would they gain?"

"There are multiple targets in the harbor. They could also pick the new marina. Or it might not even be Las Playas. They could be here because of the close proximity to the Los Angeles harbor. Maybe they just want to make a point." He shrugged, and Carly knew he had as many doubts as she had. But he needed to be positive Oceans First wasn't involved before he crossed the group off the list. "This wouldn't be the first time some radical environmentalists went too far. Remember that guy a couple years ago who was setting fires to SUVs?"

Carly nodded. He'd burned two Hummers in Las Playas and a whole bunch more in San Diego, protesting gas guzzlers.

Nick continued. "Mickey and I have been teamed up with a couple of ATF agents. We're going to be serving warrants and checking out every spot in the harbor here and in LA that might be a target. And tentatively, we'll be flying to Arizona to review things at the base. Fernando is in charge while I'm working with the feds. ATF is also adding agents to help with the gang situation here. They're hot to find out who gave the guns to Trey and to speak to any gangster who will talk." He gripped both of her hands in his. "I made arrangements for Cooper to cover my weaponless defense classes. I may not be around much this weekend."

Carly's disappointment bit deep. But seeing the excitement in the deep blue of her husband's eyes made her think before she spoke. Squeezing his hands, she said, "Will you be here for church Sunday?"

"I'll do my best, and I'll call you whenever I have a chance." He leaned forward and kissed her.

She wanted to grab him and hold on. When the kiss ended, he stroked her cheek and smiled. "You know I'll pop in when I can, but this is big, babe. We have to find the explosives. We'll be saving lives."

"I know." She threw her arms around his neck. "You just be careful, Sergeant Anderson," she whispered in his ear. "That's an order." She felt him smile and pulled back to look into his eyes.

"Yes, boss." He kissed her one more time, picked up his equipment duffel, and was gone.

Carly bit back a yawn as she stood in the sand, contemplating the surf, Maddie sitting at her feet. Nick's car was pulling out of the driveway before she'd realized she hadn't told him about the offending blog posts or Wiley's second visit. It was just as well. She wanted him focused on his job and his safety, not her complaints or dilemmas.

Dropping her towel, she told Maddie to stay and headed into the waves. In spite of the fact she wasn't training for anything in particular, she swam hard. As she churned out the first mile, it occurred to her that she should decide on something to train for, some goal to work toward. She rarely let a lot of time go between competitions, but her last big race had been the Maui Channel Swim months ago while on her honeymoon. The 9.5-mile swim had been a wonderful challenge, and she had finished with a respectable time. But it had also taken a lot out of her. The current had been tough, and she was stung numerous times by jellyfish. She'd felt sick and swollen for two days after the race.

Nick suggested she just enjoy swimming for fun for a while before thinking about the next race, the next challenge. He'd also tossed out the idea of training for a triathlon, and then they could do a lot more training together.

Carly gave that some thought. She liked to run and had no doubt she could train for a triathlon, but her bottom had an expiration time when it came to sitting on a bike, so she wasn't sure a fifty-plus-mile bike ride was in the realm of possibility. Still, it might be fun to train at all three sports with Nick. Talk about together time.

Right now, one of her days off was spent

volunteering at the local YMCA, teaching swim lessons to disadvantaged children. Carly liked the kids and loved teaching. If she decided to train for something competitive, she'd have to give that up.

She'd have to give that up and probably a lot more training time if she joined the task force. Carly pounded the water harder to clear her mind.

Once finished, she sat on her towel letting the sun dry her off. The water had worked its magic and the prick of Masters's blog had lessened to a tiny annoyance. She prayed again, asking for perspective and wisdom about both Masters and Dean Barton.

She prayed for Nick, too, a niggling fear still in the back of her mind. Oceans First was annoying and vocal, but they had never physically hurt anyone. Guns and explosives just didn't fit that equation.

13

Carly slept for about six hours and then met Andrea for dinner. She declared the subject of Ginny Masters off-limits, leaning on an academy training principle that officers were targets, but they were to react professionally to taunts and name-calling. She'd faced angry crowds before and heard many aspersions tossed her way. This was no different, and she'd have to leave Ginny Masters — and Dean Barton, for that matter — in the locker room with her uniform. *Don't take it personally.*

"Agent Wiley came to talk to you twice in person?" Andrea raised an eyebrow and looked at Carly. "He wants you on that task force."

"Well, the second time he came to ask about Trey and the guns."

"Still."

"It would be a great opportunity, an exciting gig, but . . ."

"Nick."

"Don't say it that way. I already feel like I don't get enough time with him. Especially with him being on gangs now. And he's adjusted his weaponless defense schedule not to interfere with our time together. How can I take a job that will take me away from him more often?"

"It wouldn't be forever. Has he said he doesn't want you to take it?"

"No, but we've only had a short time to sit and talk about it. The truth is, I don't know what I want — much less what he wants. I would have been happy to work with Joe in a black-and-white forever." Carly drained her coffee and then refilled it from the carafe on the table.

"You have time. You don't have to decide right now."

"That's true. By the way, when do you think Alex will be home?" she asked as the waitress set dessert in front of them. They were at Ruby's on the end of the Huntington Beach pier. Every so often, the floor shuddered as an ocean swell rolled beneath them.

Andrea gave a long-suffering sigh. "I hope soon. I miss him. But his dad is really having a difficult time coping with the loss. Alex is afraid he'll hurt himself the first chance he gets."

"Has he thought about moving his dad down here?"

"Briefly, but he's never been close to his dad, so —" she shrugged — "he's just at a loss."

Carly smiled.

"What?"

"You really like him, don't you?"

Andrea did something Carly couldn't remember ever seeing her do: she blushed. "I do; I do. I never, ever thought I could like any guy this much." She put her elbows on the table and rested her chin in her hands. "There's never any games with Alex. He says what he thinks. I never have to guess with him or . . ." Her voice trailed off.

Carly finished for her. "Play games yourself?"

Andi laughed. "You know me too well. Guys used to be a game for me, just a way to pass the time." The smile faded. "I don't want to toy with Alex, and it's scary."

"Don't worry," Carly said with a wave of her hand. "If he hurts you, I'll just shoot him, and he knows that."

They both burst out laughing and then finished their meal.

■ ■ ■ ■

Carly saw Nick briefly on Friday, when he came home around 3 a.m., slept for a couple of hours, then showered and left again. They'd discovered that besides offices on the coast, Oceans First also had an office in Arizona, so his trip to Arizona was confirmed. The ATF was set to serve warrants on the Phoenix office, and he was going along for the ride. He wouldn't be back until late Saturday but planned to be at church on Sunday.

There was movement on the protestor front as well. An appeals court judge had ruled for the city and given the okay to evict them from the park. The city and the PD were now working to determine how to evict them in a manner that would lessen the chance of violent confrontation. Carly and her shift had been given notice that they might be called in on overtime to assist.

"Things have been quiet in Las Playas as far as the gang stuff is concerned," Nick said over coffee before he left Friday.

Carly had been listening to her radio and had come to that conclusion herself. She was glad Nick agreed.

"But Harris told me that the coroner has

released Rojo and D.'s bodies for burial. One funeral is set for Sunday, the other for sometime next week, so we may have problems then. Jacobs has canceled all holidays and unscheduled vacation, anticipating needing extra hands for both the eviction and the funeral. Have you thought any more about your next career move?"

Carly shook her head. "No, I've been trying not to think about work this weekend." She told him about Wiley's second visit.

"They want you," he said with a tilt of his head. "You should be flattered."

She studied him, still not able to read him. "I am, I guess. But that makes it hard to say no."

"Are you sure you want to say no? I've been thinking a lot about it. Since I'm working with the feds on an impromptu task force, I'm getting a small taste of what they're offering you."

Carly raised her eyebrows. "Do you want me to take it?"

Now she saw conflicted emotions cross his face. "I still need to read the information. At first, I would have said no because it would mean a lot of time away from home. But if the shoe were on the other foot, I'd jump at the opportunity. Everything you do with them will be cutting-edge. It won't be a permanent gig in any event. Bottom line, I want my wife to be happy and certain that she's where God wants her."

"Aw . . ." She grabbed him in a hug, loving the feel of his strong arms around her. "I don't know what I want. Thanks for reminding me to pray for what God wants. I did pick up some flyers for detective division openings."

"Really?" His face registered surprise. "So that's something you're considering as well?"

"Yeah, my incredibly intelligent and good-looking husband made the suggestion, and after I considered it, I decided it was a good one."

He took her hand, brought it to his lips, and kissed her palm. "Whatever you choose, it's time. You need a change. Which openings are you looking at?"

"I picked up three flyers. We can talk about it on Sunday."

He nodded and looked at his watch. "Sorry to be leaving again, but I am learning so much from the feds. This experience has been very illuminating."

"Since you like it so much, are you thinking of going federal?" Carly asked.

"No, I love working in Las Playas. But I will take the next lieutenant test when it comes around. I like the idea of running the whole show. I think I could do a good job."

"I know you could."

He smiled the smile that always melted her heart. "Walk me out?"

Together they walked to the front door, arms around one another. At the door they shared a tight hug, and then Nick prayed for both of them and the investigation. Carly added prayers for safety and wisdom.

"I love you," Nick whispered in her ear.

Carly watched his car until it disappeared from view, feeling his warm breath on her ear for the rest of the day.

Friday was Carly's swim class day at the Y. She was a little apprehensive this particular Friday because the eight ten-year-olds in her class were from gang neighborhoods. They were almost entirely divided between Ninjas and Playboyz.

But thankfully the ten-year-olds were more interested in the water than in any gang disputes. And she had unexpected help: Londy showed up in his bathing suit. He was talking to Mary Ellen when Carly arrived. She was used to seeing Mary Ellen at the Y; the girl was required to do a certain number of hours of supervised community service as part of her conditions of probation and fulfilled some of them by helping with a senior citizens' water class. But Londy was a surprise — welcome, but a surprise nonetheless.

The children were doing well. They could float, swim one lap across the pool, hold their breath underwater, and do reasonable dives from one knee. Most important to Carly, they were all having fun and they weren't afraid of the water. The boys respected Londy, and his help and encouragement brought some big smiles. When they were finished, Carly decided to thank him with lunch, and she asked Mary Ellen to join them.

"Thanks, Officer Edwards," Londy said as they hopped into Carly's car for the trip to Taco Surf. No matter what Carly said, she couldn't get Londy to call her anything but *officer*.

"Thank you for showing up today. Those kids loved your help."

"I like kids. That was fun. I'm trying to get Victor, Crusher's little brother, to come learn to swim." He looked out the window.

Carly could tell something else was on his mind, but she'd learned that Londy usually had to work up to what he had to say. He was always thoughtful, always thorough. She figured chips and salsa would loosen his tongue.

"I like helping at the Y," Mary Ellen said. "It's the best part of my community service. It's not work; it's fun."

Once they were seated and eating their tacos and chips, Carly nudged Londy. "So what's on your mind? You worried about the funerals? Crusher?"

He gave a small smile. "You can tell I'm worried?"

"Sure, I'm a trained observer. What's up?"

"I am worried about the funerals. I don't want to see anyone else get hurt. And Crusher . . . well, he's doing better." He looked at Mary Ellen.

She smiled. "They did surgery to stop the bleeding in his head and it worked. He's getting better, and they hope he'll wake up."

"Really? That's good news." Carly felt a little guilty that she'd been so busy she hadn't taken the time to check up on Crusher, and she was surprised to hear good news. At least she hoped it was good news. Crusher would never be the same, no matter what.

"That's what I wanted to talk to you about," Londy said. "I've been talking to Victor a lot. I figure the little brother would know what Crusher was up to more than the mama would, you know?"

Carly nodded, remembering her encounter with the ten-year-old. "I met Victor."

"Here's the thing: he wants to be a Ninja. Always wearing the colors. I tell him it's bad, but he don't listen. He claims he knows who shot Crusher and he's gonna kill 'em."

14

"What?" Carly set her taco down and pushed the plate away. Londy was serious, and she assumed Victor was too.

"Victor copies everything Crusher does. Even when Crusher wouldn't let him, he followed him around. He saw Crusher talking with some dudes."

"Back up, Londy. When was this?"

"About a week before he was shot. Victor says Crusher left the house late at night, and he followed him to the train. They both got on and rode to where it ends at the transit mall. Then Crusher walked down to Seaside, to where there's a building all fenced off. I figure he meant the Bluestone. Anyway, he squeezed through a hole in the fence and Victor followed. Crusher was all by himself; he didn't even have Rojo with him. He met these guys who gave him drugs to sell. Victor heard one of them tell Crusher he didn't want Trey or anyone knowing.

And he heard the guy asking if he was sure no one knew he was coming to the meeting."

"Did Victor tell you what the guy looked like?"

Londy nodded and then shifted in his chair, all of a sudden looking uncomfortable. "There were three guys, all white dudes. One dude never said anything, and Victor didn't get a very good look at him. The other two . . . well, one had a beard and the third . . ."

"What, Londy? What did the other guy look like?"

"You know how in the Bible it says not to falsely accuse people? I didn't see this; I'm just saying what Victor said. The third guy . . . well, Victor said he was ugly, that his face was scarred and his ear half–chewed off. That could be Mr. Barton's brother."

Carly brought a hand to her mouth, as much from shock as to keep from saying something she shouldn't. That Dean Barton could be giving kids drugs to sell didn't surprise her. That there was a possibility he killed two kids did. But she had to stop. What if this was just wishful thinking on her part? She thought of the man who'd been waiting for Barton at the white van the first night she saw him. He had a beard, and she remembered now that he'd looked familiar. But she hadn't really gotten a good look at him.

She changed her line of questioning. "Why does Victor think these guys who were giving his brother drugs are the same ones who shot him?"

"Because they shot Rojo and D., too. Victor thinks Crusher told Rojo and D. something he wasn't supposed to and the white dudes shot them all."

Carly considered his logic, or rather the logic Londy was relating that came from a ten-year-old boy. *Why would these men pick someone like Crusher from the Ninjas in Las Playas to sell drugs for them and then insist it be kept secret from the rest of the gang? And then when Crusher lets something slip, they shoot three gang members? It's plausible they'd try to cover up the murder by making it look like a gang shooting. But in covering it up, they also wanted to start a gang war?* She rubbed her temples. None of this made sense. She was missing something important.

Lunch turned into an interview as Carly grilled Londy for every bit of information he'd gotten from Victor.

"Did Victor say how long Crusher knew these guys?" Carly struggled to remember her last contact with Crusher and realized he'd been under the radar for a while, maybe two or three months.

"I asked him that. He said Crusher's been squirrelly for about a month — you know, disappearing till early in the morning, then showing up with cash. He gave Victor an iPod Touch. Only Victor can't show it to his mom 'cause she don't want nothing in the house that was bought with drug money."

"How did Crusher meet them?"

Londy shook his head. "Don't know. Victor says he tried a couple of times to follow Crusher and got caught or ditched."

Carly finished her Diet Coke and thought for a minute. "Someone from gangs will have to talk to him," she told Londy.

"He don't like police. He won't talk. He wants to take Crusher's place in the gang, thinks it will make him a man."

Carly knew thinking like that was prevalent in Victor's neighborhood. And she remembered his attitude when she had him in the back of the patrol car.

"We've both tried to talk to him," Mary Ellen spoke up. She'd been so quiet Carly had almost forgotten she was there. "I've spent time with his two sisters. But the gang call is so strong for Victor. He thinks it's his job to get revenge for Crusher. It's very sad."

"Sounds like you both have spent a lot of time with the family."

Heads nodded. "We want Crusher to wake up," Londy said.

"We have his little brothers and sisters write letters — you know, about what's going on in their lives," Mary Ellen continued. "As soon as we can, we want to read the letters to him."

"They'll let you in to read to him?"

"Yeah," Londy said. "His mom gave us permission. We're both over eighteen, so since Tuesday we've been able to visit and talk to him. We pray, too. This morning I asked him to squeeze my hand and I think he did. He'll wake up soon; I know it." He cast a glance at Mary Ellen, who was watching him with undisguised affection.

Carly processed their look. She certainly hadn't seen that coming.

"We think God will heal Crusher. He's alive for a reason," Mary Ellen said. "He'll wake up. And I bet he'll tell us who shot him."

Her tone was full of youthful optimism. But Carly remembered the shooting scene, remembered how she'd had to stop Crusher's bleeding, and was hard-pressed

155

to muster the same optimism.

After Carly dropped Londy and Mary Ellen off, she parked and called Peter Harris in homicide. She wanted to call Nick and almost punched in his number, but he was working with the feds and she didn't want to interrupt whatever they were doing.

Harris was in, and he listened while she relayed what Londy told her.

"I remember Victor," he said. "Londy is right; he doesn't like cops. He took the shooting the hardest, really wants to be his brother's avenger. We'll go back out there and talk to him, but I doubt he'll tell us what he told Londy. But you should know that we just had a bomb threat callout."

"What?"

"At your coffee shop, Half Baked. Bomb guys rolled out there about an hour ago."

Carly rushed to the coffee shop, only to be stopped a block away. Barriers surrounded the large black van used as the command post and kept traffic off Broadway. She leaned out of her car window and spoke to the officer at the barrier.

"They evacuated this far out?"

He nodded. "It was the real deal, not some bogus, fake device. One of the coffee shop owners found a bomb wired to the safe in the office. I think it's all code 4 now. There's just some cleanup left. I can't let you drive in until I get the all clear, but if you want to walk to the command post, I'm sure that would be okay."

She thanked him and parked her car. The command post was a block away from Apex Court, and Carly saw Ned and Erika standing outside. There were also several agents with *ATF* in big yellow letters across their jackets milling around.

"Hey," she called out to Ned.

He saw her. "Carly, thanks for coming by."

"What happened?"

Ned and Erika exchanged a glance. "I found the device," Ned said. "I worked in bomb disposal in the service, so I knew immediately what it was."

"It would have taken out the whole shop," Erika said, grabbing Ned's hand. "Ned's not the one who usually opens the safe. If I had . . ." Her voice thickened and she stopped.

Carly folded her arms, stunned. "First the newspaper stand, now this. What? Who?"

"It was Dean; I know it." Erika spit the words out.

"That would be my guess as well, but we can't prove it," Ned said with a heavy sigh.

"You told the bomb guys?"

"Yeah, even though part of me knows it was him, another part of me can't believe it. We had a falling-out the other day, right after I told you we were working things out. We've had our differences, but I'd really hoped Dean had changed." He shook his head sadly. "Obviously not if he was trying to murder me and anyone else in close proximity. And in Iraq, there was always a secondary device, so I asked the bomb guys to do a thorough inspection of the entire area. I don't want anyone to get hurt because of our feud."

Carly thanked them for the information and then went into the command post to find Captain Jacobs.

"Is there anything you can tell me?" she asked.

He leaned back in his chair. "Well, the ATF is handling everything. Since the substance they found in the device is not commonly available, they're certain the plastic explosive used here is part of the loss from Arizona, but a small part."

"So there's a lot still outstanding?"

"It's a good thing Ned Barton was the one to try to open the safe today. He saw something off and knew exactly what it was. What they have pieced together is that someone broke into the shop early this morning and set the device. Had it gone off, the whole corner would be gone."

"What about the alarm? The cameras?" Even as she asked, Carly knew that security systems could be circumvented.

Jacobs pointed to a diagram on the desk in front of him. "They have a camera at the back entrance, but the lens was spray-painted by someone wearing a ski mask. As for the alarm, it was bypassed. They don't have a state-of-the-art system; it's just a run-of-the-mill alarm."

"And Ned thinks his brother did this."

"Yep. ATF is trying to find him now."

15

By Saturday morning Carly had talked to everyone she could to get information on the ATF investigation into the bomb. The feds had contacted Barton, but she hadn't heard whether or not he'd been arrested. Tired of thinking about it and talking on the phone, she took Maddie for a walk and on the way home decided it was a great day for a swim.

When she got home and changed, she turned on her handheld radio to listen to police activity in the city. She was greeted with active, nonstop radio traffic. Her pulse sped a bit. Something big was going on. Was it more gang stuff or something related to the bomb?

The phone rang just as she figured out that there'd been a shooting in the new marina.

Joe was on caller ID.

"Hey, Joe, how are you doing?"

"Good, Carly, good. Knee surgery is scheduled for next week. But that's not why I called. Are you following the shooting?"

"I just turned the radio on. Do you know the details?"

"Yeah, I heard a blurb on the news radio and I called dispatch. The Oceans First people hit the new marina from the ocean side."

"What?"

"They launched a couple of boats from the rec launch, motored around Sandy Park, and then jumped off the boats to swim into the construction site. A couple of them handcuffed themselves to equipment. One or two had red paint, and they were tossing it everywhere. It's a mess. But the worst thing is that a few of them headed for the old marina to occupy Walt's, and marina patrol tried to stop them. Jarvis shot one of them."

"You're kidding. Was the protestor armed?"

"No details yet, but from what I gather, he was in the water. I don't know how Jarvis will justify his actions. Anyway, I know we won the lawsuit to evict those people, but the city is dragging its feet to actually kick them out. This was probably a desperation ploy."

"Nick's in Arizona looking into just how crazy Oceans First is." She told him about the investigation into the guns and about the bomb at Half Baked.

"Wonder if his brother was the one who threw the newspaper rack through the front door last week."

"You're probably right."

The radio traffic had calmed quite a bit.

"So tell me about your surgery."

"It's supposed to be easy. I have torn cartilage in my left knee. The doc will go in arthroscopically and cut it out. No big scars, just two small holes. It's outpatient, so I'll be walking the next day."

"I'm glad to hear that. I'll pray that everything goes well."

"Thanks, Carly. You take care."

After he hung up, she listened to the radio a bit more and understood from all the traffic that Oceans First was still creating havoc at the construction site. Joe was right — they knew they'd be kicked out soon, so why not go for broke? As she listened to the environmentalist-created mayhem, she had to give them credit for originality. Though she was surprised they hadn't thought of it sooner. The ocean side was the only way to circumvent all the security and fencing. Since they'd completed a successful swim,

Carly found herself giving them a little more respect.

Details about the shooting wouldn't be aired since Jarvis was a city employee. Carly hoped, for Jarvis's sake, that the shooting was justified and the injuries were minor.

The phone rang, and her heart sang when she saw it was Nick. After making sure he was well and happy, she told him about Oceans First's latest gambit.

"Well, that's interesting because nothing's panning out on the Oceans First front here in Arizona. I also heard about the bomb at the coffee shop. Have you talked to Ned?"

"Briefly. He thinks Dean did it."

"And the ATF agents with me were glad to have a name to work with. But Dean was in prison when the original theft occurred."

"Doesn't mean he's not working with whoever stole it. I saw him with another man."

"That's why we'll be here a little longer. We're taking part in a conference call with prison authorities in Florence, Arizona, about Barton. But I still plan on being home in time for dinner tonight, and we'll go to church together tomorrow."

"Good. I miss you."

"Miss you, too. Love ya, babe."

Carly played his last words over and over

in her mind while she swam. She was overjoyed to know he'd be home soon. After her swim, she got busy taking care of household duties she'd been neglecting.

Nick, true to his word, arrived home in time for dinner, and the house was sparkling. He wrapped her in a hug she would have been happy to have lasted forever.

"Sorry you didn't close the case with Oceans First in the suspect column," she said as he held her at arm's length so he could look at her.

He gave a tired shrug. "Environmentalists as cold-blooded killers didn't really track for me. Those people are annoying and they do damage, but they don't kill people execution style. Jarvis is going to be in a world of hurt for shooting the one who tried to get into Walt's. The guy wasn't armed with anything other than spray paint."

"Oh, I stopped listening to the radio and didn't turn on the news. Have you heard more?"

"I talked to Fernando. He said the guy was just trying to climb onto the old dock near Walt's when Jarvis shot him. He would have drowned if the other marina patrol guy hadn't jumped in and pulled him out while Jarvis did nothing. The guy is in critical condition."

"What does Jarvis have to say for himself?"

"Not talking. He's suspended pending a shooting board. It doesn't look good."

"I didn't care for the guy, but I'm sorry to hear that."

"I'm sorry as well, but we have our own pressing issues. I'm really anxious to see how things pan out with Barton as our prime suspect regarding the explosives."

"What did you learn from the prison?"

"He was a model prisoner. That's why the early release. He settled down, went to school, even earned a degree in engineering. But we still have six years of visitor and phone logs to go through."

"I can tell you're not sold on him as the suspect, while I think he's pure evil and belongs back in prison. There's too much coincidence here."

Nick yawned and gave her another hug. "I agree that the coincidence is compelling. I'm just beginning to think the people who stole the guns and explosives are the same people who shot the gangbangers and tried to make it look like a gang deal."

"Why else would they give Trey the guns?"

He nodded. "Yeah, and while I can understand Barton having a beef with his brother, what's his problem with Las Playas gangbangers? They were shot a week before this

165

bomb was planted."

"The key has to be who he's working with."

Carly had Nick sit at the table, poured him a large glass of ice water, and told him to relax while she served dinner. As she got plates and dished out the food, she told him what Londy had said about Victor.

"I know Victor. Caught him tagging the first time I was out with the gang unit," Nick said, smothering a yawn.

"He made an impression on you, too?"

"He did. He's a bright kid whose cleverness is all being channeled the wrong way. Wants to be a gangster more than anything."

"Yeah, that's what I thought. How sad. If what Victor said is accurate, then Dean Barton has two partners. Either of them could have a problem with Las Playas gang-bangers. My gut tells me Barton needs to be taken off the streets. It's not a stretch to think him capable of murder. Maybe even murder as a distraction."

"You think he shot the gangsters to distract us from him blowing up Ned?"

"It's possible."

Carly sat once everything was served. She took Nick's hand as they bowed their heads, and he said a blessing.

"Ned doesn't always open the safe," Carly

continued, thinking out loud, trying to solve the puzzle. "If he hadn't on Friday, the place would have blown with no one to point the finger at Dean."

Nick shrugged. "Praise God no one was hurt. We'll get to the bottom of this." He took a bite of dinner.

Carly knew that while Nick was away, mealtime was whatever fast food was available. So she didn't want to subject him to takeout or any food other than home cooking. There were only two dishes she made with absolute confidence, and she'd made one of them for dinner that night.

"Mmm, this is great." Nick oohed and aahed with pleasure, his mouth full of meat and cheese lasagna. He swallowed and toasted Carly with his water. "For three days I've choked down greasy hamburgers and stale deli sandwiches. This makes me forget all that junk." He grabbed a piece of garlic bread and continued eating with relish.

Carly smiled. It was so good to have him home and across the table. The gang mess seemed to have calmed down, and Carly silently thanked God for keeping him safe.

She waited until after dinner when they were sitting together on the couch to tell him about the nasty blog posts Ginny Masters had written. The sting was gone, and Carly was glad she hadn't been able to tell Nick right away when she'd felt outraged. Nick had his arm around her, and she rested her head on his shoulder. The TV was on, but she really hadn't paid any attention to what was shown.

"She thinks picking on you is going to get her a better job?"

"I guess. At least that's what Alex thinks. I haven't talked to him. Andi has. He needs prayer. It sounds like his dad is really having a hard time with the death of his wife."

"That's tough. I'll admit I miss reading his columns. Alex doesn't beat around the bush; he always gets right to the point."

Carly could tell by the tone of Nick's voice that he was sleepy, and she decided they didn't need a deep conversation right now. "Second service or first?" she asked, closing her eyes in anticipation of a nice doze.

"Second. I want to sleep in."

Carly smiled and snuggled closer. In a few minutes Nick was asleep, and Carly followed shortly thereafter.

16

They made it to second service early in two cars. Nick planned to hook up with his team and prepare for the first funeral straight from church. Today was Rojo's, and the service would be held in a small Spanish-speaking church in downtown Las Playas at 1 p.m. After church, Nick and his people would have an hour to prepare before the funeral started.

They listened to Pastor Rawling's message from Matthew 5: " 'But I say do not resist an evil person! If someone slaps you on the right cheek, offer the other cheek also.' "

Carly thought about Ginny Masters, glad she hadn't come across the woman while she was angry. The blog posts still irritated her, but she had to admit that it was at least a blessing that Masters had not gone overboard in print. And Carly knew beyond a shadow of a doubt that she had to handle the situations with both Masters and Barton professionally, not like some wounded teenager.

She squeezed Nick's hand, feeling centered and at peace for the first time in a while. His warm, solid presence next to her was a large part of the reason why. When the service ended, they walked hand in hand toward his car so she could say good-bye. They were halfway there when Pastor Rawlings stopped them.

"If you have a minute, Carly, I'd like to speak with you."

"Sure, I'll be right there." She turned to Nick. "You be careful."

He smiled. "Always." They shared a kiss and he was gone.

"What can I do for you, Jonah?" Carly loved her pastor. He'd been her mother's pastor and mentor for years and then Nick's when she and Nick were divorced. At first Carly had hated him. But when her heart changed and she and Nick reconciled, coming to church and learning from big, gentle Jonah had changed her life. Now she admired and respected him and cherished the memory of Jonah performing the ceremony that retied her marriage knot with Nick.

Jonah held his hand out, the grip engulfing Carly's hand. "How about we go to my office?" His expression was unreadable. Carly hoped this wasn't about Mary Ellen. But then if it was, all she had were positive reports. The girl was bright and helpful, and her progress since she'd been on probation was nothing short of miraculous.

Maybe Jonah doesn't like the idea of Mary Ellen and Londy dating, if that's what they are doing. Carly's mind whirled with possibilities. They reached his office, and Jonah took a seat behind his desk. Carly sat across from him.

"Do you know Pam Sailor?" Jonah asked.

Since she was expecting a Mary Ellen question, this one knocked Carly for a loop. She thought for a moment and then remembered the name from the suicide she'd handled. "I know the name but I don't know her."

"She attends sporadically because her business is — uh, was catering and she often works Sundays."

"She was related to the guy who committed suicide?"

Jonah nodded. "He was her husband. That's what I wanted to speak to you about."

Intrigued because Jonah couldn't know she'd handled the call, Carly asked, "Does she think it wasn't suicide?" Pam Sailor would have been notified about the death by the coroner's office. It wasn't likely Carly's name would have come up at all.

"No, she's certain he killed himself. He left her a note and unfortunately a lot of problems. I don't want to go into everything Pam told me, but she has questions I think a law enforcement officer would be better equipped to handle. I also thought that speaking to another woman would make it easier for Pam. So I decided to ask you to speak with her, casually, maybe?" He held his hands out, palms up. "Maybe you can help by just listening to what she has to say."

Carly thought for a minute. She could refer the woman to homicide. Though the death wasn't a homicide, it'd still been handled by that detail. They received all the autopsy information from the coroner and were the ones who officially closed the case. Or maybe the woman needed a good lawyer. Then again, she might just need to vent. Carly could listen as well as anyone else.

"Sure, Jonah, I'll talk to her."

"Great, thanks. She's tied up for the next couple of days with family. As soon as I can arrange something, I'll let you know."

Later that afternoon, Carly tried to take a nap but was only successful in dozing off and on. The first night back to graveyard patrol was always the hardest. A lot of guys didn't try to sleep before their Monday shift. They figured they'd be tired enough to sleep well the next day. Carly liked to at least have a nap, but today there was just too much on her mind. She ended up taking Maddie for a long walk and then settling down to listen to the police radio while she got ready for work. She wanted to know what was happening in the city.

Things in the new marina had calmed down with the construction company hiring extra private security to ease up on the demand for cops. Nick had called earlier and told her that Rojo's funeral had gone off without a hitch. People were sad but peaceful, he said. The gang guys were hanging out in Ninja territory. His tone was guarded, and she knew he was afraid peace would evaporate as the day wore on and alcohol took effect.

By 9 p.m. the radio traffic she listened to was routine. She hoped that when she got to work, Nick would let her know he was calling it a night and coming home to go to bed.

Carly studied the contents of the fridge, trying to decide what she felt like eating. She almost reheated some lasagna for dinner but decided it would be too heavy. Instead, she settled on a sandwich. Humming softly, she began taking things out of the fridge.

Suddenly the radio screeched with emergency traffic. She nearly dropped the mayonnaise jar when she heard Nick's voice tight with stress. His words were indistinguishable.

Pulse accelerating, she rushed to the radio to turn up the volume.

"Gang 1, 10-9 your last."

Gang 1 was Nick and Mickey. Carly felt ice form in her veins, and she held her breath.

The dispatcher had not heard the transmission any better than she had and was asking Gang 1 to repeat. Dispatch started the steady code-red beep, a sound meant to keep the radio clear during emergencies so the unit in need could get through.

Beep . . . beep . . . beep . . .

Carly jumped when Nick's voice sliced through the code red.

"Gang 1, 998, shots fired! Shots fired!"

Carly gripped the radio, knuckles white, waiting as dispatch asked for a location.

"Gang 1, what is your 20?"

After what seemed an eternity, a radio was keyed, and Nick's voice came across breathless but clear and steady. "Southwest corner of Seventh and LPS. Officer down, officer down. An officer has been shot."

In the staccato stream of radio traffic that followed, Carly heard paramedics requested and numerous units announcing they were en route to assist Nick and Mickey.

She forgot the sandwich, running to get her shoes and car keys. A fear like she had never known coiled inside.

Where was Nick when the shots were fired?

And who was shot? Was it Mickey?

Was it Nick?

Odds were it was Mickey, and she hated that the thought gave her some relief. Mickey had a pregnant wife at home.

She was in her car moments later, speeding for the scene with the volume on her handheld radio turned all the way up. Her mind raced as she listened for information. And her pulse pounded with worry for Nick. He'd said Seventh and Las Playas Street — that was on the other side of the commuter rail line in Ninjas territory. It was also the area where he'd said they'd be hanging out, but that was hours ago.

Knuckles white on the steering wheel, she listened as the eerie emergency beep continued. It wouldn't stop until Nick or another officer at the scene was able to say that the scene was code 4, in control.

She had nearly reached Las Playas Street, where she would turn north toward Seventh, when she heard Nick's voice. Tense but controlled, he announced code 4, with the shooting suspect still outstanding, then asked for confirmation that paramedics were en route.

Dispatch answered that medics were on the way. Carly slowed when she heard Nick ask for homicide and a shooting team. Her grip on the wheel relaxed, and she jerked the car to a stop.

Hands shaking, Carly leaned forward to let her forehead rest on the steering wheel. Her thoughts cleared slowly, and she realized she'd only be in the way at the crime scene. Not yet 10 p.m, afternoon patrol would be working the call and the shooting. It wasn't Carly's place to be there — especially since she wasn't in uniform.

"Oh, God." She breathed out a prayer. "I was so afraid for Nick, I didn't stop to think. Thank you that he's okay. And please look after whoever went down."

Carly inhaled deep and exhaled regular as her heart rate calmed; then she sat back in the driver's seat. She could continue toward work and suit up early, probably get some dull job to do at the crime scene. Or she could turn around and be at the hospital in a couple minutes. *I can be of use there,* she thought, *even if it's only to update communications on the officer's condition until my shift starts.*

Carly needed to be involved. Whoever had gone down was a brother officer and one of her husband's team. She turned the car around and minutes later parked near the emergency room. As she got out and headed for the entrance, she called communications and told them where she was and asked who was hurt.

"I'll tell the watch commander," Charlie, the comm center supervisor, said. "It's Mickey T. Nick is okay. Medics have been on scene a couple of minutes, and from the sound of things, they want to get Mickey to the ER quickly." His voice vibrated with adrenaline and stress.

But the only words Carly heard over and over were that Nick was okay.

17

Mickey didn't look good. A few minutes after she talked to Charlie, serious-faced medics rushed the injured officer to a waiting trauma team. The watch commander had called Carly's BlackBerry to thank her for quick thinking and showing up at the hospital. Her presence allowed all the other officers already on scene, including Nick, to stay at the location and help in the search for the shooters. The commander had logged Carly into service as Adam 7 and asked her to update him on Mickey's condition and to collect any evidence the medical team might come across. To that end, Carly followed Mickey into the ER and waited outside the trauma room, watching and listening but not close enough to be an intrusion.

About five minutes later, her BlackBerry went off. Dispatch told her Jacobs was sending someone to Mickey's house to pick up his wife. Was there any more Carly could tell them about his condition?

Sighing, she said no. They let her know that Captain Jacobs was on his way.

Sliding her BlackBerry back onto her belt, she folded her arms, leaned against the doorframe, and watched as bloody clothes were cut off her fellow officer and her husband's partner.

While she waited for Captain Jacobs, Carly listened to the radio as Nick calmly directed officers to where he wanted them. He was certainly shaken and angered by what had happened, but the emotions would never intrude on his work. It was his job to find the shooter and keep everyone safe.

From what he'd said over the air, which at best was short-hand, Carly extrapolated that he and Mickey had been out walking through a neighborhood. They'd stopped to speak to a group of people when a drive-by shooting went down. Mickey had probably been trying to get the innocent people out of the line of fire when he was hit.

Suddenly more emergency traffic blared from her radio. A unit had spotted a vehicle fitting the description of the shooter's car. The officer recited a license plate, and his voice went up an octave when he said the car split.

The radio was then a clash of people trying to talk at the same time. Carly tensed. Finally the dispatcher got through with the news that the car was stolen.

The first unit came back on the air, sirens wailing in the background, asking for another code red.

Carly turned up her radio. She didn't realize she was holding her breath until the ER doctor stepped out to tell her that Mickey was losing a lot of blood and they needed to get him to surgery.

She nodded and said she'd stay in the waiting area.

The steady emergency beep putting her on edge all over again, Carly walked out of the ER. As the double doors closed behind her, she nodded to the security officer who monitored them. He needed to push the lock release to allow admittance to the ER. Memorial Hospital had doubled its security measures after Joe's son, A.J., had been kidnapped right out of the nursery about a year ago.

"Something happening?" the security officer asked. Carly remembered they were called facilitators, not officers or guards.

"They think they got the shooter."

The facilitator held a thumb up.

"We have the vehicle stopped, Magnolia and Sixth." An excited voice interrupted the code red.

The beep continued. Carly pictured the stop in her mind. Units fanned out behind the stolen vehicle, emergency lights flashing, cops behind open doors, weapons drawn, focused on the vehicle and occupants in front of them.

"Driver and passenger have exited."

They'd be pronged out between the black-and-whites and the stolen car, the driver first, then the passenger.

Beep . . . beep . . . beep . . .

"Occupants in custody."

They'd be handcuffed and moved out of the way so an officer could make certain no one was still in the vehicle.

And a minute later: "Code 4. Vehicle occupants and weapon in custody."

"Yes!" Carly said with a fist pump.

"Great," the facilitator said. "How's your officer in there?"

"He needs surgery."

"He'll get the best here."

Carly knew he was right. The doctors here were the best. But that knowledge didn't stop her from praying while she paced and waited for the captain.

■ ■ ■ ■

Mickey was in surgery by the time Jacobs arrived. Sergeant Barrett and a press officer were with him.

"Update?"

Carly shrugged. "He was losing a lot of blood. They said they had to operate to stop the bleeding. We can go back and check with nursing staff for any news."

She wanted to ask about Nick. She wanted to see Nick and to hold him close for a long time.

Jacobs pulled out his BlackBerry to read a text. He then turned to the press officer. "Reporters are on their way. We need a quick snippet to give them."

As if on cue, Carly heard a voice that made her skin crawl.

"Captain Jacobs! Captain Jacobs!"

When she turned, Carly saw that the high-pitched, nasal tone belonged to Ginny Masters.

Jacobs turned as the slim, curvy, bleached-blonde reporter approached them, her stiletto heels snapping crisply on the hospital floor. The heels were attached to calf-length black boots that gave way to skintight black pants. A snug red blouse and a large

182

black purse slung over one shoulder completed the outfit. A tall, skinny man with his hair in a ponytail followed her. He had a camera around his neck and one in his hand.

Carly struggled to keep her expression neutral. The photos on the blog were not a fluke. Duncan Potter had teamed up with Ginny Masters.

She worked to ignore Potter and concentrated on where she felt the real threat was — Ginny Masters. A jolt of anger shot through her, and Carly knew she needed to forget the nasty blogs and not let the woman or Potter get under her skin.

"I heard an officer has been killed by a gang member," Masters said. "Can you tell me the details?"

Carly almost lost all her reserve right then, and her mouth dropped at the callousness of the question and the excited gleam in the woman's eyes. She was spared from having to respond as Jacobs nodded to the PIO. He then put a hand on Carly's shoulder and turned to the security facilitator, who hit the door buzzer. Barrett, Jacobs, and Carly went through the door while the PIO intercepted Masters and Potter.

"I never would have made it as a PIO," the captain told her in a quiet voice.

Carly felt tension melt away, glad Jake was in charge. The doors closed behind them, and Carly's anger at Masters dissipated. It was a great relief that they could leave her out in the waiting area. The sound of Masters arguing for information reached her ears, and she could only shake her head.

"I have a right to the most current information. You can't suppress the news."

The threesome continued to the nursing station. A nurse there said she'd try to get an update for them.

While they waited, Jacobs turned toward Carly. "What's the matter, Trouble?"

Trouble was his nickname for her. Jake, as he was often called, was an old friend, only recently promoted to captain.

"I know you have to give her something," Carly said, "but that woman is obnoxious."

"All members of the press are obnoxious. You're just used to Trejo."

"I guess. Suspect in custody?"

Jake smiled. "Looks that way. Nick will be down here to brief me as soon as everything out there is squared away." As if sensing her unasked question, Jacobs put a hand on her shoulder. "He's okay. From what I heard, Mickey pushed Nick and some bystanders out of the line of fire."

She nodded, not trusting herself to speak.

When his phone buzzed again, he pulled it off his belt to read the text. "The sergeant I sent to pick up Mickey's wife, Ann, should be here shortly."

The ER nurse came back with an encouraging report about Mickey. She suggested they wait upstairs outside recovery, where he'd be taken after surgery, so the three of them walked to the elevators. While they walked, Jake texted the new location so Ann would be brought to the correct place.

On the recovery floor, the group moved toward the waiting area to the right of the elevator. Jake was again busy with his Black-Berry.

"Edwards," Barrett said, "why don't you go change? We'll need someone posted here indefinitely. Might as well be you tonight."

Carly agreed with Barrett. If she had a partner, she'd want to be out searching. But a solo officer would just be a scribe or something. At least at the hospital she'd be close to the most current information. "I can be back within a half hour."

"I'll give you forty-five minutes if you bring back some coffee."

18

Carly returned in forty minutes with coffee. While initially she hoped to see Nick at the station, radio traffic told her he'd gone to the hospital to check on his partner. She warily hurried through the lobby, not wanting to run into Ginny Masters. Thankfully Carly didn't see any sign of her. She did see Duncan Potter snapping photos of all the officers in the lobby. A lot of officers, both on duty and off, were here asking if they could help in any way. In these kinds of situations, the hospital often requested blood donations. Carly figured Memorial would set something up, but it would probably take time. She avoided Potter and got on the elevator.

While at the station she'd heard about the arrest of the shooter. Only fourteen years old, he was a cousin of the Garnets, the leaders of the Playboyz. The driver of the stolen car was an eighteen-year-old Playboy with an extensive record.

She'd also learned that Londy Akins had been with the group of people Nick and Mickey were talking to when the shots rang out. That didn't surprise her because she knew Londy considered the gang neighborhoods his mission field. He was always out there trying to talk kids out of gangs and into church. What did surprise her was the buzz around the station that Londy's group was the target of the shots and that Mickey had saved Londy's life and been hit in the process. She couldn't wait until she had a chance to talk to Nick and find out exactly what happened.

When she arrived at the second floor, the group in the recovery waiting area had grown. She stopped short.

There was Nick, deep in conversation with Jacobs. She saw dark stains on his jeans and knew it was blood. He caught her eye, paused, and said, "I'm all right."

She managed a smile. As she looked around, she recognized Ann, Mickey's wife, and steadied herself to hand Barrett his coffee.

"Mickey still in surgery?"

Barrett sipped and nodded. "But the doc was out a few minutes ago. They were able to stop the bleeding. The bullet hit him in the gut just below the vest —" he pointed to the space there — "and did some damage, but they think they can fix it." His face crinkled with disgust. "Cops' luck. Half an inch higher and he'd be fine, just bruised."

Carly shook her head. It always seemed as though a bad guy could get shot five times, all in nonvital areas, and be fine, while an officer would get hit once and it would be fatal. She sipped her coffee, feeling steadier now that Nick was in front of her, and moved to where she could hear what Nick and Jacobs were talking about.

Nick was updating him on the shooting and the search. "It was another odd deal that looks gang-like on the surface," he said. "The shooter says he was given the gun and told to shoot up Ninjas. He was promised fifty bucks if he hit anyone and a hundred bucks if he hit Londy."

Carly perked up when she heard this and almost blurted out "Who?" to be certain she'd heard correctly.

But Nick was still talking. "Captain, I was there. With the exception of this stupid cousin, most of the knuckleheads on both the Ninjas and the Playboyz seem to sense someone is stirring this pot. As unlikely as it sounds, they realize this fight is being orchestrated."

"By who?" Jacobs asked.

Nick held up his hands and Carly saw the frustration in his tired face. "No one can say. I'm afraid only that kid upstairs knows, and he might not ever be able to tell us."

Carly's thoughts also turned to Crusher. Nick was right; Hector Macias could answer a lot of questions for Nick and everybody else, if he were able.

Carly heard the squawk of the security facilitator's radio. She couldn't make out the message, but immediately the facilitator was animated.

With a shrug, Jacobs looked at Barrett. "How is that kid doing? Do you have an officer on his room?"

Barrett shook his head. "Last report we got, he was in a drug-induced coma. We didn't think he needed a guard since he's in intensive care and not talking."

Jacobs blew out a breath. "I want someone on him 24-7 from now on." He pointed to Carly. "Why don't you start us off? Better to be safe than sorry. I agree with Nick; that kid has the answers we need. He may or may not be able to tell us, but either way, we need to keep him safe."

Carly didn't want to babysit Crusher, especially since there was so much security at Memorial as it was. She wanted to be near Nick. But hospital security wasn't armed, and she did agree that their only witness needed to be protected.

She nodded, glanced at Nick, then turned for the elevator.

"I'll come up there as soon as I can and sit with you for a bit," Nick said.

Intensive care was up one floor. Carly thought about Londy and Mary Ellen's confidence that Crusher would wake up soon. If he did, would he be able to give them the answers they needed?

She remembered what Nick had said about Crusher's mother. Carly knew from her own contact with Lupe Macias, when she drove Victor home, that the woman had her hands full with her other children and two jobs. She was relieved to let Londy and the police look after her oldest. The only people barred were his fellow gangsters and the press. Thinking of the press reminded Carly of Ginny Masters, which made her cringe. She said a quick prayer that Trejo would be able to return to his job soon.

Carly stepped off the elevator and stopped, back straightening, her hand reflexively going to her gun. There stood Dean Barton and Ginny Masters. They'd been leaning over the security station, talking to the facilitator. Off to one side was

Duncan Potter. When Carly entered the lobby, everyone turned her way.

"What are you doing here?" Carly ignored Masters and glared at Barton. Out of the corner of her eye, she saw Potter begin to snap photos. She thought about the bomb at Half Baked but hadn't heard what else was going on or how that investigation had progressed.

Barton smirked, pointed at Carly's gun hand, and said to Masters, "See that? She's ready to shoot me. What did I tell you about police brutality?"

Forcing herself to relax and ignore the photographer, Carly dropped her hand. "Answer my question."

"He's not doing anything wrong. You have no right to question him." Masters folded her arms and stepped between Barton and Carly. "What are *you* doing here?"

Carly took a deep breath, willing her anger to calm so she could think clearly. But it chafed that Barton was able to irritate her like this. "Miss Masters —"

"Ms."

"Ms. Masters. You're not supposed to be here either. I believe hospital policy bars reporters from intensive care."

The facilitator, a middle-aged, heavyset woman, piped up as she stood. "They wanted me to let them in to see the young man who was shot in the head. I was trying to tell them the same thing. I cannot let them in."

Carly didn't miss the threatening look Barton shot the woman. But the facilitator stood her ground. "My supervisor is on the way up."

"Look, I am a credentialed member of the press. I have a right to access. That boy in there might have a story to tell. What are you trying to hide?" Masters stamped her foot for emphasis.

Carly sighed and ignored the question she knew was meant to bait her. "Your access is not my problem. You need to take that up with hospital administration. And I doubt anyone is in the office this time of night." She directed her attention back to Barton. "You're not press. What's your interest here?" She pulled out her handheld radio and keyed the mike, asking for Jacobs.

Barton cursed, clearly livid. "I don't have to tell you jack. But maybe I'm a friend of the kid's mother. What about that?"

"Captain, I have Dean Barton and Ginny Masters up here. Do you know if ATF wants to talk to Barton?"

"Your frame-up didn't work," Barton sneered while Carly waited for an answer.

He grabbed Masters's hand. "I was with my lady all night, not setting up a bomb."

The radio cackled, and Jacobs told her the investigation was ongoing, but she could let Barton go.

Carly refused to look away from Barton, irritated that she couldn't arrest him, and doubted that he was a friend of Hector's mother. She started to speak, but before she could answer him, the facilitator said evenly, "You all need to come back during normal visiting hours if you have permission to visit the boy."

The woman was so brave now, Carly could have hugged her. But the tension in the room thickened, and she wondered how far Barton would push her. Just then the elevator opened and two more hospital security people stepped off. Carly recognized the older one as a graveyard supervisor. He'd helped her break up a fight in the ER once.

"Officer Edwards, thanks for coming to help," the supervisor said, interpreting her presence as being there by request, "but we have everything under control. I'm not sure how these people got up here, but I'll be happy to escort them back to the lobby."

Masters sputtered, but the supervisor hit her with some legalese that a lawyer would've been proud of. Potter even stopped taking pictures. Carly made note of the fact that Barton kept silent. Finally, after losing her fight with the supervisor, Masters turned to the tattooed parolee.

"Come on, Dean. We can find our own way downstairs." She jabbed the elevator call button with a wicked fingernail.

"That may be," the supervisor replied calmly, "but it's our job to show you out."

Carly stepped aside for Barton to get on the elevator. She held his dark eyes as he shot her a hate stare to end all hate stares.

"This ain't over," he muttered as he walked past.

19

Carly said nothing as Ginny Masters, Dean Barton, and Duncan Potter entered the elevator and the doors closed.

"You came in at the right time," the facilitator said, sounding relieved as she sat at her desk again.

"What were they saying when I walked in?"

"The man — boy, he sure gave me the creeps — he was trying to tell me that they just wanted a minute to see the boy and that no one would know. I tried to explain about policy, but neither of them cared. Then you walked in." She straightened her shirt and closed a book that was open on her desk. "Are you here about that kid?"

Carly nodded. "I'll probably be sitting with him for the rest of the night. We'll be watching him 24-7 for now."

"Good," she said. "Glad to know you'll be around." She hit the buzzer to open the door to the intensive care ward.

Once inside, Carly blew out a breath, wondering what on earth Barton or Masters would want with Crusher and what unholy alliance the reporter had formed with him. She lowered the volume on her police radio, respectful of the quiet atmosphere in ICU.

Lights were dim in ICU. The nurse at the main desk looked up, and Carly recognized her as a friend of Andi's — Robin. When she saw Carly, Robin pointed to the room to the right of her station.

Carly walked there and looked in on Crusher from the doorway. Tubes and wires were everywhere. His face looked swollen and puffy.

Robin came to stand next to her. "He's holding his own."

"Will he wake up?"

"Well, he's healing, his vitals are good, and the swelling has been controlled, so now it's a matter of wait and see." She shrugged. "Those two who come to visit him said they saw him react the last time they were here."

Carly remembered Londy telling her he thought Crusher had squeezed his hand.

Robin continued. "They said he twitched when they reminded him his mother loved him. If he does wake up, we'll have a better idea of how well he'll recover."

Carly looked at Robin, whose expression was thoughtful.

"He's the same age as my son, and he has a lot going for him. The bullet did enter and exit, but the damage was minimal. And he's young, strong, and help got to him quickly."

"Is that a yes?"

Robin smiled. "Head injuries are difficult. Only time will tell. I heard that you did some first aid for him on scene. You probably saved his life."

Carly flushed. "It's my job. Couldn't let him bleed out at my feet."

"Not every cop would have done that for a gang member," Robin said over her shoulder as she returned to her station.

Carly pulled up a chair and took a seat outside the room. She thought about that night when she and Joe had rolled up to the shooting. Stopping the bleeding had seemed like a small thing considering Hector's wound, and she admitted to herself that at the time she didn't think he'd make it.

"He's come this far, Lord," she prayed. "I have to believe you'll bring him all the way back."

She'd been sitting for about an hour when she heard someone enter the ICU area. Sergeant Barrett walked toward her.

"Barton give you much trouble?" Barrett asked as he shoved an unlit cigarette into his mouth.

"No. I just hadn't heard how his involvement in the bomb investigation had panned out."

"He's still a suspect, but they have no hard evidence linking him — or anyone for that matter — to the bomb. ATF is all over it." He pulled up a chair. "Apparently he has an alibi for when they think the bomb was set. Now that they're certain the thieves who stole the C-4 are in Las Playas and ready to use the stuff, there are likely to be more ATF agents in town than cops soon."

"Have they figured any connection? I mean, it makes no sense for someone — even Dean Barton — to steal all that stuff just to blow up a coffee shop."

"Nick might know more about it than I do. He and Mickey were point men with the ATF. He'll be up later." He shook his head. "I hate it when a cop goes down. Seen it too many times in my career."

Carly nodded in agreement, so thankful that Nick was okay.

They sat in silence for a few minutes. "You don't need to hang around," Carly said finally, gesturing toward the door. "No one is going to get in here."

"I wanted to talk to you for a minute," Barrett said, looking at the cubicle where Crusher lay.

Carly shrugged and followed his gaze. The place was quiet but for the beeping of machines.

Barrett faced her, elbows on his knees. He took the cigarette out of his mouth and played with it as if he had a pen in his hands, rolling it between his palms.

Carly wondered what he wanted. As the minutes ticked away, fear rose that he wanted to talk about Andrea. She prayed that wasn't his concern.

Finally he looked up — not at Carly, but toward the nurse's station. "I've been wanting to ask you something. It's a little personal, but I hope you'll talk to me."

Carly sucked in a breath and braced herself. "Talk about what?"

Sergeant Barrett seemed as uncomfortable as she'd ever seen him. She'd had a problem with him ever since his affair with her friend. She knew Barrett was married with five kids, and it made her angry that he treated his wife so shabbily. She'd confessed to Nick that when Joe had told her Barrett had been suitcased, she'd decided he'd gotten what he deserved.

He studied his feet. "It's just that I know

199

what happened with you and Nick. I mean —" he sat up — "I know he cheated on you and you divorced him but then took him back even though you knew all about the affair. I just wondered . . . what did he do to convince you to take him back? It must have been difficult . . ."

Carly relaxed immediately. She had no problem talking about the reconciliation. It was a huge blessing, the biggest in her life to date. "Yeah, it was difficult, but Nick and I are Christians now. We're different people. I forgave him because I believed him when he told me he was sorry and it would not happen again."

"Him going to church — that changed your mind?"

"It wasn't just church. I could tell that he'd really changed. I changed as well. And I knew he regretted what happened with the other woman."

Now Barrett met her eyes. "My wife wants a divorce. She kicked me out — I'm sure you've heard — and I probably deserve it." He rolled his shoulders as if he had a stiff neck. "But I miss my kids. I hate how they look at me . . ." His voice broke.

Carly turned away, hoping he wouldn't start crying. She couldn't dredge up much sympathy. She'd been in his wife's shoes.

When she had found out about Nick's affair, she thought she'd die.

After a minute Barrett composed himself. "I see Mickey and think that could happen to me. I don't want a cloud hanging over my marriage or my kids." He cursed. "I don't know if I can change her mind, but I've got to try. I haven't been to church since I was a kid. Would it be okay if I came to your church?"

"Of course." Carly resisted the urge to pat his shoulder. "You'd be welcome at church. In fact, why don't you talk to the pastor, Jonah Rawlings? He's a great guy; you'll like him."

"Did he help you forgive Nick?"

"By the time I talked to Jonah, I had already forgiven Nick. What he helped me with was the spiritual change in my own heart and life."

Barrett shrugged. "I'm willing to try anything."

Carly told him where she and Nick went and gave him the service times. While she was happy to hear that he seemed completely sincere, she was relieved to see him go. After praying for Sergeant Barrett, she leaned back to think about her own problems and dilemmas, thankful that none were as serious or painful as Barrett's at the moment.

20

It was a couple of hours before Nick could join Carly in ICU. By then, Mickey had been moved to an ICU cubicle down the hall. Fernando, Mickey's academy classmate and close friend, was with Ann outside the room. The doctor said that while the surgery had gone well, Mickey was still critical, and he wanted him monitored in ICU. But the doctor did believe that the worst was over.

When Nick walked into ICU with a drink carrier, Carly felt her heart race. He knew her too well and gave her a smile that said, "I'm fine; don't worry" before he dropped off two coffees to Fernando and Ann. He came back her way with two coffees and a bag of what Carly hoped was something sweet. She hadn't eaten dinner, and her stomach was reminding her of that. But she also needed something more than food.

"I need a hug," she said when he returned. It hadn't escaped her notice that he'd changed. The bloody jeans were gone, and in their place were clean, black tactical pants.

"Me too." He held his arms open and Carly fell into them. It wasn't a real hug since they were separated by Kevlar vests and a myriad of traditional police accoutrements, but it did Carly a world of good.

After a minute, he said, "Why don't we sit, drink our coffee, and I'll tell you what happened."

They walked to the small waiting room across from the nurses' station and sat. Nick opened the bag and pulled out two pieces of Mexican sweet bread. Carly sighed with contentment. There was a place on the west side that started baking sweet bread early, to put on a fleet of food trucks for their breakfast business. It was now almost 5 a.m., and the bread was still warm.

"Oooh," Carly moaned, "you read my mind."

"I know my wife. A sugar high after stress is the prescription."

She smiled and, with her mouth full, indicated that he needed to tell her the details.

"Things were going good, quiet. Mickey and I ran into Londy doing his thing with a group of Ninjas." He sipped his coffee.

"That guy is bold. He was preaching the gospel to all these kids who just saw their homeboy put in the ground. I was moved. Then, without warning, someone yells, 'Drive-by!' " He shook his head. "You know how that goes."

Carly did. In a group on the street, it would create chaos.

"I saw the car out of the corner of my eye and turned to Victor — he was in the group — but he was already running. Then I heard the shots — five or six — and the next thing I knew, Londy fell into me and we both hit the ground." He sucked in a breath. "The car went past, and when I got up, I saw Mickey. He pushed Londy into me and probably saved both our lives."

Carly reached out and gripped his hand. "Thank God."

For a minute they sat, holding hands and letting it sink in.

"But there is some good news in all this," Nick said.

"What?"

"Not only do we have the kid who shot Mickey in custody; he's talking. And sitting in jail has loosened Trey's tongue. He told the jailer he wanted to talk to me after he heard about this latest incident. We were right."

"Right about what?"

"Someone is trying to start a gang war, and it's not Oceans First."

She took another bite of her sweet bread and washed it down with coffee. After she swallowed, she asked, "Did Trey tell you who is trying to start the gang war?"

Nick shook his head. "All he knows is that he was approached by a guy who told him that he had guns for the Ninjas, guns that would help him even the score after the shooting of his three homeys."

"The guns in the stolen car he was driving?"

"Yep. Trey says this guy set him up with the car and the guns. Told him they were untraceable. Not surprisingly, the guy who gave the Garnet kid the gun said almost the exact same thing."

Carly sat back and thought about this. "Same guy?"

"Most likely."

"Did he offer Trey money for actually hitting someone as well?"

"That's where it gets hinky. Trey's benefactor didn't charge him or offer him anything. Said he just wanted to see scores settled and thought it was cowardly the way the three Ninjas were shot. When I asked Trey why he trusted this guy he'd never met before, he said that at the time he was mad and wanted revenge."

"So he took the guns and was all set to do business?"

Nick nodded. "He couldn't tell me why the Playboyz would start a war in the first place. They had no beef. And when he realized he was the one we caught driving the stolen car with all of those guns, and he was the only one being charged, and that more people were getting shot, he couldn't be helpful enough." Nick finished the last bit of his sweet bread and wiped his mouth.

Carly sipped her coffee and thought about what Nick had said and the implications. "And it's the same supplier in both cases?"

"Descriptions are similar. We arranged for a sketch artist from the sheriff's department to come in tomorrow — or today, I guess — and talk to Trey. But from what both gang-bangers have said so far, you may know the guy."

"What?" She frowned. "It's a local guy?"

"Not sure how local, but the guy Trey described is nearly what you said Victor described. He has a scarred face, lots of prison tattoos, and a scratchy voice."

Carly's coffee stopped halfway to her mouth and her eyes widened. "You're kidding? Dean Barton?"

He nodded. "Tell me about your confrontation outside ICU earlier."

She filled him in. "I would have held on to him because of the bomb in the coffee shop."

"He was questioned and cleared for the time being regarding that, when Masters vouched for him. But everything is pointing to him being the gun fairy. What a coincidence that he'd be trying to get in to see Crusher. I haven't seen the guy, but Trey's description sounds an awful lot like yours."

"Add this to what Victor said. Maybe the boy was spot-on about the guys Crusher was selling for being the shooters. But . . ."

"Why?" Nick asked the $64,000 question.

"Yeah, these guys are here causing trouble, but why?" She pulled a small notebook and pen out of her pocket and began to write. "Look what we have so far. Three kids shot made to look like a gang shooting and start a war. Gang leader given guns to keep war going." She wrote down those details, making them points one and two.

"Next, a bomb planted at Half Baked — appears unrelated, but explosives were stolen when the guns were stolen." This was number three.

"Shooting tonight," Nick injected, "but

not certain how that fits because Londy was the money target, and he's not a gang member anymore."

"He was a Ninja and Ninjas were the first victims." Carly chewed on the end of her pen. "Except for the bomb." She looked at Nick, eyes wide. "Maybe the bomb was meant for Londy. He works at the coffee shop. Maybe this war is against the Ninjas, some kind of revenge for something that happened in the past."

"But how would Dean Barton fit in that scenario? He's from Arizona."

"But we know he has a partner, maybe two if Victor is right." Carly described the bearded man, though she couldn't give many details.

Nick leaned back, thoughtful. "We have one name, a visitor for Barton, who logged in several times over the years — Michael Carter. ATF is trying to track him down. It's possible he's the partner. Maybe our answers will come when we find him. Maybe he was victimized by the Ninjas. In any event, once we get a sketch of the guy Trey says gave him the guns, if it looks like Barton, it will be easier to get a judge to sign a warrant for him. When I go back downtown, I'm going to dig deeper into this Michael Carter."

"And we have to find Barton to find his partner. I knew he was trouble with a capital *T,* but . . ." Sighing, she thought of Erika and Ned.

21

At the end of Carly's shift, though she was tired, she volunteered for another shift. Nick was planning to watch the sketch artist work, and she wanted to stay and be a part of things. The station was buzzing with ATF agents. Trey's decision to talk had injected new life into the federal investigators, and they were clamoring to talk to him.

And there was good news from the hospital. Mickey was alert and talking, and while he was still in ICU, his condition was upgraded to serious.

Since Nick was still working, Carly didn't want to go home, but there was no slot for her on any of the teams working overtime.

"Sorry, Trouble," a tired Captain Jacobs told her as he finished up a press release on the shooting and then denied her request to keep working. "We're straining the overtime budget as it is. And we'll need even more when we evict Oceans First. You know that

211

if I had something for you to do, I'd give you a job."

"Yeah, I know. Call me if anything comes up."

He nodded and punched Print for a hard copy of his release.

Carly left him to his work. With a yawn she stepped out of the police station and headed for her car, careful to avoid the cadre of press setting up in front of the station. Once across the street, she paused before entering the parking structure and looked for Ginny Masters on the off chance Dean Barton was with her. She realized it was a long shot since she had no idea the nature of their relationship, but she had a minute.

And there was the bleached-blonde head across the street, touching up her makeup in a mirror. No sign of Barton.

Carly continued to her car and then headed for Half Baked and Almost Grounded. Time to talk to Ned about his brother.

Even though she remembered Ned saying he'd kicked Dean out for good, as she entered the shop, she did a quick survey, looking for him just in case. Relaxing when she saw only the usual patrons, she turned to the counter. She did a double take when she saw who was behind the counter. Londy. She knew he'd been talking with homicide for hours.

"Londy, you okay?"

He nodded and she saw his bloodshot eyes. "I couldn't miss work. They depend on me. How is Officer Mickey?" His genuine concern didn't surprise her. Londy was a caring soul.

When she thought about what this kid had been before he became a Christian, tears pressed her eyes. She blinked them back. "He'll be okay. He lost a lot of blood, but his surgery went well. What happened out there last night?"

"Not sure. I was talking to some guys after the funeral. I saw Sergeant Anderson and Officer Mickey, said hi. Things were cool. Then a few minutes later someone screams, 'Drive-by.' People started running and ducking . . ."

Carly nodded. This was pretty much what Nick had told her.

Londy continued. "Officer Mickey saved my life. Pushed me out of the way. If he hadn't . . ." His voice broke, and he took a moment to compose himself. "I'm praying for him. So are Mary Ellen and Pastor Rawlings."

Carly cleared her throat. "Me too."

"Can I get you something?" Londy asked.

"How about a large French roast."

"Sure thing." He turned to pour the coffee.

"Is Ned in today?"

Londy handed her the coffee. "Yeah. He and Erika are in the back. You want to go back there?"

"If I'm not interrupting, I'd like to talk to them."

Londy reached under the counter and hit a buzzer so he could lift the counter and let Carly in. "I think they want to talk to you."

Carly sipped her coffee and walked through, Londy closing the counter behind her. She stepped through the double doors. The office door was open and she could hear Erika and Ned. Erika was seated at the desk, facing the office door.

She looked up when Carly appeared in the doorway and rolled her eyes with a smile. "Wow, were your ears burning? We were just talking about calling you."

Carly smiled and stepped inside. Ned sat leaning on a desk in the back of the office. The space was large, with two desks, several file cabinets, and four chairs. He raised a hand in greeting.

"Let me guess the other part of your

conversation," Carly said as she sat in a chair Ned pointed to.

"He's my cross to bear," Ned said, running his hand down his chin. "I wanted to apologize for that morning I let Dean call you stupid. I should have decked him right there. But I was so shocked to hear he was out of prison and more shocked when I found out he was in town asking to see me."

"We probably owe you an explanation," Erika added. She looked at Ned with such love and protectiveness that Carly almost sighed.

"You don't owe me anything. But I am worried because Dean has enough anger toward you to plant a bomb in here. But if we can't prove it . . ."

"The ATF guys are working with the device. Dean may have an alibi now, but something in the device will trip him up, I'm certain," Ned said. "He always messed up when we were kids."

"Did he show up here to avenge some wrong he perceives you did to him?" Carly asked, holding off on telling them about the possibility that Dean had smuggled guns into town to start a gang war.

Ned folded his arms across his chest. "Probably. I didn't realize he hated me enough to commit murder. But I better start from the beginning." He blew out a breath. "And the beginning was a long time ago. Dean is actually my half brother. His mother, my dad's first wife, was killed in a car accident when Dean was about eight. A couple of years later my dad married my mother and I was born a year after that. To hear my dad tell it, Dean never recovered from losing his mother and has been acting out ever since."

"He's been abrasive and difficult for as long as I've known him," Erika added.

"Anyway," Ned continued, "he's been in and out of jail for years. Growing up, it seemed like every day my folks were fighting about Dean. My mom hated him and apparently the feeling was mutual. She wanted him out of the house and wanted my dad to stop bailing him out every time he got in trouble."

He paused to take a deep breath. "My parents are wealthy — my dad is involved with several successful business ventures — and he always helped Dean out of whatever scrape he was in. This caused constant friction with my folks. When I was seventeen and counting the hours until I could enlist in the service and get out of the house, Dean crossed the line. He'd been arrested for selling crack, and my dad bailed him out. Mom was furious, didn't want Dean in the house, but my dad couldn't turn him away. I'd just gotten home from school. Mom had been to the market and was putting groceries away. Dean had been sleeping all day and got up demanding breakfast. Mom lost it and basically told him he was good for nothing and to leave. Dean cursed her and slapped her in the mouth."

Ned closed his eyes. "I didn't really know Dean. We grew up in the same house, but he was older and never gave me the time of day. When I saw him hit my mother, I snapped. I was bigger, played football, worked out with weights. Even though he was older, he wasn't all bulked up like he is now, and it wasn't much of a fight; he had no chance.

"Anyway, to make a long story short, the cops came. They knew Dean was the troublemaker, and in spite of the fact that I'd given him quite a beating, they took him back to jail. When Dad came home and saw my mother's face . . . well, that was it for him, too. He refused to take any calls from Dean, got a restraining order, even cut him out of the will. Basically he disowned him. We were living in Rancho Palos Verdes at the time. That was when my dad relocated to Arizona. And that move probably saved my parents' marriage, but Dean just got into more trouble."

Carly's interest was piqued at this information. "You mean you grew up here on the coast?" Rancho Palos Verdes was an expensive coastal community, a suburb of Los Angeles not far north of Las Playas.

"Yeah, we lived there until I enlisted in the Marines. My parents moved to Arizona shortly thereafter."

"Ned and I met in Rancho," Erika said. "My dad was stationed here for a couple years while I was in high school. My family moved to Germany just before graduation. Ned and I crossed paths years later when he was stationed in Germany." Erika got up and went to lean next to her husband, holding his hand in both of hers. "It was love at second sight." Then her smile faded. "I've always remembered Dean as mean. When I saw him after Ned's injury, it was at Walter Reed, during Ned's physical therapy. He showed up out of the blue and found me. And do you know what he said?"

Carly shook her head, touched to the core by this story and the two people in front of her.

"He grinned and said, 'The little brat finally got what he deserved.' Then he laughed."

"A short time after that he went to prison," Ned said. "You know the rest. Erika's family moved to San Diego, and we eventually ended up here to open the shop. I never thought I'd see Dean again."

"What did he want here? Was he after money?"

"That was the odd thing. He had lots of money. He kept flashing rolls of hundreds."

"Hmm." Carly digested this for a moment. "Where would an ex-con get that kind of money?"

"Claimed he had a partner and they bought a business," Erika said. "I hoped he'd changed. He is still family. And after spending six years in prison . . ." She hiked a shoulder. "When he showed up here, even after his run-in with you, for Ned's sake I hoped he was different." She and Ned shared a look.

"But he wasn't," Ned continued. "He pulled money out of his pocket and some crack fell out. Same old Dean. I asked him to leave and he tried to start a fight. It was Londy who kept us from getting into it. Then he left, screaming that we'd be sorry because he was going to hold all the cards soon. He must have come back that night after we closed and set the device."

"What did he mean by holding all the cards?"

Ned arched an eyebrow. "He claimed that the woman he'd hooked up with — you saw her, that blonde — he said she was going to break a big story and eventually write a book and have a television show that would make millions. And he was along for the ride."

Carly thought of Ginny Masters and her brow furrowed. "How long has he been here? He told the guys who talked to him the other night he'd just gotten into town. How did he have time to hook up with anyone?"

"He told us he'd been here a couple of days," Erika said. "I think he knew her from before."

"Before he went to jail?"

"Maybe. They seemed too close to have just met." Erika held Carly's gaze and smiled. "I know what you're thinking. Dean looks quite beat-up and dangerous. But he's never had a hard time attracting women. With Ginny . . . well, he must have known her in Arizona. She was obviously quite devoted to him."

"And if Dean knows anything, it's how to exploit any situation to his favor," Ned added.

"Did he say any more about his partner? Or what kind of business they bought?"

Ned and Erika exchanged glances. "No, he didn't, and I asked him point-blank about what kind of business would generate that much cash," Erika said.

"He just smiled like the cat who ate the canary and said we'd understand it all in a few days."

"What about Michael Carter? Do either of you know someone by that name?"

They both shook their heads.

Carly looked up at the ceiling before meeting Ned's gaze. She told him about Trey and the description of the man who gave him the guns.

The room was quiet for a minute.

Finally Ned said, "Well, I hate to say it, but I would not put anything past my brother."

22

By the time Carly returned to work for her shift that night, there was an APB out for Dean Barton. He still hadn't been connected to the coffee shop bomb, but the sketch drawn up based on Trey's description was a perfect representation of his face. That was enough for the law enforcement agencies involved to decide that he needed to be found and questioned.

Dean also had an extensive LA County arrest record from when he lived in Rancho Palos Verdes. ATF was looking up all his known associates, guessing that his partner was someone from his past who was still doing crime in the LA area. But none of the known associates from LA was named Michael Carter.

Carly was glad to hear about all the manpower and resources dedicated to finding the guy, but one bit of disturbing information also came with it: Ginny Masters was nowhere to be found. Had she gotten in over her head with a dangerous man?

Nick had come home around four in the afternoon and was still sleeping soundly when Carly left for work at nine thirty. She took pains not to disturb him because she knew he needed to rest.

She drew a solo car again because even though Kyle was at work, he was assigned to work with a rookie whose training officer was sick.

Radio traffic was sparse and routine when her shift began. She welcomed the quiet because she was tired. And there seemed to be resolution in the air with the wanted poster for Barton. Maybe he was the key to all this. Maybe he and his shadowy partners had a twisted motive for all the mayhem in Las Playas, starting with the shooting of the gang members.

By 2:30 a.m., as the afternoon units logged out of service, Carly was battling drowsiness. She decided to get out and walk around to keep from falling asleep. She picked the Bluestone as the best place for a stroll. Maybe she could kill two birds with one stone — wake up and satisfy her curiosity about what Victor had told Londy about following his brother to the construction site. She knew Harris and Romo had checked the place out after she told them what Victor had said; they had come up empty, but Carly was fairly certain they wouldn't mind her poking around.

The ten-story hotel sat on the ocean side of Seaside Avenue on a rise between the new marina and the old marina. Rooms on one side of the hotel would look down on the new tourist marina and shops while the rest of the hotel would look out at the old marina and ocean. Off to the left as she drove up, Carly could see the lights of a huge billboard advertising the upcoming grand opening and pedestrian bridge dedication.

The entire property was fenced off and padlocked with a city lock, in case emergency services needed to respond to the site for some reason. Carly had an SM6 key, a master key for any city padlock. She typed in her location as code 6, out for investigation, and sent it to dispatch on the computer. When she stepped out of the car to unlock the gate, her gaze went to a beautiful full moon. It was a gorgeous June night, and the parking lot was bathed in moonlight.

Leaving the gate open behind her, she drove to the front of the hotel and parked. Several floodlights illuminated the area, but the Bluestone itself was dark. The building had been a striking piece of twenties art deco construction, but now only the bones remained. Its first major setback had been a big earthquake in 1933. It had been rebuilt and thrived for about fifty years before becoming little more than a flophouse for drug addicts by the time Carly was hired on the force. Now it was stripped nearly to the frame and wrapped in opaque industrial plastic so no asbestos fibers would escape.

Carly climbed out of the car, her mind going over what Victor had told Londy about the day he had followed Crusher. Victor had admitted to entering the property through a hole in the fence. Carly was surprised Oceans First hadn't found it. She made a mental note to stop by in the morning and tell the foreman he needed to secure the lot better.

She shone her flashlight toward the dark building, then started around toward the back, not wanting to search for a hole in the fence in the dark. Victor had said his brother met the three white guys on the back side, near a small building.

Boots crunching on bits of plaster and rocks, Carly skirted the corner of the building, shining her light ahead of her. Above her a slight breeze ruffled the plastic here and there and made a flapping noise. The property was littered with various forms of construction equipment. Three huge aerial work platforms were lined up, blocking her view of the harbor. A large storage container, which probably served as the job office, sat on the other end of the terrace.

She moved closer, only to realize the container was nothing more than a storage unit. Frowning, Carly considered that maybe Victor thought it was a small building. Then something shiny caught her eye.

At the far corner of the container she bent to pick it up. It was a bullet — a 9mm round. Not something needed for a construction site. An interesting find, but not worth much in terms of evidence. An unspent round couldn't be tied to a gun.

She moved the beam of her light and spotted a worn trail in the dirt between rows of ice plants that ran down the embankment. *Where does this go?* She started down the path and ended up at the construction yard for the new marina.

Huh, Carly thought. *The construction company working on the Bluestone isn't the same company working on the marina, so they wouldn't need to go back and forth. Why is there a path here?*

The yard itself was well lit in the middle,

but shadows along the fence created some completely dark places. Her light bounced up against the fence and she saw the hole.

Down on one knee, Carly could see that the fence had been cut and then pulled together to appear as if it were whole. She stood and took out her radio to ask for backup, explaining that she wanted to investigate a hole in the fence at the construction yard. The dispatcher asked her exact location. As she looked around the area, she realized the quickest way to reach the spot was to follow her footsteps. She'd left the gate open at the Bluestone, so the responding officers wouldn't have to pause and open a gate.

A couple of units answered, and Carly prepared to wait until someone was with her. The hole was in a good spot, she thought. Especially at night, people could come and go without attracting any attention. But still, marina patrol or private security should have seen this in the daytime. Oceans First could try to occupy the place. Maybe Oceans First protestors had made the hole. *But then why not pour in through the hole? Why try swimming from the ocean side?*

She tested the spot, and the fence came open easily in her hand.

Just then a light flashed over the water by the old marina. Carly stepped through the hole and squinted, wondering if she was imagining things or if something had flashed on one of the live-aboard boats. But the light hadn't come from the boats; it had come from a boarded-up restaurant in the old marina. Walt's had closed and would have been demolished, but — in what would be Oceans First's only victory — they'd gotten an injunction stopping the demolition of the old marina until an environmental study could be completed.

Suddenly the light flashed again. This time she heard a voice in the distance, getting closer. Someone was walking her way. She saw the silhouette of a man hugging the darkness of the fence line, his hand to his ear. She guessed he was talking on a cell phone.

Thinking commercial burglary at worst and trespassing at best, Carly drew her gun and held it down at her side. She raised the beam of her light. "Police. Stand where you are."

The man stopped, squinting in the light. Dean Barton.

Their eyes locked as Carly raised her gun. "Stop right there."

"Cops!" Barton yelled into the phone

before jamming it into his pocket.

Then he turned and ran. Not the way he came. He ran toward the bulk of the new marina construction and into the light, zigzagging around construction equipment.

"Stop!" Carly spit out in frustration as she started after him.

In the back of her mind, she knew she should wait for backup. But a surge of anger toward the fleeing man pushed her forward, and she disregarded common sense.

Barton disappeared around some equipment.

Gun in one hand, radio in the other, Carly charged after him, telling dispatch in a rush what was happening.

By the time she'd reached where she'd last seen him, Barton's feet were disappearing around the front of an almost-finished Mexican restaurant. She jammed the radio back into its holder and barreled after him.

Seeing the door to the restaurant closing, she pushed it open and stepped into the dining room as Barton bounded up the stairs to the second level. Carly followed, intent on seeing Barton in handcuffs.

At the top of the stairs, she paused, gun hand pointed ahead of her, arms forming an X, with the flashlight beam cutting through the murky darkness.

It appeared as though this would be the bar area of the restaurant. The room was large and open, and she could see a finished bar ahead of her and stacks of tables and chairs. She'd lost sight of Barton and strained to hear anything that would give his location away.

Off to her left, she saw movement and shone the light that way.

"There's nowhere to go, Barton. More cops are on the way." Carly followed the noise of footsteps with caution, knowing her help should be arriving any second.

Along the perimeter of the mezzanine were piles of drywall, cans of paint, an assortment of tools, and stacks of wood. There was no wall behind her, only a partially finished railing so the view of the downstairs would be unobstructed.

"No way I'm going back to jail." The voice was more to her left, but he wasn't far ahead of her.

Carly's anger had been doused by the fear of an ambush. She moved slowly, cautiously. Time was on her side; there was no need to rush.

"We have a lot of questions for you." She wanted to keep him talking, pinpoint his location. He could see her light coming, so Carly wanted a level playing field.

She stepped around a scaffold in time to see Barton double back to her right. Frustrated at the game of cat and mouse, Carly wanted to call in her backup but hesitated to put down either her gun or flashlight.

Suddenly Barton jumped from behind a stack of drywall.

Carly stepped back, startled. She hit the half-finished railing and felt it give way. Dropping the flashlight, she tried to grab something, but there was only air.

The last thing she saw before she hit the ground was Barton's grinning face.

23

Carly came to slowly, hearing sounds but not processing what she heard. She started to move, and pain snapped through her body in a spiderweb of unpleasant sensations.

"Whoa, take it easy. Stay still until medics get here."

Carly's eyes focused on Kyle Corley's face looking down at her. It was harder to focus her mind. She could hear the cackle of a police radio and the sounds of voices and people walking around. The area was bright with artificial light.

"What happened? Where — ?"

It came back in a rush — Dean Barton, the fall. She tried to sit up, but Kyle's hand stopped her before the pain did.

"Dean Barton. Where is he?"

"Stay still. He's been taken care of. You fell quite a distance and were out cold when I got here. Don't move; you might hurt something."

"I —" Carly's gaze traveled up to the gaping hole in the railing above her. It seemed a mile away. She realized she must be in the restaurant's entryway. "I fell that far?"

Kyle nodded. "Looks like you hit flat on your back, then your head. Vest probably saved you, but you still hit hard enough to get knocked out. Though I don't see any blood."

He looked away as new sounds entered the area. Carly could tell the paramedics had arrived. Her mind felt full of cotton.

She did her best to relax as the medics replaced Kyle and went to work assessing her. They removed her gun belt, and Kyle said he'd hang on to it for her. They began to do what she'd seen them do to countless accident victims — check her for injuries, apply a neck brace, and then roll her carefully onto a backboard — while they asked questions to assess her level of consciousness.

"What's your name?"

"Do you know what day it is?"

"How many fingers do you see?"

Carly did her best with the questions and could move her arms and legs, but her head hurt and she had been unconscious, so they

233

would take precautions until a doctor saw her.

"Kyle?" she asked as the medics raised the gurney from the floor.

"Yeah?"

"You call Nick?"

"You bet. He'll be waiting at the hospital."

Carly closed her eyes for the ride to the hospital. She struggled to remember what had happened. *Did Barton lead me into a trap? But how could he have known I was going to be there? And where was he coming from?*

She had trouble thinking clearly and thought about how dazed boxers looked as they tried to get up off the canvas after a hard blow. Carly figured she must look like that because she certainly felt like she'd been dealt a knockout blow. The only consolation was that the arrest of Dean Barton was bound to clear things up.

As promised, the first face she saw when she was taken out of the ambulance was Nick's.

"What happened, babe?" he asked, worry crinkling his brow as he took her hand in his.

Carly felt tears threaten at the thought of causing him so much worry. "Guess I wasn't looking where I was going" was all she managed.

The medics began to wheel her into the emergency room.

Nick walked alongside, holding her hand. "How bad does it hurt?"

"I've got a killer headache, but other than that, I think I'm okay. Can't wait to hear what Barton was doing in the construction yard."

Nick stayed close while Carly was examined. As soon as it was determined that nothing was broken, the neck brace and spine precautions were removed. But Carly's head pounded, and the doctor pronounced that she had a concussion. He repeated a lot of the questions the paramedics had asked, and Carly admitted to feeling a little fuzzy. He checked her grip, asking her to squeeze his fingers, and made no pronouncement but seemed satisfied. He wanted to do a CAT scan and keep her under observation for several hours.

Carly found she didn't have the strength to argue. Besides, the doctor said Nick could sit with her, and that made the stay bearable.

Sergeant Barrett came in as Carly sipped water and tried to remember all that had happened at the construction yard.

"I told them your head was too hard to be hurt by that little fall," Barrett teased. "It was only about fifteen feet."

"Fifteen feet?" Nick stared at her.

"Nothing broken," Carly said, squeezing his hand. "Did Barton say why he was there?" she asked Barrett, wanting to change the subject.

Barrett frowned. "Barton doesn't have much to say. Didn't you know?"

"Know what?"

He hitched up his gun belt. "Carly, Barton's dead. Bullet wound to the head. We'll have to wait for the coroner, but we assume it was your bullet. Homicide wants me to bag your hands for a GSR."

24

"Dead?" Carly felt as though she'd left reality. Maybe she was still out cold. She couldn't recall shooting Barton, but patches of her memory were blank. "GSR?"

Barrett nodded. "Homicide will be here to ask questions as soon as the scene is buttoned up and —" he cast a glance at the doctor — "and the doctor says it's okay."

The doctor shrugged. "Her memory is likely to be patchy for a bit. I've ordered a CAT scan, so as long as they don't interfere with that and as long as Carly feels up to answering questions . . ."

Carly was conscious of all eyes on her. "My head hurts, but I can answer questions. I just don't remember shooting him."

Barrett looked sympathetic. He opened the first of two paper bags and reached for her right hand. "This should have been done at the scene."

Nick stopped him. "You said her gun was

237

fired. Why do you need the GSR?"

"Harris wants it done." Barrett shrugged. "My guess is something doesn't add up, but you'll have to ask him."

"It's okay. Let him do it," Carly told Nick.

Barrett proceeded to bag both her hands to protect them until a gunshot residue test could be performed.

Nick stood with a worried frown. "What's the last thing you do remember?"

"I was chasing him. He ran through the yard and into the restaurant and ignored my order to stop, but —" She closed her eyes and leaned back, trying to picture the scene again.

"You have your gun drawn?" Barrett asked as he finished the taping.

"Yeah, my gun and my flashlight were up, but it was for safety. I mean, the guy's an ex-con; he's wanted. I tried to stop him so I could take him into custody." *And he made me so mad I wasn't thinking straight.*

"Why don't we give this a rest for now?" Nick said to Barrett. "You have to fill out her injury paperwork. Let's do that and let homicide ask the other questions. Maybe Carly will remember more when the shooting team gets here."

Barrett agreed and picked up his clipboard. Carly answered his questions about

238

the fall as best she could. They'd just finished when a nurse came to take her for the CAT scan. She heard Nick ask the doctor if she could have caffeine when she was done. The doctor said yes.

"Hear that, babe? I'll be here with fresh coffee when you get back."

The scan took about twenty minutes. Carly actually felt better once it was over. She felt even better when she saw Nick's smiling face and the steaming cup in his hand. But then she saw Harris and Romo. Beside them was the lab tech who would conduct the GSR test.

"Hey, Carly, how are you feeling?" Harris asked in a tight voice.

"Like I didn't see the truck." She scooted up to drink the coffee Nick held out for her.

"We need to do the GSR." He gestured to the lab guy, who stepped forward and started with the left hand. "There are some strange things at the scene. I'm not going to taint your recollection by telling you what we found, but this test may clear up some stuff."

"Fine. I don't have a problem."

Carly forced herself to relax as the lab tech used small circular swabs, pressing them over her hands and also her face. He was efficient and finished quickly.

As the tech packed up the test in his kit, Harris pulled out a mini recorder. "If you feel up to it, I need to know exactly what happened, and I want to tape it."

With the bags from her hands gone, Nick handed Carly her coffee and she took a sip before answering. She told Harris how she had gone to the Bluestone to walk around. But he stopped her almost immediately.

"You left the gate open?"

"Yeah, I wasn't going to lock myself in. That would be shoddy officer safety. Why do you ask?"

"Because the gate was locked when assisting units got there," Harris said. "They would have reached you a lot faster if they hadn't had to stop and unlock the gate."

"But that was why I left it open." Carly felt the blood rush to her face. Her head started to pound again. Only a green rookie would have locked a gate behind them like that.

"Calm down, babe," Nick soothed. "Someone else must have shut it."

"But who? And why?" She stared at him, doubt invading her cloudy mind. Carly pushed the doubt away; she knew she'd left the gate open.

"Let's move on," Harris prompted. "Tell

us what happened next."

Carly continued with the narrative. Details were clearer now — until she got to the confrontation with Barton.

"Was he armed?" Romo asked.

"I didn't see a weapon. I drew mine when I thought I had a burglary in progress. I'm not sure where he came from. Did you find out what he was doing in the construction yard?"

Romo shook his head. "There was no sign that anything was tampered with. But the yard is a mess of equipment. We asked the foreman to check everything out thoroughly and get back to us if anything is amiss."

"There certainly isn't anything worth stealing down there, unless you have the ability to remove heavy construction equipment." Harris rubbed his chin. "It's curious he led you to that restaurant."

"Why? What was special about that place?" Nick asked.

"That's anyone's guess," Romo said. "But he must have known the railing was only partially finished. There had been a rope with caution signs around it. We found it tossed to the side."

Carly looked away from Romo. "Barton set me up?"

"Looks that way. He intended to do you

harm. We can prove it if this becomes an issue."

Carly's voice fled. She'd let her anger at Dean Barton lead her into a trap that could have cost Carly her life. The thought froze Carly's blood, and she closed her eyes, struggling for memories that wouldn't come.

"You okay? Your face went pale," Nick said as he grasped her hand.

"I don't know." Carly opened her eyes again. "It's unnerving thinking about what might have happened."

"Be thankful it was nothing more serious than a bump on the head," Nick said, enfolding her hand in both of his.

"I agree," Harris said. "The shooting sure smells like a setup."

"But if Barton set me up, why did he end up dead?"

"I don't know." Harris checked a text, then put the phone back on his belt. "Bottom line — assisting officers heard two shots fired with about one, maybe one and a half minutes between shots. Barton was shot once in the forehead, and two rounds were fired from your weapon." He held Carly's gaze. "You carry your weapon with a full clip and one round chambered, correct?"

Carly nodded.

"You don't remember firing and shooting him?"

"No, Pete. He startled me. That's why I stepped back into the railing. And he was grinning at me. That's the last thing I remember."

Andrea arrived with Carly's mother after Harris and Romo left. Carly was glad Barrett was gone too. She didn't need any drama from an encounter with Andrea. But she hated being fussed over, and that was something her mother excelled at.

"You have a nasty bump on your head," Kay observed, frowning. "And you don't look good. Are they certain it's just a concussion?"

"That's what the doctor said, Mom."

"They did a CAT scan, Kay." Nick put himself between Carly and Kay. Carly could have hugged him. "The doctor said it looked fine. He told me what to watch for, and I haven't seen any warning signs. Her thinking is clearing up. The doctor will be back in about an hour to tell us if we can leave."

"I'm just getting tired from sitting on my butt." Carly yawned. "And I'm a little sore, but my head isn't pounding anymore." Actually, her lower back and neck hurt a lot. Carly figured it was from how she'd landed. She knew she'd ache later on.

"You haven't had any dizziness or nausea, right?" Andrea asked.

"No. And I don't feel so confused anymore. But I still can't remember everything."

"That's normal." Andi gave a wave of her hand. "The details will probably come to you when you're thinking of something else."

"One thing is bothering me. I'm not sure if it's anything to be concerned about, but has anyone heard from Ginny Masters? She was incommunicado yesterday. I may not like the woman, but I'd hate to think of Barton doing anything to her."

"I can check with Alex." Andrea pulled out her cell phone. "He'll be able to ask the newsroom."

"Kind of early to wake him up, isn't it?" Nick said, pointing at the clock. It was coming up on 5:30 a.m.

Andi gave him a brilliant smile before waltzing out the door to use her phone outside. "He loves to hear from me no matter what the time."

The comment made Carly smile, but it quickly faded when another thought came to her. "Oh, I just remembered Ned."

244

"Hmm?" Nick sat on the edge of the bed while Kay moved to the head.

"They weren't close, but Dean was Ned's brother. I'll need to speak to him, tell him how sorry I am."

"Better wait until you can say exactly what happened," Nick said, leaning down to press his lips to her forehead.

25

"You don't have to stay and babysit me." Carly patted her wet hair gingerly with a towel. She and Nick had made it to occupational health as it opened, and the doctor had put her off work indefinitely, ordering that she be reevaluated next week. As the day began, she'd showered and was ready to try to get some sleep.

Nick had kicked his shoes off and reclined on the bed. "Yeah, I do. The doctor told me to keep an eye on you today. Fernando has everything under control. Mickey is awake, and he's been upgraded to stable. My phone is on. I can stay home and watch my wife for a day."

"Hmph. I'm not an invalid," she huffed without much feeling as she hung up the damp towel. Carly loved having Nick home with her, today more than usual because of her interview with homicide and the lingering anxiety from falling and not remembering.

Struggling to quell the frustration, she smoothed her still-wet hair with her fingers and curled up next to her husband. Try as she might, there was no place in her mind where she could access what had happened in that second between when she saw Dean Barton grinning at her and felt the railing give way behind her.

"I need to remember," she said, gripping Nick's hand. "A man is dead."

Nick brought her hand to his lips. "We'll pray, and you will remember." He smiled and prayed, and in spite of everything swirling around in her thoughts, Carly went to sleep almost immediately after he finished.

The first call came around 11:15 a.m. to the house landline, and it was a tip-off that the floodgates were about to open.

"Who was it?" Carly asked with a yawn and a stretch and an *ow*. She ached all over and felt as though she'd been in a car accident. Adding to her discomfort, she hadn't wanted to eat before she went to sleep, so now she was starving. She ran a comb through her hair, wincing when she came to the knot her fall had left.

"Channel 2. They wanted a statement about the shooting."

She looked up to see Nick's brow furrowed with irritation and worry, the scar on his forehead an angry shade of red.

"What about the shooting? And how did they get our home number?"

He shook his head. "I'm not sure what's going on."

The phone rang again and he waved a hand. "Let it go to voice mail. I'm going to fire up the computer and check the *Messenger* website. Why don't you turn on the TV?"

Carly nodded and followed Nick into the living room.

The phone rang again, and a second after that, Carly's cell phone buzzed.

The caller ID said Andi, so Carly answered. "What's up?"

"How are you feeling?"

"Okay, I guess. A little sore." She rolled her shoulders. "But overall fine. Why?"

She heard Andrea sigh. "Carly, that woman is evil. I can't believe what she's done. I can't —" she sputtered.

"Who?" She looked at Nick, who was studying the computer. The scar on his forehead was the darkest she'd ever seen it. "Masters?" She spoke the name of the only evil woman who came to mind.

"Yes. You were worried about her safety.

Do you know where she was? She was out at the state prison in Tehachapi, interviewing Drake and Tucker. Now she's quoting them, calling you a loose cannon, saying you assassinated Dean Barton!"

"What?" Carly's stomach turned as she remembered how much damage a newspaper reporter could do by tossing around accusations and skewing the facts.

"Alex will call you. He has the details. Right now see if you can catch the local noon news reports. I'm so sorry."

Carly closed the phone and clicked on the TV, then moved to where Nick sat. "How bad is it?"

He shook his head. "Bad. She claims Barton told her he was afraid of you. That he knew you wanted to hurt him. She also claims that you drew down on him at the hospital for no reason and that she has the pictures to prove it. She's screaming for an independent investigation into his death."

Carly felt her knees weaken, and she sat down heavily next to Nick to look at the headline under breaking news. *"Reporter Alleges Murder by Cop,"* it blared.

Her headache returned full-force as she turned her attention to the TV screen and switched to channel 2. When the noon news report started, Carly felt jolted as if by

249

electric current.

There was her picture as the newscasters droned on with Ginny Masters's accusations. They quickly switched to a live shot of Masters standing in front of Half Baked and Almost Grounded. She announced that she'd learned there already was a federal investigation into the shooting death of Dean Barton, a man, she said, wiping away tears, who was trying to turn his life around until he ran into an unforgiving and corrupt police officer who didn't believe that anyone could change. She vowed to keep the pressure on until the feds arrested a murderer.

"Officer Edwards persecuted Dean, hounded him. She was waiting for a chance to hurt him. I just can't believe she'd kill him in cold blood. He was unarmed! It makes you wonder about every investigation this rogue officer has ever been involved in." Masters dissolved into tears.

The television reporter took over and tried to get a comment from someone in the coffee shop. Erika was there, and she firmly told them that no one had any comment. The reporter sent it back to the studio, where the anchor read the formal police statement and said that Captain Jacobs would be holding a press conference later in the day.

Carly's cell phone buzzed again. This time it was a text from the POA president, asking that she call right away.

She showed it to Nick.

He brought a knuckle to his lip. "I'll call him. He's probably going to advise we get representation."

Carly nodded and folded her arms as he pressed the number to the Police Officers Association. Numbness spread from her head to her toes. *Representation . . . I need a lawyer,* burned in her thoughts.

She heard only Nick's half of the conversation but she understood the gist. The POA president advised that she not report for any interviews until she was cleared medically. Hopefully by then more facts would surface to support her story. He also suggested an attorney be present for any talks with the feds.

Part of Carly bristled at this. She had nothing to hide; only the guilty hid behind lawyers. But she realized it was probably sage advice.

Nick ended the call and wrapped Carly in a hug. She didn't want to cry, but it was just too much déjà vu. Nearly two years ago she'd been hounded by a false press allegation that had resulted in her being yanked from patrol and hidden away in juvenile.

How can I go through this all over again?

She buried her head in Nick's chest, knowing she didn't shoot Barton in cold blood. *That couldn't have happened, could it?*

Why can't I remember?

26

By the next morning Nick wanted to pack up the dog and get out of town for a few days. Carly was on medical leave, and he had plenty of vacation hours to burn. Ginny Masters's front-page story ran that morning with excerpts from her interviews with Karl Drake and B. K. Tucker, the two disgraced police officers Carly had helped to put behind bars. They'd accepted plea agreements months ago but refused to testify against Burke.

Hardheaded, know-it-all, and *trigger-happy* were some of the phrases used to describe Carly. Not surprisingly, the two former officers didn't have anything nice to say. She wondered why Masters hadn't also gone to Burke for dirt.

When Nick checked in with Fernando, he learned that a team of FBI agents had subpoenas for Carly's personnel records. The only good news was that they were keeping a low profile, so the specifics of their investigation wouldn't be released to the media. Carly heard that Wiley was also involved in the investigation. She figured that meant the task force was no longer in her choice column, which stung more than she expected since she wasn't sure she really wanted the job.

Carly knew having the feds involved was good politically, that it would make the investigation completely impartial. But the cloud over her name was almost unbearable. The phone calls from news agencies were maddening. When an afternoon talk station with two loudmouthed shock jocks started piling on, even her mother called, disturbed by what she was hearing. The DJs didn't have any of their facts straight. They said Carly shot Barton in the back and were calling for a public arrest and perp walk.

"The investigation has just started," Kay said when she talked to Carly. "How can they say those horrible things?"

"I don't know, Mom. I'm trying not to listen."

Her mother had ended the call with a tearful prayer that the truth would come out soon. Carly had to blow her nose after talking to her mom, hating that the fallout from an incident she couldn't remember was affecting everyone she cared about. She and Nick had turned the landline off and were only answering cell phone calls from numbers they recognized. It broke her heart to see all the negative press impeding her husband from doing the job he loved.

"We can't leave now," Carly told Nick after breakfast that morning. "You have to find out why Barton wanted Londy shot."

"Fernando is doing a good job directing things. I trust my team."

Carly sat at the kitchen table, where she'd been doing a devotional and trying to beat down the anger she felt toward Ginny Masters. But the anger gushed anew, burning through her like a swath of molten lava. *I've been through this before,* she thought, *but I wasn't with Nick then. Seeing how it's affecting him is just about more than I can bear.*

Why, Lord? Why?

She'd been reading in Psalm 62, how David waited quietly for the Lord, how he counted on the Lord to fight his battles and the Lord never failed him. "My victory and honor come from God alone. He is my refuge, a rock where no enemy can reach me." Holding that thought, she closed the Bible and went to where Nick stood leaning in the doorway. She put her hands on his face and looked into his blue eyes, eyes that always calmed and grounded her.

"Hey, I have to believe that God and the truth will clear me. Until then, I refuse to hide, and you can't either. You need to be with your guys right now."

He gave her a half smile, took one of her hands from his face, and kissed the palm. "I guess that Christian stuff really took with you, huh?"

She laughed. "I hope it did. I married a guy who is a strong Christian, and it makes our marriage so special."

He pulled her close and pressed his lips to her forehead. "That guy you married still sometimes needs to be reminded of who is in control."

"Don't we all." After a minute of enjoying his warmth and closeness, she moved back and pushed against his chest. "Why don't you go to work to make sure things are going smoothly? Get home by six and we can go to church together. We haven't gone to a midweek Bible study together in a while."

This time he pressed his lips to hers before he agreed and left her to change for work.

Nick hadn't been gone long before Andrea pulled up. It was her day off, and she brought some DVDs to watch.

"Alex is on his way home," she said as she

sat on the sofa and opened a bag of chips. "He and his father left San Francisco an hour ago, so they should roll into town in time for Alex to go to church tonight. He really wants to talk to you and would have phoned but decided a face-to-face is better."

"I hope he didn't cut his trip short on account of me." Carly reached into the bag and grabbed a handful of chips, mostly to stifle a smile. Andi had been incredibly resistant to church until she started seeing Alex. Now she talked about church as if it were as comfortable to her as a hair salon. Carly was glad to see the outward change, knowing an inward change couldn't be that far away.

"Are you kidding? He's been dying for an excuse to come home. He would have flown but he can't get his dad on a plane."

"Is his dad going to live with him then? For good?" Carly opened a Diet Coke.

Andrea shrugged. "Alex is calling it a visit. Truth is, he doesn't think his dad can live by himself right now."

Carly was about to hit Play when her cell phone buzzed. "It's Joe," she said after checking the screen. Her partner had had his knee surgery the day before, and Carly wanted to talk to him.

"How are you doing?" he asked.

Joe's concerned voice brought a lump to her throat and a keen awareness of how much she missed him. He'd just had his knee cut on, and he was concerned about her. She worked to stay as upbeat as possible, reminding herself over and over that God was in control. When she hung up, she saw Andrea regarding her with a bemused expression.

"What?"

"Nothing, it's just . . . well, it's good to hear you so positive and upbeat. I don't think I would be under the same circumstances."

Carly sipped her Coke. Maddie jumped up next to her on the couch and gave her a look that said she wanted a chip. Carly fed her one.

The gravity of her situation was bearing down on Carly every minute. Masters was accusing her of cold-blooded, premeditated murder, of violating every single thing she stood for.

"I'm angry, Andi. Furious. But what do you want me do? Charge around like the loose cannon that woman is calling me?"

"No, no. But I remember a time when you'd have been more fired up. And I wish we could hit her in the face with a pie or something."

Carly laughed. "I'm afraid that right now I'd hit her with something harder. I just wish I could remember exactly what happened."

Andrea pulled a pillow into her lap and leaned forward. "Do you want to go over it? Maybe talk it through? It could jog your memory."

Before Carly could answer, there was a knock on the door. Maddie jumped down to run to the door and bark.

Carly shushed the dog and looked at Andrea. "You didn't invite anyone else to this movie party, did you?"

Andrea shook her head. "You want me to see who it is?"

"It might be a news crew or that obnoxious radio station. They've been such a pain. I can't believe they got our home number. Hate to say I wouldn't be surprised if they got our address as well."

Andrea stood up as the knock sounded again. "I can send them away with some legalese I learned from *Law & Order.*"

Carly held on to Maddie as Andi answered the door.

"Carly, it's Ned and Erika!"

Carly went to the door, not certain what to expect. She didn't see anger in their faces.

Instead, Erika smiled and held up a thermos of coffee in one hand and a pastry box in the other. "Carly, we wanted to come and say that we hoped you were doing all right."

"And that we're sorry for all the trouble Dean caused you," Ned added. "Would you accept this offering and talk with us?"

The foursome settled around the kitchen table. They'd brought Carly's favorite French roast coffee and an assortment of pastries. Even on top of the chips and Diet Coke, the sweet stuff was welcome.

"We've been chasing newspeople away from the shop since yesterday," Erika said as she plated the pastries and handed them around. "It wouldn't be so bad if they bought something, but all they do is pester."

"Even in Arizona, they were bothering my parents." Ned poured coffee. "My dad just decided to take my mom out of the country to get away from them."

"I'm so sorry," Carly said, still surprised and unsure about the couple's presence. "I mean, in spite of everything, he was your brother."

Ned set the thermos down, reached across the table, and put his hand over Carly's. "I don't blame you for Dean's death. I'd be lying if I said I felt nothing. I'm sad that Dean never could turn his life around. But one thing I learned in the military was how to size people up. And no matter what, I don't for a second believe you murdered him in cold blood like that woman is saying. That's not your style."

Tears threatened as Carly held Ned's gaze. Where she had feared she'd see accusation, all she saw was warmth and friendship. Until he'd spoken, she hadn't realized how much she'd been worried about what he thought and believed.

She swallowed. "Thanks, Ned. Thanks." She sipped her coffee.

Andrea jumped in. "Just what did your brother have going with that reporter, anyway?"

Erika held up an index finger and glanced at Ned before answering. "That was something we wanted to tell you, Carly. We think she met him in Arizona, but her name was different then."

"Really?"

"Yeah," Ned said. "After our last talk we made some calls and my dad did some checking. Apparently there was a woman who wrote a story on Dean after he was arrested six years ago. She went by the name Virginia Masterson. She was a local gadfly in city government with some kind of agenda against police officers. My dad didn't remember specifics. But the local paper did publish a three-part article on Dean."

Ned sighed. "He followed my parents to Arizona when they moved, but he never got work. He was living in his car at the time he was arrested. Anyway, this Masterson was sympathetic to Dean then, and after he was arrested, my mother remembers her calling and asking questions about why my father disowned Dean. They remember it vividly because the woman insinuated my parents were heartless and cruel to leave him out in the cold and that that was the reason Dean ended up in prison."

"Hmm." Carly sat back to digest this. "Someone else's fault, not because of his choices."

"Right," Erika said. "We don't know how or why this woman got here and became Ginny Masters, but it's too big a co-incidence for it not to be the same woman."

"Alex can find out," Andi said. "But she's been in California for at least a year because she worked at the *Times* before she came here."

"There are probably more opportunities for reporters here than in Arizona," Carly said. "It doesn't surprise me that she'd come here to work for a paper like the

Times. I just want to know what got her fix-
ated on me."

"Dean probably has a lot to do with that,"
Ned said. "Before I kicked him out of the
bakery and then found the bomb, he
brought her to the shop twice. She seemed
to idolize him, advocate for him." He shook
his head. "I think I told you before that he
was a master manipulator. He was surely
taking advantage of her."

Carly frowned, cutting her bear claw into
bite-size chunks but not putting any of it in
her mouth. "Some pieces are starting to fall
together. If they've had a long-term relationship and she considers herself an advocate
for him, maybe that's why she's picking on
me. She was blogging nasty stuff about me
for a couple of weeks." She paused, remembering the dates on Masters's blog posts.
"But it started before I ran into Dean, so
there's more than advocacy going on. Something is missing. I don't understand why
they both wanted to give me a bad time."

Ned leaned back in his chair. "Dean
always hated cops. Don't take that personally. From what I heard, he complained
about being misunderstood by police his
whole life, and that woman just took his
side. We saw the blog. We didn't believe any
of it. In fact, we don't believe what she's

saying now. She tried to drag us into a wrongful-death suit, and we told her to pound sand."

"Don't worry," Erika said, leaning forward. "We came to tell you that we believe in you. And we want to help."

"You've helped just by being here."

"We'd like to do more," Ned said. "I've been talking to Mickey and the ATF agents. They told me about the missing plastic explosive. I was an EOD technician before this." He held up his stump. "I know how dangerous that stuff is. And it wouldn't surprise me at all to learn that my brother had it squirreled away somewhere."

"That's great, Ned." Carly put down her fork and held out her hands. "But I'm not involved in the investigation. I can't be. But I bet if you can help them figure out who this mysterious Michael Carter is, that would be a big help."

"You mentioned him before." He looked at Erika, who shook her head. "The name is not familiar."

"I'll find out from Nick if he's been identified."

Ned sighed. "I need to help. I hate feeling useless. And since the cause of a lot of trouble seems to be my brother, I feel obligated." A weariness in his face made him seem older than his years.

Nick got home from work in time for dinner before church. Andrea planned to stay for dinner, but as they were finishing up the preparations, Alex called to tell her he'd gotten home. She left in a hurry to help him get settled in with his father. In the time before dinner was ready, Carly filled Nick in on what Ned and Erika had told her about Ginny Masters.

"That's interesting," he said. "I looked at the visitor logs. There was a Virginia Masterson listed several times. The prison noted she was press, so I didn't think anything more about it. You don't think she's involved in the killings and the gun theft, do you?"

"No." Carly blew out a breath. "But she could be a useful idiot, doing things for Barton and the two mysterious partners, thinking everything is on the up-and-up . . ."

"When it's not?"

"Yeah. You and I have both seen women like that, infatuated with someone to the point that even when you show them evidence the person is involved in illegal activity, they don't believe it." Carly had seen that a lot during her short time in juvenile. Some parents never wanted to believe their little darling was a crook.

Nick nodded. "Maybe we need to investigate the investigative reporter."

"And I think it's something Harris should know."

"Agreed." The timer for dinner rang, and Nick looked from Carly to the oven. "Right now I'm starved."

Carly smiled and gave him a kiss before removing the meat loaf from the oven.

"The second funeral is tomorrow," Nick said after he'd blessed the meal.

"Diondre's?" Carly took a bite and swallowed. "Hate to say it, but I'd forgotten he still needed to be laid to rest."

"You've had a lot on your mind." He smiled, making oohing and aahing noises. "Great dinner."

"You have to remember to thank Andrea. She went to the market for me and put some stuff in there that I never would have thought of. How are things on the street?"

He shrugged. "Quiet, actually. Londy has been a huge help. They had to raise money to bury D. That's what took so long. Every chance he's gotten, he's been out talking to kids, soothing tempers. Even after he got shot at." He cocked his head. "He's a great negotiator."

"Has Mary Ellen been with him?"

266

"As a matter of fact, she has. Why do you ask?"

"I think she's sweet on him."

His eyebrows arched. "Mary Ellen and Londy?"

"Uh-huh."

"Didn't see that coming," he said with wonder in his voice.

27

Carly feared the radio shock jocks would be covering the church grounds. She'd read that they were planning on doing a rally — a "Justice for Dean" rally or some such nonsense. But it turned out her fears were baseless. The crowd at church was simply made up of familiar fellow worshipers, many of whom stepped up to give her a hug and a show of support.

She got the surprise of her life when she saw Sergeant Barrett walking across the parking lot.

"Nick." She jabbed him with an elbow and pointed.

Nick smiled and moved to greet the man. "Hey, Hal, good to see you here, man."

Barrett looked surprised and then relieved. "Nick, Carly. I admit I feel a little out of place."

"No need." Nick shook his hand. "Want to come sit with us?"

"Uh, sure."

The three of them entered the church together. Carly's mother was already inside, and she gave Carly a tight hug. Nick introduced Kay to Barrett and they all took their seats. Carly wanted to ask Barrett if he knew any more about the shooting investigation. But because the service was about to start, she did her best to push all the turmoil from the past few days out of her mind and concentrate on the message. She felt more at rest than she had since being released from the hospital. It was fortifying sitting between Nick and her mother, surrounded by love and listening to Pastor Rawlings.

She'd hoped to see Alex, but Andrea had said he was exhausted, so Carly guessed he opted to stay home and get his dad settled.

Jonah was going through the book of Psalms on Wednesday nights. Carly had forgotten that since work had kept her away from the midweek study recently. It amazed and moved her that he reached Psalm 62 about midway through the message. That was the psalm she'd studied that morning in her devotional.

" 'My victory and honor come from God alone. He is my refuge, a rock where no enemy can reach me. O my people, trust in him at all times. Pour out your heart to him, for God is our refuge.' "

Carly read the words of the seventh and eighth verses over again and closed her eyes. She felt a great peace. God was her refuge. No one could reach through his protection; not even Ginny Masters could knock her down. *If I could just remember.*

Barrett left immediately after the service. Carly couldn't gauge if he'd been moved or not. He had listened and followed along in the Bible. After the message, she wanted to find Jonah and tell him how the message had touched her. She didn't have to look for him, though; he sought her out, and right behind him was a trim, dark-haired woman Carly didn't know.

Jonah shook Nick's hand and gave Carly a hug. "How are you doing?" he asked, his face crinkled with concern.

"I'm good. Psalm 62 says it all." She went on to tell him what a coincidence it was that she'd read the psalm earlier that morning.

He laughed. "I don't believe in co-incidences. If you need anything, don't hesitate to ask." He then gestured to the woman who'd followed him over. "Carly, Nick, I'd like you to meet Pam Sailor."

After they'd said their hellos, Jonah turned to Carly. "This is the woman I told you about. I was hoping you could speak to her."

Carly looked at Nick. "I have to find Londy and talk to him about the funeral tomorrow," he said. "I'll meet you in Heavenly Grounds."

He left and Carly turned to Pam. "Want to get some coffee or tea?"

She shook her head. "No thanks. But maybe we can find a place to sit."

The church had finished construction on a beautiful fellowship hall last year. It had a kitchen, a large area for tables and gatherings, a coffee shop and espresso bar named Heavenly Grounds, and a bookstore. Carly and Pam walked together to the coffee shop. If this had been a Sunday, the place would have been packed, but crowds were always smaller at midweek. They found a table right away.

"I want to thank you for talking to me, Officer Anderson."

"It's Carly, and it's no problem. I hope I can help."

Pam lowered her head and studied her hands. "I'm sure you know that my husband committed suicide last week." She looked up and Carly nodded. "Well, at first I thought it was all a mistake, that my husband wouldn't kill himself." She paused. "I was probably like the woman who's been cheated on — you know, in denial that my

271

husband would ever cheat."

She turned away for a moment. When she spoke again, her voice dripped with biting sarcasm. " 'My husband would never kill himself; he had so much to live for. . . .' Yeah, right. He had a lot of secrets to keep hidden. All the secrets are out in the open now that he's gone."

"I'm sorry. Was he having an affair?"

She shook her head violently. "If that's all it was, I could live with it. No, Keith wasn't having an affair. We'd been in business for fifteen years, started the catering outfit out of our own kitchen. And we built a big, strong business. At least I thought we had." She sighed deeply and rubbed her brow with two fingers. "I'm sorry. You must think I'm rambling."

"No, take your time. I can't imagine having to deal with what you're dealing with right now."

Pam hesitated before continuing. "You see, Keith had a passion for gambling that I knew nothing about. He was in debt — no, *we* were in debt to the tune of about a quarter of a million dollars. I didn't know that. I also didn't know that Keith had taken a loan out on the business. I was stupid enough to leave all the money matters to him. I'm the cook and planner." She stopped for a moment, then went on.

"He signed on a partner in order to have the money to keep the business rolling through the bridge dedication ceremony. Here I've been working myself to the bone to prepare for the biggest catering job we ever landed and . . ." Her voice broke.

Carly reached out, but Pam waved her away. "No, I need to finish. Argh, you think you're numb and that you've cried all the tears you can cry, and then they suddenly grab you by the throat." She composed herself and blew her nose.

Carly knew exactly how Pam felt. She waited patiently.

"Keith not only took a partner; he sold the business right out from under us. It seems the moneyman who bailed him out accepted the business as collateral. When Keith died, the business reverted to this man. I have nothing. I can stay and be an employee, but the business is no longer mine."

Carly's chest felt tight. Her problems faded away in comparison to the pain of the woman in front of her. "I'm so sorry. And you're sure it's legal? I mean, have you had a lawyer look at it?"

"It's legal. My lawyer says it is."

"How can I help?"

"This man — the man with the funds — his name is Michael Carter. All I want —"

"Michael Carter?" Carly stared at Pam Sailor.

"Yes. Do you know him?"

"No, but I've heard the name a lot lately. What do you know about him?"

"Nothing. All I want to do is talk to him, but he won't return my calls. I fired my lawyer because not only do I not have the money to keep him on, but he helped Keith with the paperwork behind my back. Look, I know there's probably nothing you can do, but I just want to find out if we can work something out so I can get the business back. Sailor's Catering was my life. Is there any way you can ask him to talk to me?"

Carly looked into pain-filled eyes. It wasn't the oddest request she'd ever gotten. There were people in the world who thought the police could solve any problem. And when they were desperate, the lines between criminal problems and civil problems blurred. This was definitely a civil problem, not a police problem. But she couldn't tell Pam Sailor that right now. Neither could she tell her that this elusive man by the name of Michael Carter was someone a lot of people wanted to talk to.

What she did say was, "All I can do is ask

him to talk to you. I can't force him."

Relief flooded Pam's face. "Thank you." She opened her purse and slid a business card across the table. "This is the only number I have for him. I've left several voice mails, but he never calls me back. A man calling himself Carter's assistant has spoken to me, firming up the plans we have for the bridge dedication, but that's it."

"The bridge dedication?"

"Yes, the assistant says that Mr. Carter is anxious to be certain everything is perfect for that event."

Carly looked at the card. It was a cheap white card with black printing on it, just *Michael Carter* and a phone number. Odd, inexpensive choice for a supposed money-man.

As Nick walked up, Carly promised Pam she'd call the number in the morning. Pam asked Carly to let her know what she learned and thanked her again.

"What was that about?" Nick sat, and they watched Pam leave the fellowship hall.

Carly held up the card.

"What?" Nick took it and studied it. "She knows him?"

"No, but he bought her business." She told Nick about Sailor's Catering and the suicide of Keith Sailor.

He frowned and rubbed his chin with his hand. "What is going on?"

28

Carly wanted to talk to Nick, but he was at work. He'd relayed what Pam Sailor had explained about Michael Carter to the ATF agents since they had the resources to track the man down.

When he'd gone to see Barton in prison, Carter had signed the visiting log with an Arizona driver's license. A little digging into the catering business purchase uncovered the same address as his ID. The phone number on the business card belonged to an untraceable burner phone. There was no California identification for the man.

Nick also promised to dig deeper into the shooting investigation at work that day.

As self-pity began to envelop her, Carly knew she had to do something to stop it. Nick always said that when the negative began to pile up, concentrate on the positive. She stood to pace and do just that.

The worst of her soreness had faded, and

she wanted to be at work — or at the very
least out defending her reputation, not stuck
in the house.

When the phone rang and she saw a work
extension, she nearly let it go to voice mail.
But she needed a distraction, any distraction. It was Captain Jacobs calling to see
how she was doing.

"I still can't remember."

"Relax, Trouble. I'm sure it will come
back. I wanted to see how you were doing
and to ask you a favor."

"I . . . umm, I'm fine. Considering everything going on right now, I'm okay. What
can I do for you?"

"Come in and talk to the department
psychologist. She may help with your
memory issue. I'm not going to order you.
But I'd like you to do it. Charlotte Linder is
light-years ahead of Floyd Guest. I'm
certain she'll help you."

Carly hesitated before agreeing to see
Linder that afternoon. In the end she
trusted Jake and understood what he was
saying about Guest. The old department
psychologist had been a partner in the corruption that resulted in the previous mayor's
murder. He'd tried to kidnap Carly from
the hospital. Linder wouldn't have to do
much to be an improvement.

After speaking with Jacobs, Carly debated calling Trejo but wasn't certain about the situation with his father. The phone rang before she'd decided. An unfamiliar work extension this time.

"Officer Edwards?" It was internal affairs.

"Um . . . hello."

"I'm calling to see if you can come into the office for an interview today at 1 p.m."

"Is this about the shooting?" Carly frowned. There'd been no shooting board.

"No. This is about a citizen's complaint. It's simply a routine interview."

Carly sighed and began fiddling with a pen, tapping it on the table in front of her, remembering that the POA president had told her to hold off on interviews until she was cleared of the head injury. But this was in-house, not the feds. *And I have nothing to hide,* she thought with a stamp of her foot.

"Yes, I'll be there."

Ending the call, she knew she needed to get out of the house. Carly pocketed her cell phone, grabbed the dog's leash, and headed for Dog Beach with Maddie. Reporters or no, she couldn't hang out in the house for two and a half hours until it was time to leave for IA. She'd climb the walls. What she really wanted to do was jump into her swimsuit and swim without stopping for a few thousand meters before surfacing to face the world. But Nick had expressly requested that she not swim by herself until the doctor cleared her. As much as she wanted to argue with him, she had to admit it wasn't an unreasonable request. So she'd just play fetch with Maddie for a bit.

She and Maddie were a block from the beach when her cell phone chimed with a call from Alex.

"I was going to come by. Where are you? At home?"

"On my way to Dog Beach. Meet me down there?"

"Sure."

She and Maddie had been in the sand for a few minutes when Alex showed up. He opened his arms and gave Carly a hug. As he apologized for what was happening, Carly fought to keep her composure.

"It's not your fault, Alex. You have your hands full. I'm sorry about your mom. How's your dad doing?"

Alex shoved his hands in his pockets and looked down before meeting Carly's gaze. "He's a broken man. My mom doted on him for over forty years and he treated her badly. Now he's all remorse and regret. Says he loved her but never told her. It's eating him up."

"You can't ever go back."

"No. But enough about my problems. I do feel responsible for yours. You know that Masters has hired a publicist? She's trying to get spots on all the big national news programs." He kicked a pile of sand. "I hate to say it, but people are nibbling and it's just making her more aggressive."

Carly took a deep breath and tossed a stick for Maddie. It was a struggle not to give in to all the negative emotions she felt. "What do you know about her? How'd she hook up with Duncan Potter?"

"I know you don't like Potter and his motives bug you, but he takes great pictures. Everyone wants his work. As for Masters, she fancies herself the next Katie Couric, and she'll do whatever it takes to get herself there."

"Do you know anything about where she was before she was hired by the *Times*?" Carly outlined what Ned had told her about Virginia Masterson.

Alex frowned and rubbed his chin. "I knew she was from out of state, but I only paid attention to what she did at the *Times*. They liked her work, or at least they said they did. She was let go because of layoffs. Last hired, first fired — that kind of thing."

"How long has she been in California?"

"She's been with us for six months, and I think she was with the *Times* for at least a year." He stopped. "You're not getting paranoid on me, are you? Do you think there's more going on here than a dead parolee?"

"I don't know, Alex. All I know is that I did nothing wrong — nothing. And she's trying to make me sound like Drake or Tucker. Maybe that wouldn't be so bad, but the FBI might be listening to her."

"They're just being polite."

Carly snorted.

He reached out and gripped her shoulder. "I know things are bad right now, and I want to help."

"I'm not sure what you can do. I'm off at least until I see the occupational health guy on Monday. The feds are in on the shooting investigation, and I have to talk to internal affairs today."

He put an arm on her shoulder as they strolled down the beach, and Carly felt the comfort of a friend.

"Are they going to suspend you?" he asked.

"The investigation is ongoing, so no, I don't think so. I think it's just routine. But then I don't know how much political pressure is building. Mayor Hardy was elected because he promised a scandal-free city. And then, of course, there's the Burke trial."

His face scrunched with worry. "Brace yourself. Scuttlebutt in the newsroom is that there's a lot of pressure building. Masters seems to have her finger on the pulse and she's exploiting that. Something may come up about the trial."

"I was afraid of that. Which brings me back to the big question: why me?" She stopped and turned to face Alex, hands on her hips.

He tossed another stick for Maddie. "You're a name. Let's face it — everyone in Las Playas has read about your work. By just doing your job, you made national news. You already brought up the trial. And next week you'll be honored at the bridge dedication. Masters saw you as a target; if she can topple you, think how much news that would make. And how many job offers she could conceivably generate."

"So this is all about her career?"

"From what I've seen, everything is about her. Now, about this Barton guy. I can only tell you what the newsroom gossip is. The more I think of it, this fits with what Ned told you. Masters seemed to indicate she had this long-distance relationship with him that only became a close physical relationship a month ago —"

"A month ago? He told officers the first night I saw him that he'd been out a month but had only just gotten into town."

Alex shrugged. "An ex-con lied to the police — imagine that. Masters said when she met him, it was love at first sight but they weren't able to be together. It wouldn't surprise me if she was one of those sick women who falls for someone behind bars and becomes a pen pal and that was their long-distance relationship."

"Ned said he thought they met when Dean first got arrested. She went from reporter to groupie to girlfriend, I guess, in six years." Carly rubbed her hands together. "While I'm certain Barton was behind the shooting and guns, do you think she has any connection at all to that?"

"I wouldn't put anything past her. She's a climber."

Carly said nothing and they started back the other way down the beach.

"I really do want to help," Alex said. "I can be the anti-Masters. Tell me what happened that night."

"That's the problem. I don't remember the most important part." Carly told Alex what she could recall up to the point where she saw Barton grinning at her.

"Is it possible your gun went off when you fell and it was just dumb luck the bullet hit him?"

Carly wrapped and unwrapped Maddie's leash around her wrist. She didn't tell Alex about the GSR. Homicide was trying to prove or disprove something with that; she could only speculate. "I don't know. I was in a haze when they took me to the hospital, so I didn't get a good look at the spot I fell from. But Barton was hit in the center of his forehead. If I'm falling down . . ." She stopped and tried to envision falling with her gun in her hand. "I guess it's possible. I just don't know for sure."

Alex shook his head and frowned. "I wonder if I could get in there and take a look at the scene."

"I doubt it. It's probably still sealed. Jacobs mentioned that the construction company was going to do a thorough inventory."

"I heard that the contractor is having a cow about how far behind that will put the restaurant opening."

They'd reached the walkway leading up and out of the beach. Carly unraveled the leash she'd been fiddling with and bent down to hook it to Maddie's collar. "You've already tried to get in, huh?"

Alex smiled. "I really mean it when I say I want to help. Let me ask you this — are you sure Barton was grinning at you?"

"What do you mean?"

"Well, you don't think he wasn't there by himself, right?"

Carly nodded and Alex continued. "Suppose he was grinning because he knew something you didn't? Maybe that you were outnumbered in there?"

Carly brought a hand to her forehead, trying to picture Barton's face in her mind. What had he been so gleeful about? "But even if there was someone else there — someone who was working with Barton — they had the advantage. They could have just killed me."

"Maybe Barton irritated more people than just you. Maybe the man who pulled the trigger was in the restaurant and he wanted to sever the partnership with Barton and saw the perfect opportunity to frame you."

They'd reached Alex's car. Carly looked at him and arched an eyebrow. "Maybe you read too many novels. I do know he was working with at least one other person, maybe two. I saw him with someone, and he told Ned he had a partner." She told Alex about Michael Carter. "And someone did lock the gate behind me, which slowed down my backup. But I'd need to know more about what Barton and his buddies were doing at the old marina."

He folded his arms and leaned against the side of his car, cocking his head to the side. "Boy, I go away for a little bit and this whole city falls apart. Wild parolees, gang wars — what's next?"

"I hope truth and closure. You know, before this happened, when Barton was implicated in the stolen guns, Nick and I sat down and tried to figure out what was going on."

"You mean with the gang shooting?"

"We're not sure it was a gang shooting. We think Barton was trying to instigate a war, but we don't know why."

"I haven't had a chance to review everything. If I'd been here, I would have been covering everything. As it is, I have to go by what's been published."

"We were thinking it had something to do with the Ninjas — Londy specifically. He was shot at and he used to be a Ninja."

"Maybe Barton's partner had a beef with the Ninjas?"

Carly shrugged. "Not sure. We were hoping Barton would answer questions and fill in the blanks. I didn't want him dead." She shook her head in an attempt to shake away her uneasy feeling. "I have to get going. Thanks, Alex, for being a friend."

"No problem. But you still haven't told me how I can help you the most."

"I don't know." She turned to leave and then stopped. "Maybe if I knew for certain why Masters hates me."

"I'll find out everything I can about her," Alex promised. "And . . ."

"And what?"

"This mysterious Michael Carter has piqued my curiosity."

"The feds will find out about him soon, I'm certain."

"So you say. One more thing."

"Yeah?"

"I don't think Londy and the Ninjas are the only targets. Something tells me Officer Carly Edwards fits into that equation as well. Watch yourself."

29

"Watch yourself."

Carly considered Alex's words while she got ready for her meeting. But for the life of her, she couldn't remember anything controversial she and the Ninjas had been involved in. And as for Londy — she had helped clear his name, but that was about the mayor's murder; it had nothing to do with the Ninjas.

The whole thing was giving her a headache, so she pushed it away to concentrate on her appointments.

She decided to dress casual for IA, settling on jeans and a blouse with flats instead of tennis shoes. She also called and asked the union for a representative to be with her during the interview. On the way to the car she debated texting Nick about the IA meeting. She'd been listening to the police radio and knew the funeral was in full swing. She finally concluded that it would be better not to distract him. If he called her, she'd tell him, but she wasn't going to take the chance of throwing him off his game at all.

IA was in a building across the street from the police department. Though she wasn't surprised, the sight of protestors on the station's front steps still gave her a shock. Just about any police shooting brought protests out of the woodwork; the fact that a man was dead amplified the dissent. She didn't dwell on the crowd but did read a couple of signs as she pulled into the lot across the street. One read *End Police Brutality* and another said *Send killer cops to prison.*

Carly saw Sergeant Cooper as she parked. She was a day sergeant, a union rep, and a welcome presence. Cooper had been a cop for about fifteen years and was highly respected. She was Nick's substitute weaponless defense instructor when he couldn't teach a class. She'd also passed the bar and did law work in her off time. While Carly doubted she needed a lawyer at this stage of the game, it never hurt to have experience on your side.

"Hey, Carly, how are you doing?" Cooper held out a hand.

Carly shook it. "Okay. Feeling healthy.

290

Hoping to be cleared for duty next week."

"Good. Glad you weren't hurt bad. I guess you noticed the cheering section." Cooper jabbed a thumb toward the protestors.

Carly nodded. She could also see now that a podium was set up for a press conference. She wondered if one had already been given or was going to be given soon. "I hope the protests aren't making life hard for the guys on the streets."

Cooper shrugged. "Don't worry about that. Things will settle down once we get more information on the whole incident. Captain Jacobs might have some information. He's giving a press conference later."

Carly thought about that. Jacobs hadn't mentioned a press conference to her. She wondered if something had happened since she spoke to him. Regardless, she found herself hoping she'd be home before that circus started.

"I guess we should head in," she said to Cooper. Together the two of them entered the IA office.

"I talked to Granger — he's the investigator assigned to you," Cooper said.

Carly silently groaned. Granger was a much-hated old-timer. Though he was known as a relentless investigator with the nickname Headhunter, he didn't play dirty as far as she knew. She'd always felt that if cops were doing wrong, they needed to be weeded out. Guys like Granger were a necessary evil. But rumor had it he was angry that Drake and Tucker had managed to be involved in so many illegal activities and yet had escaped notice. Some guys said he made up for that oversight by being especially hard on everyone who now came to his attention.

"This meeting has to do with a couple of IA complaints filed by Dean Barton and Ginny Masters," Cooper said. "Granger assured me he just wants your side of the story. Since no shooting board has been convened yet, this doesn't have anything to do with the shooting."

"A couple? I only knew about one."

"His words were 'a couple.' Don't stress; let's hear him out."

Carly puffed her cheeks and blew out a breath. "Well, let's get this over with."

The secretary directed them to Investigator Granger's office.

Carly saw three complaint forms spread out on Granger's desk and struggled to keep surprise from her face. Her palms got clammy.

Granger waved her forward and passed

the three complaints to her. "Read through them," he said, his expression pure cop.

She quickly scanned the first and only one she recognized, then picked up the other two and saw that Barton had filed one after Carly saw him in the coffee shop the second time and that Barton and Masters had filed the third jointly after the incident at the hospital.

"We just hadn't gotten around to contacting you about these two," Granger explained. "The complaints were coming in fast and furious and we got a little behind."

Carly did a double take to see if he was joking but saw only hard eyes. She certainly saw nothing humorous in the situation but knew getting angry and upset would do nothing for her cause.

"I wasn't persecuting him, and I never drew down on him at the hospital." Immediately Carly hated sounding defensive.

"I'll write that down, but you sure seemed to cross paths with this guy a lot." Granger sat back in his chair and fixed a stony gaze on her. When he spoke, his tone said he'd not tolerate any fabrication. "Just tell me your side. You know the drill. I'll be talking to all of the witnesses in each incident. You can also tell me who you remember being present at each confrontation."

Carly refused to be intimidated and took a deep breath. She told her side of the two incidents, speaking as dispassionately as possible, as though she were on the witness stand and relating only the facts. Granger interrupted her.

"That's all? Just coincidences here?" he asked with one raised eyebrow. "Sure there's nothing else?"

"What else would there be?" Carly tensed.

"This reporter claims your body language was threatening."

"I was alert. By then I knew Barton was an ex-con. Officer safety dictated my body language."

"Relax, Carly." Cooper put a hand on her shoulder and addressed Granger. "Thought all you wanted was her side."

Granger gave a half shrug. "If this is what she wants down, this is what I'll put down."

Cooper stood and Carly followed suit. Granger regarded her with suspicion, and it hurt. But she couldn't think of anything to say without sounding more defensive, so she followed Cooper out.

"You can see where he gets his nickname," Cooper said wryly.

Carly managed a half smile. She was glad for the walk across the street to talk to Dr.

Linder because it helped loosen up residual tension.

Carly said good-bye to Cooper as the sergeant went back into service, then watched the crowd of protestors for a minute. For the time being, they'd taken the spotlight away from Oceans First. They walked in a circle on the sidewalk in front of the steps chanting, "Justice for Dean." They couldn't block access to the station, but they had the right to organize on the sidewalk.

Two news trucks pulled up as she watched, probably to set up for the press conference, and Carly decided discretion was the better part of valor and crossed the street at the far corner to enter the station from the rear.

Carly arrived at Linder's office a few minutes early. Linder ran things differently than Guest. Carly knew from departmental memos that she didn't have a secretary and there was no nameplate on her office door. Her rationale was that she wanted officers to know that when they came to see her, it was in strict confidence. Her waiting room was furnished with comfortable, homey furniture, and Carly took a seat and picked up a magazine she paged through but didn't read.

Her phone chirped with a text from Nick. He and Fernando were keeping an eye on a couple of gangbangers after the funeral gatherings. If all stayed mellow, he'd be home early.

Carly sighed, praying quiet would rule the day. She sent back a text that she loved him and asked him to stay safe.

Carly hadn't heard anything negative on the department grapevine about Linder, so as she waited, she realized anxiety was absent and she'd come to the meeting with an open mind. About five minutes passed before the door to Linder's office opened.

A petite Asian woman smiled at her. "Officer Edwards, come on in."

Linder immediately put Carly at ease. She seemed genuine, and the vibe Carly got from her was totally different from the vibe she'd gotten from Guest. She'd never really cared for Guest, even before she knew he was corrupt. But the more she spoke with Linder, the more she saw a woman she'd like to socialize with, sit down and have coffee and pastries with at HBAAG. They chatted for about twenty minutes before they finally got to the shooting at the construction yard.

"Everything goes blank after I see Barton grinning at me," Carly said with a sigh.

"The next thing I remember is Kyle. I don't remember landing or firing my weapon, but I understand it was discharged twice."

"It's not unusual after a concussion to experience a loss of memory. Your memory could return suddenly, or you may never recall exactly what happened that night."

Linder talked more about head injuries as Carly listened. Considering that she might never remember what happened that night was sobering. She recalled Alex suggesting she'd killed Barton accidentally. *How do you live with accidentally taking a life?* she wondered. *That speaks of incompetence of the highest level.* And she thought of Granger looking at her as if she were a dirtbag criminal.

Carly left her appointment with Linder feeling frustrated. Police training was deeply ingrained in her — a cop didn't fire her weapon unless there was a threat to her life or to an innocent bystander. Barton had been annoying, but he hadn't been a threat. Maybe that was what bothered her the most. Barton had gotten under her skin. He'd rubbed her the wrong way from the get-go and had made her so angry she'd disregarded basic officer safety to chase him. In truth, she'd wanted to kick his behind all the way back to prison.

A thought popped into her head, and she frowned as she waited for the elevator, trying to remember the full Bible verse. Somewhere she was sure it said that even being angry with someone could lead to judgment. She wasn't only angry with Barton; she hated him.

"Officer Edwards, did you hear me?"

"What?" She turned and saw DA Martin, head of the team who would be trying the Burke case, trying to catch her attention. "Sorry. I was thinking."

"Yeah, I guess. You have a minute?"

"Sure." She followed him to a small conference room, her gut still churning with thoughts of murder.

He closed the door. "There's an awful mess going on in the press right now."

"You're telling me."

He fidgeted and wouldn't make eye contact with Carly. "We might have to make some adjustments."

"Adjustments to what?"

"Well, maybe offering a plea deal to Burke would be the best way to go — I mean, in light of what's happening right now."

"I thought you tried to come to a plea agreement earlier and it didn't work out."

He nodded. "Yeah, we did, but that was with the murder charges and the death penalty. We're considering dropping the murder charges altogether and just going with embezzlement and fraud."

"What? Burke is responsible for his wife's murder! He ordered the killing of a police officer and you're going to let him skate on that?"

Martin raised his hands as if to calm her down. "Look, Burke is guilty of only what we can prove. And most of the firsthand witnesses are dead. You —"

"I'm the only witness. Are you accusing me of lying?"

"No, no, not at all. All I'm saying is that reasonable doubt will get Burke off on all counts. Would a plea where he at least serves some time be better than nothing?"

Carly couldn't believe what she was hearing. "Have you already made this decision?"

"No, not yet, but I thought you should know that it is a possibility."

Carly felt numb as she left the station. Burke had been charged with two murders, one of them her fellow officer Jeff Hanks, but she knew he was responsible for more. It floored her to think that he would get away with them because her credibility as a witness was being tarnished. But then a thought entered her mind that made her face flush with shame.

Is it possible I shot Barton accidentally because subconsciously I hated the man and wanted him dead? If that were the case, am I any better than Galen Burke? And even if the shooting is declared accidental, how could I put on a uniform to uphold the law ever again?

30

Carly slunk past the growing crowd of reporters and climbed into her car. She'd meant to ask what the press conference was about but was so disturbed by the discussion with Martin, and the condemnation in her thoughts, that she needed to get away.

Did my hatred of the man make me pull the trigger?

Of all the horrific incidents Carly had seen in her eleven-year career, nothing shook her to the core like what she was thinking about this shooting. All that percolated in her brain was what horrible ugliness there must be in her heart that she would let the gibes of a low-life parolee drive her to murder. Tears burned at the corners of her eyes, and for a few minutes she couldn't think of where to go or what to do. Finally, after wiping her eyes and swallowing the bile in her throat, she directed her car to a sure sanctuary.

By the time she parked in front of her mother's house, the worst of the sick feeling inside her had passed. But she was still reeling with the knowledge that she might have taken a life in anger.

She could smell the homemade cookies before she opened the front door and remembered that it was Thursday. Her mother and a group from the church fed the homeless on Fridays. Kay always baked cookies to pack in the lunches they made.

There was praise music playing. Carly called out so as not to startle her mother. "Hello, Mom, anyone home?"

"In the kitchen."

The aroma of baking chocolate chip cookies was strong and soothing as Carly entered the kitchen. Kay already had several racks of cookies cooling, and she was mixing a large bowl of fresh dough. Carly tried to unwind and work the knots of stress out of her neck. This was a safe haven.

"I was going to call and ask if you wanted to come over and be a cookie taster today." Her mom's smile faded and she stopped stirring. "Oh, Carly, what's wrong?"

Carly sat at the kitchen table and put her head in her hands. "Mom, I think I've done something horrible."

Kay left the bowl, wiped her hands on a

dish towel, and sat across from Carly. "What on earth can you have done that was so awful?"

"I think I *did* murder Dean Barton. I think I wanted him dead and . . ." Her voice broke.

Kay moved to sit next to her. "I don't believe that for an instant. Tell me why you would think such a thing."

The words tumbled out. "I hated him, Mom. I let him get under my skin and I wanted bad things to happen to him. Now he's dead. I may as well have shot him on purpose."

"Let's take a step back here and look at what actually happened." Kay handed Carly a Kleenex. "Blow your nose while I take the cookies out of the oven. You're not a murderer."

Carly composed herself and felt steady by the time her mother sat down again. "Mom, you're not listening to me. I hated the man. The Bible says being so angry with someone could lead to judgment. I arrest guilty people who face judgment for their crimes. I hated Barton and now he's dead. How am I better than the people I arrest?"

"Carly, look me in the eye and tell me you could shoot a man — any man — in cold blood."

Carly shook her head. "That's not the point."

"It *is* the point. I understand what the Bible says. That passage in Matthew is meant to show you — show us — that we need a Savior. We're none of us perfect or able to save ourselves. We need God's grace. And in Romans it says that condemnation is not from God. You're coming down awfully hard on yourself when you don't really know what happened. Even if you hated the man, there's no way you wished to see him dead."

"That's true. But I did want to see him back in jail. I knew he was up to no good. I'm just afraid that subconsciously my negative feelings turned into some kind of self-fulfilling prophecy. And I'm supposed to be a professional, always in control."

"Carly, you're human. No human being is in control all the time. I understand where your heart is in this. You're looking deep inside and recognizing that there was something wrong there. But your wariness of this man, even your hatred, was only a human response; it doesn't mean it made you shoot him. At the very worst, this shooting was just a horrible accident. And you said he'd baited you, tried to hurt you by leading you to the weak spot in the railing. You are not a murderer."

Carly took a deep breath and considered her mother's words. "I just wish I could remember what happened." Turbulent unrest still swirled inside. And now Martin's words sank in. Galen Burke was going to get off because of her. It was too much to think about at the moment.

Kay squeezed her hand. "I'm sure you will. Just give it time. Now, how about some warm cookies and milk?"

Suddenly Carly's phone buzzed. She looked at the screen and saw a text from Nick: ON MY WAY HOME.

"It's Nick. I'll tell him I'm here. Can you spare a couple of cookies for him, too?" A little darkness lifted. She could tell Nick about Martin.

"Always," Kay said.

Nick arrived with news. The purpose of the press conference, he said, had been to announce that Mayor Hardy and the city council had voted to postpone the bridge dedication. The mayor read a prepared statement giving the reason for the postponement as the triple shooting and the upcoming eviction of Oceans First. They wanted more resolution in the case and a clean Sandy Park before celebrating with the dedication. The restaurants and shops ready to open would still stage a grand opening, but the city's ceremony was on hold indefinitely. The mayor then left Jacobs to be peppered with questions about the status of the gang shooting investigation.

"Ouch," Carly said, feeling Jake's pain.

"He did okay," Nick said, mouth full of cookie. "Jake eats that stuff up. He thinks fast and gives good answers."

"Did he get any questions about my shooting?"

"You mean about your fall? All Jake said about it was that he wouldn't comment on an ongoing personnel matter. You know nothing's going to happen there until after the shooting board."

The phone rang, and Carly braced herself, fearing the press would start bugging her mother. But when Kay answered, it was obvious the call was from a friend.

"I have to take this. Will you listen for the timer and take the last tray of cookies out?"

"Sure, Mom," Carly said as she relaxed. Kay went to the other room, and Carly told Nick about IA, Dr. Linder, and Martin.

His scar darkened, and he gave a look that told her he was irritated.

"What?" she asked.

"You really need to stop doing that."

"Doing what?"

"Trying to spare me. Not calling and telling me about your appointment with IA or the shrink or other happenings in your life. I'm your husband. Don't you think I'd want to know these things? Pray with you about them?"

Carly sat back, speechless. "I don't know what to say. I didn't want you to be distracted."

He blew out a breath. "I'm not distracted by your life. I want to be part of it. Gee, Carly, for a smart woman, sometimes you're exasperating." He rubbed his face with his hands and then looked at her. "I know that you're tough and smart and that you can handle yourself, but you're not supposed to go rogue from your own husband."

Carly fought for composure. "I wasn't going rogue. You're out there in the line of fire. All I wanted was to make sure you were concentrating on your job and not worrying about the mess in my life."

"Your life?" He stood and turned away from her, hands on hips, then spun around. "Listen to you! When we were married the first time, it was *my* life and *your* life and we both did a lot of lone ranger stuff. But now I thought we were a team — a partnership — and here you want to shut me out from what's hurting you." He held his hands out, palms up.

Carly saw the moistness in his eyes and lost it. The tears fell before she could stop them. "I was trying to protect you." She let out an exasperated huff and stood, wiping her face with the palms of her hands. "I couldn't forgive myself if something happened to you because you were worried about me."

"Are you the same woman who told me a couple of days ago that God is in control?"

She held his gaze and saw only love and a little bit of pain in his eyes. Her throat was thick and her voice heavy with emotion. "I couldn't bear to lose you like Elaine lost Jeff." She crossed her arms as a sob escaped.

Nick grabbed her in a hug and kissed her head while she squeezed her eyes tight and forced the tears back. "Babe, you're using tomorrow's strength for today's troubles and trying to bear everything by yourself. I'm here for you and I'm not going anywhere. Please don't try to spare me and deal with heavy stuff all by yourself, okay?"

Carly kept her eyes shut, head buried in his strong shoulder, determined to speak to him in a clear voice, not a weepy, whiny one. She held his shirt in her fists and swallowed the lump in her throat before she felt okay to speak.

"I love you, Nick," she breathed into his neck. "And I promise from now on I'll call you about everything," she whispered before gently pushing him away and grabbing a napkin to wipe her face.

Just then the oven timer rang.

Nick smiled. "Thanks, I appreciate that. And I'm sorry for getting so upset."

Carly gave him a quick kiss and hurried to get the cookies out of the oven.

He moved to a chair while she slid the cookies onto the cooling rack.

"If I can't talk, I'll tell you or let it go to voice mail."

Carly nodded. "I'll call you. I will — I promise."

Nick grabbed another cookie. "That really chafes about Martin."

"You don't think they'd really do it, do you? Drop the murder charges on Burke?" Carly took the last hot cookie off the sheet and sat at the table to finish her milk. She realized she felt better than she had since her fall. It was as if a weight had been lifted off her shoulders even with bad news pending.

Nick sighed. "Hate to say it, but next year is an election year. That's all the big DA would need, to lose a huge case like this.

With a plea, at least he'd have half a win."
He drained his milk.

"But Burke is guilty as sin!"

"I know. Guess we'll just have to trust that
God is in control there, too."

Carly clicked her teeth, chagrined.

Kay came back into the kitchen. "Thank
you, Carly. What's the verdict on the cookies?"

"Great!" Carly and Nick said at the same
time.

Carly laughed and then realized that even
though she'd had three cookies and a glass
of milk, she wanted real food. She looked
from her mother to Nick. "Are you hungry
for dinner?"

Nick shrugged. "Why not? We had dessert
first. Want to take your mom out?"

Carly nodded and turned to where her
mother was washing up.

"Mom, do you — ?" She stopped as a
memory flashed through her mind.

Her mother looked at her with a frown.
"Yes?"

"I remember." She turned back to Nick,
excitement coursing through her like an
electric current. "I remember what happened." Clear as day, there it was. "I stepped
back, the railing gave way, and I dropped
my flashlight first. Barton was grinning like

he was happy to see me fall. But I didn't fire my gun." She shook her head. "I know I didn't! I dropped my gun. Even if I had fired, there was no chance for me to aim; I was falling, not trying to shoot someone. I didn't shoot Barton. But . . ." She looked at Nick again.

He finished her thought. "If you didn't shoot him, who did? And why did they want it to look like you did?"

31

Carly and Nick took Kay to Sancho's Ocean
Tacos for dinner. Carly listened while Nick
and Kay chatted. Her mother was as outraged as she and Nick were about Martin
and his talk of a plea deal for Burke. But
now that Carly remembered what had happened that night in the half-built restaurant,
one thought consumed her: getting back
inside the construction yard and figuring
out what Barton had been doing there.

It also occurred to her that Barton had
been coming from the old marina — Walt's,
to be exact. She had assumed that when
Victor followed Crusher, the meeting he
witnessed had been at the Bluestone. But
what if it had been at Walt's? Walt's was also
a fenced-in building under construction.

Since they had two cars, Carly walked Kay
to her door while Nick headed home.

"Thanks, Mom," Carly said as they
stepped onto the porch.

"For what? Nick bought dinner."

"I think coming here and talking to you helped me remember. So thanks."

Kay smiled and gave Carly a hug. "I know you're not a murderer. Good night."

On the way home, Carly's mind churned in frustration because she could not think of any way to justify entry into the construction yard. The investigation was out of her hands. She would call Pete Harris in the morning and tell him what she remembered. She wondered about the GSR test, what it was they wanted to clear up. Maybe now that she remembered, he'd tell her. But since she knew now she hadn't killed Barton, finding any evidence that would clear her was important.

As she pulled into the driveway next to Nick's car and saw the glow of lights from the kitchen and living room, she realized that this was the first time in almost two weeks she and Nick were home together with no plans to go out and nothing pressing. She bowed her head and thanked God for her husband, knowing now more than ever that they were meant to be a team, a partnership, and that she could have peace in the knowledge that God was in control of what happened to both of them.

Prayer finished, she smiled as all thoughts

about the construction zone and mysterious partners fled, and then she hurried inside to find her husband.

"Michael Carter doesn't exist." Nick hung up the phone the next morning and picked up his half-finished cup of coffee. "The Arizona driver's license was bogus, and the Social Security number used to obtain it belongs to a dead guy."

"But he injected money into the catering business."

"The money came from an offshore account, a foundation. Guess who the trustee of the account is."

Carly's coffee stopped halfway to her mouth. "Who?"

"Duncan Potter."

"Huh? That doesn't make sense. Potter doesn't have money. He complained to Alex that he couldn't pursue a civil case against me because he didn't have the money for an attorney."

Nick arched an eyebrow. "That's what Mickey and the ATF dug up. They're trying to find a connection to Barton but have come up empty so far."

"Potter is connected to Masters."

"But that's through work, not through Barton." He sighed. "In any event, Potter is on our list today. We need to talk."

After Nick kissed Carly good-bye and left for work, Carly called Harris with the news of her returned memory.

"Pete, I remember."

"Hey, that's great. Fill me in."

Carly did and took a cleansing breath when she finished.

"Your account fits well with what we found at the scene," Pete said. "The lab results should be in later. If you don't mind, I'll wait until I get them before I go into any specifics."

"I guess I can wait. I know what happened and that makes me feel great. But something else I heard yesterday really upset me."

"You talked to Martin about Burke."

"Yeah! What's up with that?"

"It's politics and it really frosted me. The problem is, we had hard evidence against Drake and Tucker, but the cases against Burke and even Correa were more circum-stantial — at least where the murders are concerned. We've got Burke and Correa dead to rights on the embezzlement and fraud, so the DA wants to play it safe."

"We wouldn't be in this situation if Drake or Tucker had agreed to testify against him."

"Maybe," Pete said. "At least they could testify about firsthand knowledge. But it would be a struggle not to make their testimony look self-serving. Romo and I are going to pay them a visit, appeal to any conscience we can find. Maybe they'll change their minds."

"There's nothing in it for them."

"I know, but I can't let Burke get off, so any straw I can grasp, I'm there. Tucker and Drake avoided the death penalty and maybe it was a good thing to spare the city those two trials. But for Burke to get off easy would be the worst miscarriage of justice," Harris said. "I'll do everything I can to keep the DA from backing off."

"Thanks, Pete." Carly hung up, glad there was a united front against going easy on one of the biggest criminals in Las Playas history.

She paced her living room, trying to practice patience, not her strong suit. The phone calls from news organizations had slowed as time had moved Carly and the Barton shooting investigation off the front burner. It was a blessing and a curse for Carly. As long as Masters was screaming about her in print, at least Carly knew what direction she was being attacked from. But when she saw there was no new Masters column in the paper and no new blog posts, she found herself worrying about where and when the next attack would come.

Her BlackBerry buzzed. Alex Trejo.

"Hey, glad you called. I've got a lot to tell you."

"I've got some news for you as well. Are you home?"

"Yeah, but I need to get out. How about meeting at Heavenly Grounds, at church? They're open."

"Sure. What time?"

"I have to walk the dog and shower. Be there in an hour?"

Alex agreed. Carly ended the call and grabbed Maddie's leash. She and Nick had done a devotional that morning in the book of Joshua, and Carly kept seeing the phrase *"Be strong and courageous"* over and over in her mind. She wasn't at all superstitious, but she found herself wondering if it was an omen.

32

Heavenly grounds was open whenever the church bookstore was open. There were only a few cars in the parking lot, and Carly figured that since it was early, she and Alex would probably have the fellowship hall to themselves. Alex was waiting outside when she arrived.

"You look a little less stressed than you did the last time I saw you," Alex said.

"I remembered," she said.

His eyebrows arched. "Really? I want to hear."

Carly gestured toward the coffee shop. Alex held the door open for her.

Once they'd settled at a table with coffee, Carly told Alex about her memory suddenly returning.

"Good for you. I knew you wouldn't shoot someone for just being a jerk. If that were your MO, I'd be dead."

"Ha. On a more serious note . . ." She

told him what Martin had said.

Alex shook his head, but his eyes said that he was expecting the news. "That's why I hate politics. I had a feeling something like this might happen. I told you pressure was building, and when pressure builds in city hall, it spreads everywhere. The big DA would rather see a plea than a loss."

"But you and I both know how guilty Burke is. He can't get off."

Alex held up his cup in a mock toast. "Here's praying that he doesn't." He took a sip.

"Okay," Carly said, "it's your turn now. What have you got? Where has Masters been? No column, no blog?"

"One at a time, one at a time." He sat back and rubbed his chin. "I'm going to start with the oddest thing first. It doesn't really have anything to do with the new marina or Masters, but it's strange. It's Michael Carter."

"Michael Carter? Nick found out this morning that he doesn't exist." She told him what Nick had learned about the nonexistent Carter and about Duncan Potter's unexpected role.

Alex looked defeated but still intrigued. "Well, that fits with what I found. This guy is a mystery I couldn't stop thinking about, so I spoke to Pam Sailor."

Carly sipped her coffee and indicated that he could keep talking.

"I saw all the paperwork she'd copied from her lawyers. I could write a novel. This guy calling himself Michael Carter somehow got wind that Keith Sailor had a gambling problem."

"How long ago?" Carly interrupted.

"At least a year. Pam is a sweet person but completely naive. She trusted her husband." He shook his head. "Anyway, Carter swooped in to rescue him, but Sailor was in too deep. He didn't stop gambling, and it wasn't long before he'd dug such a big hole that he lost the company. Apparently he couldn't face his wife with the news, so he killed himself. The lawyers then dropped the bombshell on Pam that the company was no longer hers, that because of the money Carter gave her husband to keep the business solvent, upon his death Sailor's Catering became the property of Michael Carter."

"But if there is no Michael Carter, how could that be legal? How could a fake Michael Carter take over the company?"

"He paid all the company's outstanding debts through the foundation. I didn't know Potter was the trustee." Alex frowned.

"Hmm . . . Potter a trustee for a lot of money? That just doesn't make sense. I've got to get to the bottom of this. Pam allowed me to copy everything her lawyer gave her, and I sent it to our legal department. I even talked to the city's community relations division because they arranged the catering contract. But the bid they approved came from Keith Sailor, not Michael Carter. Carter took over after that contract was signed."

He shook his head. "And now the bridge dedication has been postponed. They told me they have a call in to Carter to reschedule, but they haven't heard back from him. Talking to employees of Sailor's Catering, I learned Carter canceled all their other jobs. He wanted the bridge dedication to be their priority. They're afraid they'll lose their jobs because in catering you have to keep scheduling work or . . ." He held his hands out.

"Business dries up. Why would a guy invest money to take over a catering company just to let it die?"

Alex hiked a shoulder. "I thought maybe he had a grudge against Keith Sailor, but I can't find any connection. Ditto Pam Sailor. You gave me a true mystery, and I plan to keep digging."

Carly drained her coffee and decided she

might help him dig after all the dust cleared regarding her situation. "What about Masters?"

"Ah, interesting news there. She did used to be Virginia Masterson. Apparently Dean Barton started her career as a newspaper reporter."

"Started? How on earth?"

"Patience, Edwards. Let me finish. She wasn't a journalist; she was something of a community activist. It seems her father was killed in a shoot-out with the FBI — he was a bank robber — about ten years ago. After that happened, she became a one-note song dumping hundreds of letters to the editor on newspaper after newspaper. The topic was always police brutality. She believes her father was assassinated, even though he had a gun and shot at agents."

"Well, that explains a lot."

"It does. What got her a job at a newspaper was a three-part article she wrote about Barton. She can write — I'll give her that. After going through her stuff, she's best when she's passionate about a subject."

"And misguided?"

Alex cocked his head with a smile and went on. "She happened to be in Yuma when Barton led the entire PD there on a high-speed chase. At one point his car almost hit hers and that so piqued her interest in his case that she followed his arrest and subsequent trial. Coincidentally, he was sentenced to serve his time at the state prison in Florence, where she lived."

"Small world."

"Yeah. I read the three-part article she wrote. I didn't agree with her points, but it was actually pretty good. She won an award and a job at a paper in Tucson. I talked to a guy there. Seems Masters considered Barton her good luck charm. Her constant petitioning for him was part of what got him released early — not to mention that he behaved himself while behind bars. Her next big gig was the job at the *Times,* and I guess she went Hollywood when she got here and changed her name."

Alex paused to drink some coffee, his expression telling Carly he had more information. "I nosed around the *Times* and found out that while she did good work there, it was patchy. Seems the only stories that interested her were police brutality pieces. She always took the side of ex-cons and would say things like, 'He was probably framed like my Dean.' "

"So she really did love the guy. I doubt she's involved in any of the ugly stuff Barton was."

Alex crinkled his nose. "What? You think because she loves him, she's not involved in anything illegal?"

"You think she helped steal guns, kill an Army reservist, and then came here to start a drug war, all the while wanting to be an award-winning journalist?"

"I just don't want to jump to conclusions. The Dragon Lady can't be trusted."

"That's an unbiased statement if I ever heard one," she said with a roll of the eyes. "How'd she hook up with Potter?"

"She met him here. Like I said, he does good work. And I guess the fact that he hates you as much as Masters does cemented their relationship."

"Birds of a feather."

"I told you I've talked to Potter, tried to convince him you're not the evil person he thinks you are. But —" he shrugged — "he never saw his brother for the dirtbag he was."

"Just like Masters can't see what a dirtbag Barton was."

"Yeah, they're kindred souls in more ways than one."

"She's been quiet lately. What is she cooking up?"

"She's gunning for you with all she's worth. She was all set with a front-page hit piece on you, complete with more quotes from those losers Drake and Tucker, when I came across some information that made the editors ask her to hold off."

"What information?"

Alex got smug. "Well, it just so happens that a guy I know from high school is with the ATF. He's here looking for the explosives. He leaked part of an unofficial report to me that says the GSR indicates a high probability that while your weapon was fired, it wasn't by you that night."

Carly stared at Alex, who was now smiling. "You should have told me that first thing!"

"Why? You already knew. You got your memory back."

"Yeah, but that makes it official, tangible, probably what Harris was waiting for. And that was quick. I'm amazed all the labs were in so fast. And surprised Nick doesn't know."

"He'll probably know soon. Apparently they were suspicious because when they found you, your weapon was in your right hand."

"What?"

"Yep, someone was trying to frame you. But your backup officers were close. Maybe in his haste to kill Barton and plant the gun on you, he shoved it into your off hand."

Relief flooded Carly's entire body. Her shooting had just officially become a non-event. She should be able to get back to work as soon as she saw the occupational health doctor on Monday.

"I know that's a relief to you, but it does open up a whole new can of worms, doesn't it?"

Carly nodded. "It sure does. But if Barton had a partner, why did he shoot Barton?"

"And what was going on at the old marina? I'd love to get in there and take a look around."

Shifting in her chair, Carly fought the urge to rush right over and do just that.

33

After she'd said good-bye to Alex, Carly went home to get ready for swim class. Nick phoned and told her about the ATF report.

"I should have known that that hound dog reporter would find out first. This pretty much clears you of any wrongdoing, but it's not going to be made official for a while. Can you live with that?"

Carly knew this was coming. "They don't want whoever shot Barton to know that they're onto him." She made a mental note to tell Alex that. Masters would probably get to publish her hit piece. While Nick talked, she put together her pool bag.

"Right. We're investigating Barton as thoroughly as we possibly can. Fernando and a couple of ATF guys are in Rancho Palos Verdes now. Even though we went through everything once, they're going through it again. They're combing through all of his prison records, arrest records, contacts, etc. Fresh eyes, that kind of thing. I couldn't find Potter when I looked for him. Harris and Romo are on his trail now. He's done a Houdini. They're working on a search warrant for his boat."

Carly remembered that Duncan Potter lived on a boat in the old marina. "I never thought of him as a criminal. He just idolized his brother and couldn't come to terms with Derek being a dirty cop. I kinda feel sorry for him." Blowing a silent kiss to Maddie, she locked up the house and walked to her car, phone at her ear.

"I agree, but they'd like an explanation about the money and Michael Carter. While they're there, I'm taking another team to the construction yard and the old marina in a bit, turn it upside down. Wanna come?"

"Oh, Nick, you know I want to!" She sighed and looked up at the sky. "But I have swim lessons today, and I can't disappoint those kids."

"Ah, I forgot about that. What time do you finish?"

"Around two."

"Well, call me. Maybe we'll still be there."

After the conversation ended, a painful thought occurred to her. Would all the publicity about the shooting mean she'd have to cancel her swim class anyway? Most inner-city parents distrusted the police to begin with, and they might be inclined to believe the horrible stories. She prayed not, because she knew the kids did love the pool and their lessons. She arrived at the Y early to swim laps. She'd promised Nick she wouldn't swim alone, but there was a lifeguard at the pool.

Everyone greeted her like normal, so she hoped that would be the template for the day. People at the Y knew her. They couldn't believe all the bad press, could they?

By one o'clock she'd finished with her laps and was doing a lazy sidestroke while waiting for her class. At five after, she began to worry. At ten after the hour, she got out of the pool and grabbed her towel.

Just then Mary Ellen burst out of the locker room, the three girls in Carly's class trailing behind her, chatting and giggling like typical ten-year-olds.

"Sorry the kids are late, Officer Edwards. But they were waiting for Londy. Have you seen him?"

"No, I haven't. Maybe he's working today?"

Mary Ellen frowned. "No, he wanted to do the lessons. His shift starts after. He told me he was meeting with Victor to see if he could get him to come to the lesson. But when Londy didn't show up where the van picks the kids up, I called Victor's house and they told me they hadn't seen Victor or Londy. Mr. Teagle happened to be off work today and volunteered to help with the boys."

"Have you tried calling him?" Carly asked as the group of rambunctious boys burst from the locker room. They were followed by a large black man — Mr. Teagle, she guessed. She recognized him but wouldn't have remembered his name.

He came toward her and Mary Ellen.

"I call his number, but it goes straight to voice mail." Mary Ellen was borderline hysterical.

"Officer Edwards." The man extended his hand, and Carly took it, trying not to show the anxiety she felt. "I'm Marcus Teagle, Jason's father. I just wanted to tell you that we're behind you. We don't believe all that trash in the paper."

A lump formed in Carly's throat as she relaxed. "Thank you, Mr. Teagle. That means a lot."

"It means a lot that you take so much of your time and give it to our kids. Thank *you.*" He turned back to supervise the boys.

Carly's attention returned to Mary Ellen.

"It's not like Londy to turn his phone off, is it?"

She shook her head. "It's not like him to not show up where he's supposed to be. I'm scared."

Carly put a hand on her shoulder. "I'll call Nick before we start and ask him to have one of his gang officers look for Londy and Victor. Right now, why don't you head over to your assignment? As soon as the class is over, you and I will look for Londy if he hasn't turned up by then, okay?"

Mary Ellen bit down on her bottom lip and nodded before turning to her duties with the senior citizens.

As Carly pulled her phone out of her pool bag to call Nick, a pang of dread struck her gut. It wasn't like Londy to disappear. What could have happened to him?

When the lesson ended, Carly showered and changed quickly. She combed her hair but left it to air-dry.

Mary Ellen was already waiting by her car when Carly jogged out to the lot. "I just tried again. No luck," she said.

"Hang in there, Mary Ellen. We'll find him."

They were climbing into Carly's car when her phone buzzed. "It's Nick," Carly said as she answered the phone.

"My guys just called me," he said. "Something weird is going on. Victor Macias is missing also. He was supposed to be home so his mother could take him to see his brother. The doctor was going to let the little kids in for the first time, and he's nowhere to be found. He's only ten, so this is a critical missing."

Carly considered this. A critical missing meant a command post and a lot of resources thrown into the search. "Do you think Victor is with Londy?"

"Victor's five-year-old brother thinks he saw Londy talking to Victor earlier, but he's only five and doesn't communicate very clearly. Anyway, juvenile is on it, and we're leaving the yard now to pitch in."

"I'm with Mary Ellen. We're going to head to Half Baked and see if Londy talked to anyone there."

"Okay. I'll be there in a few. We didn't finish here, so maybe when we come back, you can ride along."

"Did you find anything?"

"Just puzzles. It's obvious someone other than the construction crew has been in here. We've decided to seal up the scene for one more day in case the shooting team wants to do another walk-through. I'll tell you more when I see you."

Carly filled in Mary Ellen while she drove.

"That's bad," Mary Ellen said. "Victor couldn't wait to see his brother. He wouldn't have missed that for the world."

Carly said nothing, just continued to the coffee shop. When they got there, the place was packed; in fact, the whole Apex shopping complex was busy. She could see that the coffee shop was short-staffed. Ned was emptying a trash can, and she walked over to help him. Besides garbage from the outside can he was emptying, he also had a bag of trash from inside the shop.

"Thanks, Carly," he said as she took the bag from him. "Nice surprise to see you here." He frowned when he saw Mary Ellen. "Hey, where's Londy? His shift started ten minutes ago. He's always early. This is the first time in six months he's a no-show."

Mary Ellen paled.

Carly answered for her. "Londy's missing. That's why we're here."

"Missing?"

"Yeah, he didn't show up at the pool either. A boy is missing as well — Victor Macias. He's only ten. We were hoping maybe Londy called you or something."

Ned shook his head. "No, it's been crazy here today. Jinx is sick, so we were counting on him coming in. I know Victor. Londy's brought him in for cinnamon rolls from time to time. I haven't seen him either."

"Do you want me to work for Londy, Mr. Barton? I don't want him to get in trouble for not being here."

Ned put his hand on Mary Ellen's shoulder. "Hey, I can tell that you're upset. We'll manage." He picked up his bag of trash, and Carly grabbed the one she had taken and followed him to the Dumpster in the alley, leaving Mary Ellen at the front of the shop.

"Is this serious, Carly? I mean Mary Ellen looks terrified."

"You said yourself it's not like Londy to be a no-show."

"No, it's not." He set the trash down to open the gate to where the Dumpsters were.

A horn honking followed by the sound of tires screeching to a halt made Carly look up. She stepped around the Dumpster for a view of the street.

There was a kid running toward them.

Carly motioned for Ned to join her. "Ned?"

He stepped up to follow her gaze. "What the . . . ?"

Carly dropped the trash bag as Victor

crossed Broadway and was nearly struck by a car.

"Ned! Ned!" he yelled, breathless.

He was almost upon them. Carly thought he looked dirty and a little bloody.

"Ned, help, help!"

Carly took one of the boy's arms and Ned the other.

"Whoa, what happened?"

"Please." He bent at the waist and sucked in air. Up close, she could see his face was streaked with tears. "He took Londy and now he's after me." His small voice quaked.

Carly looked at Ned. "Go get Mary Ellen please."

As Ned moved away, Carly knelt down. Victor was at the stage of sobbing where the whole body shakes. He was filthy, and there were cuts and scrapes all over his arms.

"Who?" Carly asked. "Who took Londy and who are you afraid of?"

"Don't know his name."

Mary Ellen came running over. "Victor! What happened?"

The boy stood up straight and swallowed. "He got Londy."

"Who?" Carly and Mary Ellen asked simultaneously.

"The white dude. The one who shot Hector."

34

"He's dead, Victor. The man who shot your brother is dead," Carly said, still down on one knee.

Victor shook his head. Now that he'd gotten his breath back, the words came out in a rush. "The other white dude — the one with the beard. I seen him. Londy was taking me to swim, and the van came by. Londy told me to run 'cause he thought it was a drive-by. I ran, but I saw the van go after Londy. The man jumped out and snatched him. Londy couldn't fight him off, and he put him in the van. Then he came after me, but I hid until I could come here." He reached into his pocket and pulled out a smashed cell phone. "It's Londy's phone. They smashed it when he tried to call for help."

Carly took the phone and stood. "Mary Ellen, take Victor into the shop."

"But we have to find Londy!"

She held the girl's frantic gaze. "We will. I have to make some calls, get Nick over here and some help from juvenile. Get Victor cleaned up and calmed down so he can tell us everything he remembers."

By the time Nick arrived, they'd moved Victor into the coffee shop office. Ned gave him some water, and Mary Ellen cleaned his face. Erika made him something to eat. After a layer of grime was cleaned off, Carly saw that while his arms were cut, scratched, and bloody, everything was superficial.

"Where were you when this happened?" Nick asked the boy.

"Up by where people catch the train. When they came for me, I jumped the fence and hid in the tow yard. I came here as soon as I could but then got scared that they were still looking for me."

Victor's hiding place must be near the second commuter stop for the metro rail. It backed up to the police tow yard and was near where he lived.

"Describe the van, Victor. What did the van look like?"

"It was white and it didn't have no windows. I'm sorry, Mary Ellen. I couldn't help him."

"Oh, Victor, he'll be okay. I know it. We

just have to pray." Mary Ellen bent down to hug Victor.

Carly nodded to Nick. Together they left the office and walked out the back door of the shop.

Nick had his radio with him. He'd already contacted the juvenile team that was handling the critical missing pertaining to Victor. Nick relayed everything Victor had told them about the white van and Londy.

"He'll be okay," Nick said, replacing his radio on his belt.

Carly closed her eyes and shook her head as dread clamped on. "I'm sorry. I don't believe that. Whoever is after him has already killed two." Opening her eyes, she looked into Nick's blue ones and saw a steadiness there.

"If they'd wanted him dead, they could have shot him in the street. No, something else is going on here."

"But what?"

One of the juvenile detectives came on the air with a license plate. Someone had written letters and numbers down, but they said it was a funny plate and couldn't tell which state it was from.

Carly grabbed Nick's sleeve. "Tell them to run it as Arizona. Everything seems to be coming here from Arizona these days."

He smiled and made the suggestion to dispatch.

"Good call, Gang Sam 1, R/O info returning now. Chevy van, no want or warrant, registered to a Virginia Masterson, Tucson, Arizona."

Nick stared at Carly and she didn't know what to say. The juvenile detective said that he would call auto stats and ask that a BOLO be entered into the system for the van.

All Carly could think was that maybe Alex was right — Masters was a Dragon Lady. But was she also a killer?

35

"Well, we have a call into the *Messenger,* but no one seems to know where Masters is right now." Nick sat down across from Carly. "Victor didn't see a woman."

"But someone had to be driving." Carly drummed on the table with a combination of impatience and anxiety.

She and Nick were seated in the coffee shop, waiting for Victor's mother to pick him up. A juvenile detective was with Victor and had even coaxed a smile out of him. The boy had calmed down and eaten the sandwich Erika had made for him.

Mary Ellen was alternating between prayerfully assured and inconsolable. Carly had called Jonah to come get her. The search for Victor had switched to a search for Londy. With Victor's information about what had happened, Londy's status of "missing" turned into "kidnapped," and homicide was assisting patrol and gang officers with the search. As best they could determine from Victor's narrative, the white van had snatched Londy about two hours ago. Carly did not want to think about what could have happened to the teenager in two hours.

"I'm going to call Alex. He might know how to get ahold of Masters or where she is," Carly told Nick, who had been busily texting back and forth with the officers searching for Londy. Victor said he picked up Londy's phone in the street after he was sure the van was gone. Nick had his guys checking the street in the area on the off chance there was more evidence on the ground.

Carly stood and walked outside to use her phone. Before she punched the number for Alex, a small black sports car screeched to a stop at the curb. Carly's gaze was drawn that direction by the noise, and she turned in time to see an angry Ginny Masters climb out of the driver's seat.

Oh, Lord, help me, she prayed as the woman focused on her like a laser beam. The air cracked with each stomp of Masters's high-heeled boots on the pavement as she strode toward Carly. Sliding her phone in her pocket, Carly prepared to face the woman.

"You have nerve showing up here after what you did to Dean." Masters squared off in front of Carly. "It's my mission in life to see you drummed out of police work and in prison, where you belong!"

"I didn't kill Dean."

Masters's index finger shot up as if spring-loaded. "Don't you lie to me! All cops are power hungry. It's a job requirement. You fired your gun and Dean is dead."

"Someone else was in the restaurant with us, and that person shot Dean. Maybe they used my gun, but I didn't shoot him."

Masters's hands flew to her waist and she stood up tall, assuming a posture officers called "chicken-chested." It was meant to intimidate, to make the person you're facing step back.

Carly didn't budge, just held the angry woman's gaze with as calm an expression as she could muster. From the corner of her eye, she saw Nick come out of the coffee shop, but she didn't look away from Masters. He was in his gang uniform: black tactical pants, nylon gun belt, and police Windbreaker. Masters might see him as an authority figure and chill, but Carly doubted it.

"Now it's a cover-up! Who did you pay off to hide your murder?"

"Ms. Masters —" Nick began as he stepped up behind her.

She whirled around. "Don't you try to do anything to me!" She held up a small flip camera. "This records video. You won't be able to hide." Her voice was shrill.

Nick held up both hands and spoke calmly. "I'm not going to do anything. We've been looking for you. We have some questions for you."

Carly kept silent, knowing Nick should handle this. He moved to stand next to her so Masters would face both of them. He probably didn't want her to feel surrounded, Carly thought.

"Are you going to try to pin something on me?"

Nick took a deep breath and asked his first question in the least accusatory tone he could, as far as Carly was concerned. "Do you own a white van?"

The question seemed to throw Masters for a loop. "A white van?" Something erased the indignation in her face for a split second, something that told Carly she knew exactly what Nick was talking about. Then it was gone, again replaced by outraged indignation. "No, my car is there at the curb." She gave an angry wave in that direction. "Why?"

"Because a white van was involved in the kidnapping of a young man earlier today. We have the license plate of a white van, written down by a witness, and the vehicle is registered to you in Tucson, Arizona."

"I . . . uh . . ." Masters deflated as if pricked with a pin, and her eyebrows scrunched like an accordion. "I helped Dean buy a van. He couldn't get credit when he was released. The van was his. If someone was driving that van, then it must have been stolen."

"We could be wrong — your van might not be the one we're looking for — but we'd like to check. Do you know where his van is? Or if anyone else had access to it? Maybe Dean gave it to a friend?"

She jerked her head away and would not look at Nick. "There you go! He's on parole, so you assume he'd have friends who would kidnap someone."

"I'm just touching all the bases. It's possible it's not Dean's van we're looking for. Do you know where the van was parked? We can go check and see if it's there. If not, then we'll know it's stolen."

"Maybe he gave it to his brother."

"We're certain Ned doesn't have it."

"Hmph. You assume Dean was the bad guy and you don't take a second look at his brother. How do you know that man isn't the criminal you think Dean is?"

That question took Carly by surprise, and she could see Masters read her expression. The woman threw her hands up theatrically. "No, of course, you wouldn't consider him!" The index finger shot up again. "I think you better look hard at that man! Accusing Dean of planting a bomb. He cheated Dean out of his inheritance. Any man who is that money-hungry is capable of anything."

Ned came out of the coffee shop. Masters turned her scathing gaze his way and crossed her arms. "You need to look long and hard at that man and let my poor Dean rest in peace." She stomped back toward her car, with Nick following.

"What was that all about?" Ned asked.

"Long story." Carly watched as Nick tried to talk to the woman, to get more information about the van and who might have it or where it should be. "I don't know why she came here. Hey, do you remember seeing Dean driving a white van?"

Ned scratched his chin. "No, the only times he came here, he was with her in that little sports car."

They both started when Masters burned rubber away from the curb.

Nick walked toward them, shaking his head. "That lady has a chip on her shoulder." He nodded toward Ned. "She's really created this image of your brother. He was Gandhi, Nelson Mandela, and Martin Luther King all rolled into one."

Ned sighed and started to say something when Erika poked her head out the front door and said he was needed inside.

"Did she tell you anything about the van?" Carly asked Nick.

"No. All she would say is that they always traveled in her car. She wouldn't even tell me where Dean stayed when he wasn't with her. I did try to convince her that someone else killed Dean and tried to make it look as though you did it."

"Is that what made her angry enough to burn rubber?"

He shook his head. "I told her Dean must have had a partner who doubled-crossed him and shot him to frame you. That wound her up."

A plain car pulled up to the curb, and Fernando stepped out.

"We canvassed a couple of blocks where Victor says Londy was snatched." He shrugged. "A few people remember seeing the van but not the kidnapping." Frowning, he faced Carly. "That kid made someone mad enough to go to all this trouble?"

"I don't know," she said. "I don't know."

He looked at Nick. "Harris is getting ready to serve a warrant on Potter's boat. You want to help or stay on the search for the kid?"

Nick folded his arms, a thoughtful expression on his face. "Well, if Potter's involved in all of this, there might be answers about who took Londy and why if we can talk to him." He turned to Carly. "I think we'll assist Harris. Let me know if you hear anything else?"

"I will. You too."

He gave her a casual salute and left with Fernando.

Carly paced outside, worried about Londy. It was going on two and a half hours. So much could have happened in that period of time.

Her phone rang. It was Andi.

"What's up?"

"Have you talked to Alex?"

"No, we've kinda got a situation going here." She filled Andi in on what had happened to Londy.

"I'm so sorry to hear that, but it makes me even more disturbed that I can't reach Alex. I'm really worried. His phone goes right to voice mail, which is odd. He never turns his phone off." Andi's voice was uncharacteristically tight with stress.

Here we go again, Carly thought, anxiety ramping up anew. "I haven't talked to him. I was going to call and ask him a question, but that question was answered. When did you last speak to him?"

"This morning. He said he was going to be out following clues and leads but that he'd call me before lunch. No call."

Carly frowned. That wasn't like Alex at all. "Did he say where he was going to be following these leads?"

"No, and that's what scares me. He said he didn't want to tell me because he didn't want me to get in trouble."

Carly hit her forehead with her palm. "Oh, man. I think I know where he may be. Andi, keep trying to get ahold of him, though."

"Swell. You're not going to tell me either, are you?"

"I think he went to the restaurant where Barton was shot."

"That's still off-limits, isn't it?"

"Yep."

She heard Andi sigh. "I hope he doesn't call me to bail him out of jail."

Carly ended the call and was about to try Alex's number when Jonah walked up, face lined with concern.

"Any word on Londy?"

"Sorry, not so far. Mary Ellen is pretty upset."

"Not surprised. Just about everyone she's cared about in her short life has died. Please pray for her heart while you pray for Londy."

Carly nodded that she would, and Jonah entered the coffee shop.

A sudden weariness enveloped Carly and she sat down at a sidewalk table, holding her head in her hands. Her thoughts went to Mary Ellen and what Jonah had said. First the girl's mother had been killed in a traffic accident, and then her father abandoned her to foster care. After being in foster care for years, she ran away at sixteen and hooked up with a loser burglar who was eventually murdered. Jonah and Londy were the most stable parts of her life, and now she might lose Londy.

But why? Was everything happening in Las Playas because someone wanted revenge against Londy? For what? If it was a gang beef, he could have been taken out in a drive-by. No one else would have been involved or hurt.

Carly rubbed her forehead and thought about the Burke trial. Yes, Burke had tried to frame Londy for his wife's murder. To

Carly's knowledge the teen hadn't yet been subpoenaed for the trial, though he could be. *Is Londy a big threat to Burke?*

No, no, she decided. *Burke would have a bigger beef with me.*

Chewing on this, she phoned Captain Jacobs. She got his voice mail and left a message while an idea floated around in her head. Then she hung up and dialed Alex's number. It went straight to voice mail, just like Andi said it would.

After leaving a message, she shook her head. *Not another missing.*

Clues and leads. Alex had told Andi he was looking for clues and leads. To Carly that meant Alex was at the construction yard. She prayed she was wrong and that Alex hadn't trespassed at the site.

A lump of dread developed in the pit of her stomach as the realization dawned that that was exactly what Alex would do. But Nick's team hadn't found anything. Yet she knew Alex would want to see for himself.

As Carly pondered her next move, Ned came out of the shop and sat down at her table. "I guess by the look on your face there isn't any news."

"No, sorry. And I'm afraid that a good friend of mine may have done something stupid."

"And you're going to try to save his bacon?"

Carly smiled. She was concerned about the situation with Londy, but Nick was working on that, and she knew he'd call with news as soon as he had it. She'd decided to go look for Alex, but it surprised her that she was so transparent. "Pretty much."

"Mind if I tag along?"

"Uh, I'm not sure what I'm going to do exactly."

"Yeah, but you're going to do something and you really shouldn't be by yourself." He hiked a shoulder. "Things have quieted down here. Hey, I'm a gimp, but I can still use a phone or call out a warning."

Carly thought for a minute. *Is it wise to have Ned hanging around? Suppose something comes up? What am I worried about? Nick just came from the site.* And she didn't want to see Alex get arrested for trespassing. She decided he'd probably call her before she even got to the yard. Besides, something about Ned reminded her of Joe. He had a calm, confident presence, and she felt comfortable having him tag along.

"Sure, Ned, let's tell everyone where we're going and then take a drive."

36

Carly was about to turn the key in the ignition when her phone buzzed. It was Alex.

"Hey, I was about to come looking for you."

"Sorry, I had my phone off. I only realized it now. I know Andi isn't going to be happy with me."

"You'd better call her. Are you where I think you are?"

"Yes and no. Can you come down to the old marina, dock 15, slip 22?"

"Why? What's there?"

"Nothing right now, but I've got a lot to tell you."

Carly bit back an impatient response. "Alex, Londy is missing. He's been kidnapped. Victor Macias saw him being forced into a van and driven away."

"Kidnapped? When?" Alex sounded startled.

"A couple of hours ago now."

Alex whistled low over the phone. "Just come down here. Maybe this will answer some questions."

Sighing, she said, "Okay. Be there in about five." She hung up the phone and turned to Ned. "That's who I was going to look for. At least now I know that he hasn't done anything illegal."

"I'd still like to tag along, if that's okay."

She nodded and started the car.

"Where did you think he'd be?" Ned asked.

"I thought he'd be poking around in the construction site."

"Where the environmentalists are always trying to get into?"

"Yeah."

"I read in the paper that the protestor who got shot the other day died."

"You're kidding. I hadn't kept up on that story." *What a mess,* Carly thought. *It looks as though Jarvis really screwed up.*

Carly drove the few blocks to the old marina parking lot. She saw Alex's red sports car and was able to park next to it. Dock 15 was the one closest to Walt's, part of the old structure that wasn't being knocked down. The slips here were the smallest in the marina, so there weren't many people living aboard boats docked in any of them. All the

boat docks were gated and only boat owners had keys. It was difficult to get a slip in
Las Playas. Carly knew there was a long
waiting list. Compared to marinas north
and south of the city, Las Playas was
smaller, quieter, and more desirable to older
folks or anyone who liked a peaceful setting.

Carly had a master key to the gates, which
she used at dock 15. Slip 22 was near the
end. She saw Alex and started that way with
Ned on her heels.

"What's up, Alex?" Carly asked when they
reached him.

"I came down here and tried to get into
the construction yard. One of the marina
guys stopped me."

"Good for him."

"Yeah, yeah, but I charmed him into talking. I think something is going on in Walt's.
When I look around the area, that's the only
place Barton could have been coming from
when you saw him."

Carly nodded. "I figured that. I'm even
thinking that maybe Victor saw his brother
meet Barton at Walt's, not the Bluestone."

"Great minds think alike. Anyway, this
marina guy was telling me that Jarvis was
particularly attached to Walt's, didn't want
anyone else checking the place out or even

going near it. He even watched it from his boat." Alex pointed to dock 16, a dock with bigger slips and therefore more live-aboard boats. "See that ugly turquoise number? That's Jarvis's."

"He can watch Walt's. So? Maybe he found something to be diligent about."

"So you know him to be a slug as well? The marina guy says the reason Jarvis shot that environmentalist was to keep him away from Walt's. Now the guy is dead. Isn't killing someone to keep them away a little too diligent?"

Carly folded her arms and looked at the boarded-up restaurant in the fading daylight. "I haven't followed that investigation too closely. But okay, say you're right. What is he trying to protect in Walt's? And why did you bring me to this empty slip?"

"The marina guy told me there's usually a boat docked here, a thirty-six footer. Jarvis and the guy who lives on the boat are tight. I asked him to check on who rents the slip, and he couldn't tell me."

"Why? There's no confidentiality here."

"That wasn't the problem. No one is listed as renting the slip. Yet he knows someone has been here regularly for months. But this is a dock that falls under Jarvis's sphere of responsibility. So either he's just a sloppy administrator or . . ."

"Or he's letting someone live here under the radar." Carly chewed on a thumbnail and considered the possibilities. She turned toward Walt's. "Why didn't the marina guy stick around to talk to me himself?"

"He wants to remain anonymous. He's afraid of Jarvis."

"And it's dusk now, so he's off. But we'll have to talk to him sooner or later, Alex. Who is it?"

Alex got a little testy. "He's my confidential informant."

Carly sighed and decided to leave the pressing to Harris. "Did you try to get inside Walt's?"

"The marina guy stopped me. But the three of us might have better luck now."

"Yeah." Carly started walking down the dock as the gangway lights came on. "Like I'm going to bust in there with you two. I have to give this to Harris. By the way, did your CI know where Jarvis is?"

Alex shook his head and opened his mouth to speak, then stopped. Carly followed his gaze to the gangway where Harris, Romo, Nick, and Fernando approached the neighboring dock with four SWAT guys in tactical gear.

She looked at Alex again. "Relax. They're

here for Potter. His boat must be docked over there close to Jarvis's." She turned toward the gangway and motioned for him to follow. "Let's go tell them what you found."

"If you insist," he said, falling into step with her. "But you know how I feel about storm troopers."

In spite of the gravity of the situation, the comment brought a brief smile to Carly's lips. She regained her composure by the time they reached the other dock.

"What are you doing here?" Nick asked.

"Long story, but it might be one you —" she pointed to Harris — "want to hear."

"Can it wait until after we serve our warrant?"

"Definitely. I don't want to get in your way."

"Thanks," Harris said as he slipped on a Kevlar vest and tightened the Velcro straps. "Nobody has seen or heard from Potter for days. We don't think he's here, but we're not taking any chances. Hang on, and as soon as we clear the boat, Romo will come back and listen to what you have to say."

"Happy hunting," Carly said as she leaned against a post.

The men stomped off toward Potter's boat. Proving that the living space was small, Nick and Romo returned a scant fifteen minutes later.

"No one home," Nick said with a shrug. "But they found a 9mm handgun with its serial number filed off."

"What?" Carly stared at Nick for a minute. "You think it's the gun used to shoot the gangbangers?"

Nick and Romo exchanged glances.

"It will have to be checked out. Harris will send it to ATF," Romo said.

"I can't believe Potter was the shooter!" Carly thought of the mousy man who'd been following her around for months. Could he really have shot and killed teenagers in an attempt to start a gang war? What possible motive would he have?

"Well, first the foundation money, now the gun. The evidence is piling up. Now what're you guys doing?" Romo asked.

Carly let Alex fill him in.

"Let's go check Walt's out," Romo said when the reporter finished. "We're here, and we can look around if we can get in." He radioed Harris, who was still inventorying Potter's boat, and everyone headed to Walt's.

"You guys will have to wait out here," Carly told Alex and Ned.

Alex argued, but Ned took a seat on a

bench on the dock.

"I would have gone into law enforcement if things had been different," he told Carly. "And I certainly don't want to get in the way."

Alex threw his hands up. "This is my lead, my story."

Carly patted him on the shoulder. "No one's here to scoop you."

Romo unlocked the gate around the old restaurant and then the lock on the boarded-up door. The dock beneath them creaked and moaned, and there were still remnants of the crime scene tape from Jarvis's shooting.

"Is Jarvis going to be charged with homicide?" Carly asked.

Romo nodded. "Looks like it. That kid he shot wasn't a threat. He was trying to climb onto the dock, and Jarvis shot him three times. We've tried to talk to him several times since then and he had nothing to say. He was ordered to come in and didn't show. He's not helping himself."

By now it was dark, but Romo and Nick had flashlights. Carly stayed close to Nick as they checked out the main dining room. Nick found a loose board on the water side of the restaurant. He pulled on it until it became an opening large enough for a man to slip through.

"It's been laid into place to look closed," he said, "but I'll bet someone has been coming in and out that way."

Romo began a systematic search of the old restaurant, but it was empty.

Carly began to think this was a wild-goose chase. She left Nick and was heading for the front door to apprise Alex when Nick called from the kitchen. "Look here." He shone his light on the floor, and Carly saw footprints and a clean spot in the dust. "Something was stored here recently."

A shadowy form caught Carly's eye and she grabbed Nick's shoulder. "Shine your light over here."

In the far corner near where the restrooms would be was a chair with clothing draped over it — a black shirt and black chinos.

"Those are the clothes Dean Barton was wearing the first time I saw him." Her adrenaline ramped up. Maybe there was more here than she initially thought.

The four of them moved to the corner and saw a cot folded up and leaning against the wall.

"He must have been staying here," Carly added.

"He told us he was living with his girl-friend, and she confirmed," Romo said.

They continued their search, retracing steps and looking more carefully. Romo found several bullets in various places and collected the unspent rounds. They were all 9mm.

Carly found some wiring and picked it up, not certain what it was but wanting to take it outside to study it. When they did go outside, it was fully dark but for the gangway lights.

"Where'd you find that?" Ned asked, pointing to the wiring Carly was fiddling with.

She held it up. "In the kitchen. There was a lot of stuff there. We think your brother had been staying there."

"Do you know what that is?"

She shook her head.

"That's a detonator — a military-grade detonator."

37

By the time Nick and Carly returned to their cars, it was after midnight. Ned's identification of the detonator Carly had found turned the investigation at Walt's into an ATF affair. They had descended on the dock with personnel and plenty of artificial lighting. Carly could still see the glow of the lights when she reached her car.

"Ohh," she said with a yawn, turning to Nick, "what a day." The excitement over the discovery they'd made in Walt's was tempered by the fact that Londy was still missing.

"That's an understatement." He grabbed her arm and pulled her close. "I'm starved. I haven't eaten since breakfast. You want to stop at Harbor House?"

"No," she said into his shoulder, "I just want to go home." She wanted to be alone with Nick and pray for Londy.

"Okay, we do have plenty of leftovers. Follow me?"

"Anywhere."

There wasn't much traffic, so the drive down PCH through Sunset Beach to Huntington Beach didn't take very long. Nick turned onto their street. Carly nearly ran right into him when he stopped in the middle of the street.

She looked but didn't immediately see anyone in front of him. Then he moved, pulling his plain car to the curb and parking. Frowning, Carly looked toward their house and froze. Parked in their driveway was a white van with Arizona license plates.

She swallowed as her mouth went dry. There was no one near the van, but what was it doing in their driveway?

They both got out of their cars and met at the back of Nick's. He was on the phone, calling Huntington Beach PD and asking for backup.

"They'll be here shortly," he said as he disconnected and then punched in the watch commander's number so he could apprise their department of the situation.

Wide awake now, Carly felt an icy fear seep into her veins as she considered what might be in the van. It could be Londy.

It could be Londy's body.

When the Huntington Beach unit arrived,

Nick identified both himself and Carly to the officer, who advised them to remain where they were for the moment. The officer positioned his vehicle to shine both his spotlights and his headlights directly onto the van. The advantage was theirs if someone came out of the car shooting because they would only see the blinding lights. He then got on the PA and ordered the occupants of the van out.

They waited and nothing happened. The most dangerous part of any car stop was approaching the vehicle if you didn't know who was inside or if they were armed.

Nick moved toward the squad car and told the officer that he and Carly would approach with him. The officer had no problem with that. Nick drew his duty weapon and Carly took her off-duty gun from her backpack. The three of them fanned out to approach from the rear.

Guns trained on the van, they moved to the side, and Nick gestured to the HB cop to open the side door while he and Carly kept the van covered. On a count of three, he jerked down on the handle and the side door slid open.

Nick's flashlight illuminated the interior, and Carly jumped when she saw Londy.

His eyes blinked and she saw the fear

there. His mouth was covered with duct tape, and he was tied up in a sitting position. His head moved back and forth as if he were saying, "No" over and over.

Anxiety knotted Carly's stomach, and she wanted to say, "No, what?" but he couldn't answer her.

Carly lowered her gun and stepped forward to untie Londy, but Nick grabbed her.

"No, look."

She followed the beam of his light and saw what Londy was sitting on. Two gray squares on either side of a large battery, attached with wires.

Carly had been to enough training classes that showed pictures of objects like that. While the numbness of fear and dread paralyzed her where she stood, she didn't need anyone to tell her it was a bomb.

38

A sick feeling gripped Carly by the throat. She and Nick moved back to the corner of their street to wait for the ATF bomb squad. Nick had seen a detonator, much like the one Carly had found at Walt's, and that cued him to use caution. Though Londy couldn't talk because of duct tape over his mouth, he'd been able to move his head slightly to answer questions with nods or shakes. The bomb would detonate if he were moved off the mound of C-4.

Carly had retrieved Maddie from the house right away while Nick and the HB officer alerted their closest neighbors to evacuate. Now, the sky was tinged with pink and Huntington Beach PD had the block cordoned off. Carly could see their chief coordinating with the Red Cross people to find a place for the displaced homeowners to stay, in case it took an extended time period for the bomb to be rendered safe.

Carly's eyes were heavy with fatigue when Alex's little red car pulled up as the sky brightened with sunrise. Ned stepped out of the passenger side. Alex had offered to drive Ned home from the marina. Carly wondered why they were still together hours later.

Alex bounced over to where she stood, obviously pumped full of adrenaline and coffee. "Hey, Ned and I were doing some research about his brother. Londy is on a bomb?" The reporter's eyes were big.

Carly sighed and leaned into Nick, letting him explain what they had found while she continued to pray that Londy would be saved.

"A pressure-sensitive device?" Ned shook his head. "We saw those a lot in Iraq. Booby traps — open a door and boom. Move a body — boom. But they aren't impossible to disarm." He held up a bag. "Erika heard what was happening when Alex answered his messages. She made you a couple of sandwiches, and there's coffee in the car if you want it."

"Bless you, Ned." Carly reached for the bag.

A second ATF bomb vehicle pulled up. By now the neighborhood was awash in official vehicles and news vans. Carly had moved her car off the block.

It was a Huntington Beach operation now, and Carly and Nick were asked to back off. They sat inside Carly's car with Maddie to eat their sandwiches. Alex pestered everyone he could for access, but it was too dangerous.

Carly had called Jonah to let him know about the situation. She hadn't wanted Mary Ellen to hear about it over the news. Jonah said he'd wait to tell her because she'd just fallen asleep.

"This will be a while," Nick said after they finished the food. "You can curl up with Maddie and take a nap if you want."

Carly held up the coffee. "I'm getting a second wind, and that sun is bright. You think we can watch the ATF monitor?" The ATF agents had sent in a robot with a video camera so they could study the bomb safely.

"Sure thing."

They got out and walked to the ATF vehicle designated as the command post.

The scene there was controlled chaos. There were too many agencies involved for it to be anything else. In addition to the ATF agents and bomb guys, the Orange County Sheriff's bomb squad had rolled. Plus, there were Huntington Beach officers and some Las Playas officers. Carly even spotted Agent Wiley talking to Captain Jacobs.

Carly also saw an imposing-looking bomb suit and wondered if someone was going to try to defuse the device.

Many of Carly's neighbors stood outside the crime scene tape watching and waiting. News crews were everywhere, and three news helicopters hovered above. Carly looked down the street at the white van parked in her driveway. The terrible reality of the danger broke through her fatigue, and her mouth went dry. This was personal now.

There was such a crowd around the monitor, Carly hung back.

"Don't you want to look?" Nick asked.

She shook her head. "I'll wait here." She found a car to lean against and settled in to watch the activity and sip her coffee. Praying for Londy, she surveyed the activity around her.

By noon, all of her second wind had worn off and she was yawning again.

Wiley caught her eye and walked her way. "Edwards, I hear today is your lucky day."

"I guess that depends on your perspective."

"You didn't move the kid. The ATF guys are certain there's enough explosive under him to leave a huge crater." He leaned next to her. "It's probably the loss from Arizona."

"All of it?" Carly asked, hoping the nightmare would end here.

"They won't know until they make it safe. Who has such a grudge against you and that kid that he wants to blow you both to bits?"

"I don't . . ."

"What?" He looked at her quizzically.

"There's only one incident Londy and I were both involved in. But everyone is in jail except for . . ."

"Mario Correa. I know; he's number eight on our hit parade." He stared at her and pointed to the van. "You think he's behind this?"

Carly had to find Alex. She hopped away from Wiley and searched the ranks of press until she saw him. The cadre of press had grown exponentially as the day wore on. She bit back the disgust because she knew they wanted to see blood — Londy's blood. She didn't have to look far for Alex. He'd been moved behind a barrier, and he was trying to get her attention. He wanted access. She jogged to him, ignoring all the questions yelled her way.

"Hey, any chance you can get me in there to watch the screen?"

"I'm not here in any official capacity."

"But they let Ned stay in."

"He's not a reporter. He's a bomb guy. Listen for a minute — I have an idea about who is behind this."

"You mean you know who set the bomb?"

"Maybe." She told him what had popped into her mind as she spoke to Wiley.

"Mario Correa?" His eyes narrowed.

"Yeah, Correa. Suppose he was Barton's partner and he's behind all of this because he wants to get back at me and Londy, discredit us, keep us out of the Burke trial, or just kill us. I wish I had gotten a better look at him the night I saw him."

"Unbelievable," Alex said. Then he was quiet. All Carly could hear was the noise of the crowd around him. Finally he said, "You could be right. Can't you get me in there so we can talk about it?"

"I'll talk to Jake, but I'm not making any promises." She turned to see Ned watching her.

"Sorry. Didn't mean to startle you. Just wanted to tell you that things are looking good. I think they'll get Londy out of this."

"Oh, that's great news."

"I couldn't help but overhear part of your conversation. Did you say Correa — as in Mario Correa? The fugitive who was involved in the mayor's murder?"

"Yeah, why? Do you know the name?"

"I heard that name when we moved here and it didn't surprise me that he was in trouble with the law. He went to high school with my brother. I never liked him."

39

Carly ran to find Nick. He was watching the bomb squad's video monitor as the call went up that the bomb was code 4. Nick and the guys around him cheered. One of them hailed the paramedics, who were standing by to tend to Londy.

Carly could make out Londy's battered face on the monitor and winced.

Nick turned to her, grinning. "They got it. Now maybe Londy will have some answers for us."

"I think I have some answers. It's Mario Correa. He's behind all of this."

Nick's smile faded. "What?"

She told him everything she'd learned.

Hands on hips, Nick frowned. "But why go after Londy? And why not just shoot him? Why shoot those other kids?"

"I don't know. All I know is that it would benefit him if the charges against Burke were weakened or dropped. Maybe all of this is about getting Burke off so he can join Correa wherever he's hiding."

"You would be the target then. You're the star witness."

Nick was interrupted when a Huntington Beach officer walked up and slapped him on the back. "I hate to say it, but I was holding my breath, afraid I'd hear a boom."

The three of them turned and watched as the paramedics wheeled Londy away from the van. Now that the bomb had been made safe, the bomb guys would need to safely dispose of the explosive.

Nick put his arm on Carly's shoulder. "Let's go see what Londy has to say."

As they walked to the medic van, Carly felt bone weary, not sure how long it had been since she'd seen Victor sprinting across traffic to tell her about Londy. When they reached the rig, she saw a stiff, sore, but obviously relieved Londy responding to the paramedics as they assessed his condition. He'd suffered a beating. One eye was swollen shut, and it looked as though his nose had bled. He looked at her, his good eye widening.

"Who did this, Londy?" Carly asked when the medics stepped away so she and Nick could ask questions.

"It was that harbor guy — Correa."

The confirmation jolted Carly. "You recognized him?"

He nodded. "I saw him in the harbor before. I know him. He was real mad. Mad at you."

"About what? About Burke?"

"Mad that no one is blaming you for killing Mr. Ned's brother. I didn't understand all of what he said, but he wanted to ruin your life and says he didn't and things are worse now. He was also mad at Mr. Barton, too — called him stupid, said he messed up all the plans."

Carly frowned. "Plans for what?"

"I don't know. He was in a big hurry. But mostly what made him mad was the bridge dedication being canceled. He told me I was going to die. But he said if something went wrong and I lived, I was to tell you something."

"What's that?"

"He said he's coming for you and he won't miss now."

It was dark and early Sunday morning by the time the van, explosives, and all the newspeople had cleared their block and Nick and Carly were able to get back into their house. Speculation had Carly's mind spinning as she stood in the shower, exhausted but relieved that Londy was safe.

After he'd been thoroughly interviewed, all hell broke loose. The FBI in particular were like bloodhounds on a scent at the news that one of their most wanted was in the area. They sent a team to the marina to search Walt's again. And they were going over the pedestrian bridge as well. From what Londy had heard, Correa had planned something for the bridge dedication ceremony. Bomb dogs were brought in to scour every inch of the structure. They'd also determined that there was still a fair amount of stolen explosive unaccounted for.

"Did you ask Jacobs to check into Burke's visitors?" Nick asked after Carly was out of the shower and dressed for bed.

"Yeah, I did. It was just a hunch. Why?"

"Because Michael Carter visited Burke twice."

"You're kidding."

"Nope. The most recent visit was about six months ago, right after all the explosives and guns were stolen. They're studying surveillance videos. Michael Carter appears as a bearded man who bears a close resemblance to Mario Correa. It won't be long before pictures of him are everywhere."

"That's great," she said with a yawn, falling onto the bed. "How is it you're so alert?

I'm dead."

"I'll join you after I shower. I just got an update. Potter is still missing."

He leaned over her to tuck her in, but Carly barely felt his presence. She closed her eyes and was sound asleep instantly.

Carly didn't feel normal until eleven the next morning, when she stood with her face under the shower again, relishing the warm water washing away cobwebs and the last remnants of sleep. She dressed in shorts and a comfortable T-shirt and walked into the kitchen, inhaling the heavenly odor of coffee.

Nick was on the phone and he blew her a kiss. From his side of the conversation, she could tell he was talking to someone in federal employ.

She mouthed the words, *"Anything new?"*

He nodded and held up a finger to indicate he'd tell her in a minute.

Carly went about making breakfast. She pulled bacon, eggs, and mushrooms out of the fridge and looked at Nick. He gave her a thumbs-up, which told her he hadn't eaten yet. It was omelets for two, then. By the time breakfast was ready, Nick was off the phone, and cheese and toast had been added to the feast.

"Well, Burke confirms that it was Mario Correa who visited him — as Michael Carter. But he said it as a taunt, basically saying that we'll never catch him; he's too smart. He also said that Correa took over a year to plan his revenge carefully, that the harbor gig was his dream job and you took that away. And in the yearbook from San Pedro High? Dean Barton, Mario Correa, *and* Keith Sailor were all in the same graduating class."

"The pieces fall together." Carly sat at the table, ignoring her rumbling stomach. "What nerve he has, to walk right into the jail like that."

"Well, his alter ego had no wants or warrants, and as long as he behaved himself, there would be no reason to check further. His first visit was right after Burke lost his bid for bail, and like I said, the last was six months ago.

"But let's eat." Nick leaned over and gave her a kiss. "Boy, you were out cold."

"I was tired. How long have you been up?"

"About an hour. I took the dog for a walk. Wiley called when I got back. The file on Mario Correa should be in your in-box."

Carly nearly jumped up from the table. She'd wanted to read the FBI's file on Correa last night but Nick had talked her out of it. The FBI was rather sensitive about fugitive searches since one of their ten most wanted, Whitey Bulger, had been apprehended a couple years ago. It was discovered he had hidden in plain sight for more than a dozen years in Santa Monica, living a normal life.

When the authorities learned that Mario Correa had been in Las Playas, they were determined that he wasn't going to get away, live in freedom for a dozen years, and splash egg on their faces when he was finally caught. In high-handed fed fashion, they declared the search theirs and were closely guarding the information they'd collected on him. It was Ned who said he'd try to convince them to give Correa's file to Carly. Turned out one of the agents called in to assist in the search had participated in some training with Ned when he was in the service. He was certain, in private, he could convince his friend to let loose with some info.

"I'll check it after breakfast," she said.

Nick smiled. "Then let's pray and eat." He took her hand and they bowed their heads. "Lord, bless this food to our bodies, and thank you for your love and provision. And I pray you keep Carly safe and help us put those responsible for the death and destruction in the city in jail."

Together they said amen. After breakfast they took mugs of coffee and sat together on the couch to review the file.

Mario Correa Jr., aka Michael Carter, had been born and raised in Rancho Palos Verdes. His parents were extremely wealthy; his dad founded and ran an import/export business.

Nick snorted when he saw that. "So the son is a perverted chip off the old block. His 'export business' as harbor superintendent just happened to be one that specialized in stolen and illegal goods."

Carly said nothing, just kept reading. Correa and Barton might have been good friends, but unlike Barton, Correa had no criminal record. Sailor did, though. He'd been arrested twice for offenses related to illegal gambling. Correa must have exploited a known weakness. Correa either kept his nose clean, or he'd just not been caught until the mayor's murder.

A few years before Correa became harbor superintendent, his father had sold his business and moved with the wife out to Palm Desert to retire. Dad claimed he and his son were estranged, but the feds had watched him carefully for months to determine if Junior ever contacted his parents.

They never saw evidence that he had.

The feds noted that Correa did appear to have been estranged from his parents long before his illegal activity was discovered. He didn't have a place of residence. He lived on a boat that was moored in the old marina. The boat, named the *Rex,* had been impounded and confiscated by agents. Carly remembered the yacht she and Jeff had been taken prisoner on. Searching through the paperwork, she found a reference to another boat, the *Tango.* This one had never been located, leaving the feds to speculate that Correa had sailed to Mexico and was living south of the border on the ocean.

"I'll bet it was Correa living on that boat — the one the marina guy told Alex about."

"And Jarvis has been covering for him?" Nick tapped his chin with an index finger. "There's a waiting list for slips in Las Playas. Jarvis would have had to do a lot of tap-dancing to let a guy live there without questions being asked."

"Maybe not. With all the construction going on and the Oceans First protests, I'll bet people are moving in and out or maybe even left their boats until the construction is finished. The mess and confusion may have helped to hide Correa."

"And —" Nick picked up her train of

thought — "if he's using a fake identity, he probably falsified the boat registration. Or maybe he's not living in a slip. Maybe he's just off the coast somewhere."

Nick turned to her and gripped her hand. "I know you want to get back to work, but until Correa is tracked down and put behind bars, you need to be careful."

"There are more FBI agents in the city right now than there are residents. Please don't be paranoid."

"I'm sure Jake would let us take some vacation time. Let's take a trip."

"We'd have to take Londy with us. Correa is after him as well."

"Don't change the subject."

Carly stood and faced him, hands on hips. "I'm not. Come on, I can't run and hide because of this dirtbag."

Nick rose and placed his hands on her shoulders. "Okay, since I expected that answer, will you at least promise to be careful?"

She wrapped her arms around his waist. "Yes, I will be careful. And I will keep praying that Correa is caught." She leaned back and gave him a kiss. "Now, can we go to occupational health?"

He touched his forehead to hers. "I'll drive."

40

The occupational health doctor cleared Carly to return to work Tuesday night. Then she and Nick stopped by the station to check with Harris on the status of the investigation into Duncan Potter.

"Just got ballistics back," Harris said. "The gun we recovered in Potter's boat was the gun used in the double-homicide gangster shooting. Judge issued a no-bail warrant for him."

"What's his connection to Correa?"

"If Carter is Correa, other than the foundation, we haven't found one yet."

"We still can't even find him," Romo said.

"He follows me around," Carly said. "Maybe Tuesday night he'll show up."

"We can hope."

When Nick pulled into the driveway after the visit to occupational health, Carly didn't miss the plain car parked up the block.

"We have watchers?"

"Yep. You're the target of a fugitive. You'll have shadows until it's safe."

Carly started to say something but stopped. She didn't like the idea of baby-sitters, but she wasn't going to argue with Nick about it. It was not a battle worth having. She and Nick had planned a quiet evening at home together, and she didn't want to inject any drama.

Later that night, after Nick was sound asleep, Carly struggled to follow suit. The knowledge that she was the target of a cold-blooded killer would not let her mind shut off. If she were the person Correa wanted to kill, why shoot three gang members and try to start a gang war?

Did he think she'd get killed in the cross fire?

Or was this all about discrediting her for the Burke trial?

She wanted to get up and pace, but she didn't want to disturb Nick. He was a light sleeper. They'd learned earlier that Harris and Romo wanted to interview Burke about Correa and his visits but had been shut down by Burke's lawyers. All she could do was speculate on the plans Correa and Burke had hatched. And fight the fear that threatened when she thought about all the death and destruction the missing explosives could cause if their plan involved an attempt to use it.

Carly closed her eyes and prayed they'd find Correa and stop him before anyone else was hurt or killed. She'd finally dropped off to sleep when the phone jerked her awake. Groaning, she rolled over and grabbed it, feeling Nick shift and knowing he was awake now as well.

It was Alex.

"This better be good."

"It is. Can you and Nick meet me at Harbor House?"

"When? Tomorrow?"

"Right now."

Carly sat up and looked at Nick, who was rubbing his eyes. "Alex, it's after midnight. I just got to sleep. What's so important it can't wait?"

"Trust me, please. I came by your house and saw the agents out front. Please, Carly. I wouldn't ask if it wasn't important."

Carly sighed and glanced at Nick again, who was frowning. "All right. We'll be there in about fifteen minutes." She ended the call.

"Where are we going to be in fifteen minutes?"

"Alex wants to talk to us at Harbor House.

I figure this is an important thing to share with my husband."

"Lack of sleep? Thank you very much." He swung a pillow at her before she could get out of the way.

She was laughing as she climbed out of bed and got dressed.

Nick sent a text to the agents at the house asking them to stay there, that he and Carly would be right back.

"He wouldn't say why he wanted to see us?"

"No," Carly said with a yawn. "He was being very cryptic."

Ten minutes later, they pulled into the Harbor House lot. They'd both brought off-duty weapons with them. Nick had his 9mm in a belt holster and Carly had her .380 in her backpack.

Carly scanned her side of the lot and knew Nick did likewise on his side. But the parking lot was mostly empty except for Alex's car.

When they went inside the restaurant, it took a minute to find Alex. He was seated way in the back, in the emptiest section of the place. And he wasn't alone.

Carly looked at Nick, who shrugged. Together they walked back to where Alex sat, stopping short when his companion turned.

Seated with Alex was Duncan Potter.

41

"What's going on?" Carly asked. She knew Nick's hand was on his gun. But Potter didn't look dangerous; rather, he looked exhausted and terrified. Where his brother had been buff, built like a fireplug, Duncan was thin as a rail with almost-delicate features.

Alex stood and held his hands up. "Hey, calm down," he said in a hushed voice. "Please — you should listen to what he has to say."

Carly turned to Nick, who nodded but didn't relax. He moved between her and Potter.

"You're wanted for murder, Mr. Potter," Nick said as they sat — Alex and Potter on one side of the booth, he and Carly on the other. "The evidence points to you shooting three people execution style."

"I didn't kill anyone. I can't prove it, but I'm not a killer." Potter rubbed his face with both hands and stayed silent as the waitress came with two cups for Nick and Carly and a fresh carafe of coffee.

"He showed up on my doorstep . . . kind of like someone else I know," Alex said. "And what he told me was compelling."

"Two people are dead, one is in a coma, and the gun that was used was found on your boat. If you have an explanation for that, let's hear it," Nick said.

Potter looked at Carly, deer in the headlights. "The gun? On my boat?" He uttered an oath and tensed as if to rise. Something like a whimper escaped, much like air escaping from a tire, and he deflated back into the booth. Carly nodded for him to continue.

"I didn't shoot those gang members. I was there taking photos afterward; that's all." His bloodshot eyes pleaded. "All I wanted was justice. I didn't want anyone to get hurt. I know you killed my brother, and I never believed that it was anything but murder. That's why I've been following you. I figured I'd catch you doing something wrong."

"Duncan, I'm sorry your brother is dead. But I didn't have a choice."

He dropped his head and sobbed. "I don't know what to think anymore. People who I thought were my friends have done horrible things." He faced Carly. "I miss Derek. He always knew what to do, what to say. I don't."

"Just tell them what you told me," Alex said.

Potter wiped his face with a napkin and continued. "Ginny believed me. She said I was on the right track. When she introduced me to her boyfriend and he believed me too, I got more confident. They said they'd help me prove you murdered Derek, help me get the evidence that would get you fired or put in jail. They introduced me to Michael Carter. He hated you more than I did. He scared me a little, but because he was certain you were a corrupt cop, I trusted him."

"You know he's not really Michael Carter?" Carly asked.

Duncan looked at Alex, then back to Carly. "I was afraid he wasn't who he said he was. He's the one who shot those gangsters. I think Jarvis and Dean helped him."

"What makes you think that?"

"I talked to Ginny and we pieced it together. Like I said, Carter was more obsessed with you than I was. He insisted you had ruined his life and that his best friend was in jail because you lied on a report. He kept saying he wanted you to suffer."

Carly folded her arms and sat back, biting off a sharp remark as Potter continued.

"And he was focused on the new marina dedication, said that if we didn't get you before, we'd get you then in a big way. Until the dedication, he wanted you distracted."

"You think he shot three people to distract me?"

"Ginny thinks that was what happened. She put together a couple conversations she'd heard Dean and Carter having. They talked about how small the police department in Las Playas was, that if they had a big problem to deal with, they'd be tied up in knots. He was glad Oceans First was here but then nervous about them being evicted too soon."

"Too soon?" Nick asked. "Too soon for what?"

Potter shook his head, his gaze returning to Carly. "Remember when you stopped the car? The one with all the guns?"

Carly nodded.

"Ginny said that when Carter heard about that, he screamed and yelled at Dean. They almost had a fistfight over it. She didn't understand at the time why Carter blamed Dean for that, but in hindsight she figured Carter gave the guns to Dean to give to the gangbanger. But you finding them wasn't supposed to happen. I told her that didn't make any sense unless Carter wanted to start a gang war. And then Ginny said she thought that's exactly what Carter was doing, only she thinks he was going to blame everything on Dean and that people would believe him because Dean was on parole."

"What did he have planned for the dedication that he needed the police distracted by a lot of bloodshed?" Nick asked.

"I don't know. He never confided in me. But he'd been planning something for a while. He bought a catering company just to be sure he'd be there for the dedication."

Carly started to say something, but Nick raised a hand.

"What was the relationship between Michael Carter and Dean Barton? Why would Barton simply deliver guns to gang members because Carter wanted him to?"

"They were friends — good friends at first, I thought. As much as Carter hated Officer Edwards, Dean hated his brother, Ned. From what I heard, Dean was going to help Carter get even with Officer Edwards, and Carter was going to help Dean get even with Ned."

"Get even with him? Was Carter responsible for the bomb in the coffee shop?"

"I don't know. I know he was angry when he read about it, but . . ."

"He could have been angry that it didn't explode."

"I guess."

"What about the foundation that you're trustee for? That makes it look as though you're involved with Carter more than you're admitting. Carter is using money you signed over to him. He bought a catering company. He probably gave money to Barton."

"The foundation . . ." Potter frowned. "He asked me to be the trustee, said it was just to avoid some problems he was having with the IRS. I agreed. I was never after money. When he needed me to send money somewhere, I did it. He'd been helping Sailor for months, giving him money. When Sailor defaulted on the loans, Carter needed me to write a check for the catering company."

"Why did you disappear, and why are you here now?" Nick asked. Carly heard the impatience in Nick's voice. Potter was a wanted man and he needed to be arrested.

"It's because of what happened to Dean. That night, I was driving around, waiting to hear Officer Edwards get a call. I lucked out. I saw her park at the Bluestone." He looked away from Nick. "I got out and decided to follow you." He held Carly's gaze briefly. "I felt a little peevish and locked the gate behind you to mess with you." He looked away. "I knew there was another way out of that yard. Anyway, I followed you to see what you were doing."

"I never heard you, never had an inkling I was being followed."

He shook his head. "You were concentrating so hard. It surprised me when you started down toward the construction yard. Carter always organized meetings either there or on the old marina dock, so I know my way around and where the open places in the fence are."

"Did Carter live on a boat in the old marina?"

Duncan nodded. "Jarvis hooked him up with a slip. I watched you go down to the fence and find our way in."

"Wait," Nick interrupted. "Why did Carter want to meet where everyone was trespassing?"

"He told me that people couldn't be trusted, that everyone had an angle to work. If we met in secret and kept our plans to ourselves, we'd accomplish our goals. Carter kept going on about his friend in jail, the one who was framed, so we were all kindred spirits fighting for justice. And

Dean liked meeting in dark, hidden places. He said it was because he'd been in jail so long."

"I was the main focus of your meetings?" Carly asked, feeling completely creeped out.

"Mostly we planned how to catch you breaking the law."

"How were you going to do that?"

He sniffled and ran a hand under his nose. "Set up things like Dean confronting you at the coffee shop."

"That was a setup?"

"Yeah, but you surprised them by not drawing your gun. Carter was certain that you'd draw your gun, and I was supposed to photograph the scene, get the shot of you pointing a gun at an unarmed man. But then he got mad at Dean for taking a swing at you and provoking you."

Carly frowned. "Dean was there for my benefit, not his brother's?"

"No, Dean wanted to tweak his brother as well; you were just the first project. Dean and Carter had a pact, like I said."

She sat back. "From what you're saying, Carter flaunted the law. Why did you trust anything he said?"

"He supported me. He kept assuring me we'd catch you doing something. I'm sorry, but that was what I wanted more than anything. I believed Carter until I saw him shoot Dean."

42

Dishes clattered in the restaurant's kitchen as Carly processed what Potter had said.

"You saw Carter shoot Dean?"

Potter nodded. "I followed you. You found the hole in the fence, and I was going to stop you right then; but you saw Dean, and he ran. I'm guessing he went into the restaurant to make certain you didn't head toward Walt's. Besides, he spent a lot of time in every part of the construction site after dark. He really knew his way around. I think Carter paid the security officers to look the other way."

"What was at Walt's that he wouldn't want me to see?" She remembered Dean's belongings and the clean spot in the empty restaurant that indicated something had been stored there.

"Carter kept some personal items there. Dean and Jarvis kept them safe. Dean stayed there when he wasn't with Ginny.

He said he needed space from time to time."

Carly shot Nick a glance. Potter was confirming what Alex had discovered about the boat; Jarvis was involved up to his eyeballs. Nick gave an almost-imperceptible shake of his head. Duncan Potter was either the most naive of people or a consummate actor.

Potter continued with his story. "I was going to follow you in, but all of a sudden Carter was there. He must have come from Walt's. He ran in right behind you, but he didn't see me. I stood outside the door, heard you calling Dean. The next thing I knew, you were falling."

He paused and drank some coffee. "I couldn't believe what I saw next. Carter stepped out from under the balcony and picked up your gun — you had dropped it — at the same time Dean came running down the stairs. Carter was furious. He wanted to know what Dean thought he was doing. Dean cursed him, said they got lucky and could finish things right now. But Carter was as mad as I've ever seen him, saying this wasn't the way he wanted it to go down. He didn't want your death to be quick and neat. He wanted you to suffer. Dean told him that he wasn't his boss, and all of a sudden Carter was pointing your gun at Dean."

"Dean wasn't armed?"

Potter shook his head. "He wasn't scared either. He called Carter a stupid punk. Carter said Dean had always been a moron and that he'd ruined all his plans, but finally he'd made himself useful at the end. Then he fired. He killed Dean."

"What did you do?"

"I was shocked. I jumped. Carter must have heard me. Maybe he thought it was your backup coming. I heard him curse; then he put the gun in your hand and fired it again, making your hand squeeze the trigger. That's when I saw the flashlights of more officers. I hid and assumed Carter did the same thing."

"He never saw you?"

"No, but he knew I was there. Maybe Jarvis saw me run back to my boat — I don't know, but I was scared and wondering what to tell Ginny when Carter showed up at my boat. He had a gun, and he started to harangue me about spying on him and wanted to know what I'd seen. There was murder in his eyes and I freaked. I was certain he was going to kill me. I jumped overboard and swam away. He called after me, telling me I was dead and if I went to the cops, I'd be sorry and wish I was dead."

He gulped more coffee. "I swam to the

jetty, then made my way to my car soaking wet and just drove. I got on the freeway and drove north, didn't stop until I needed gas. I've been living out of my car ever since. When my brain cleared, I turned around. I'd read in the papers about what was happening here and knew I needed to tell Ginny what I'd seen. She didn't believe me at first, but after Dean's van was parked in your driveway with a bomb, she called my cell phone and said she believed me. I tried to talk her out of it. . . ."

"Talk her out of what?"

"Going to Carter. She was going to confront him. She loved Dean and believed in him like I believed in Derek. When she accepted that I'd truly seen Carter kill him, she was so angry. I tried to tell her we needed to go to the police, but she wouldn't listen, and then she told me I was wanted, that Carter had framed me and I'd be arrested. That was yesterday, and I haven't seen her since. I'm afraid he's done something to her."

43

"Confront Carter?" Carly stared at Potter as she considered the reporter fronting off a cold-blooded killer like Correa. She was dead for sure.

"She loved Dean; what could I say?"

"You're going to have to come to the station and give a full, taped statement," Nick told Potter.

"Will I be arrested?"

"For now, yes."

"Can you get someone to look for Ginny?"

"Where do you think she went?" Carly asked.

Nick stood. "I'm going to call this in. I'll be out front."

"Probably to Walt's," Potter said as Nick made his way outside. "Maybe to Jarvis's boat because Jarvis always knew how to get to Carter."

"Do you know why Jarvis shot the protestor? Is it related to Correa in some way?"

"I'm not sure. I think it was because the guy got too close to Walt's. Jarvis was very protective of Carter's stuff."

"Did you ever see his belongings? Or what was in them?"

"I saw crates; that's all."

Carly said nothing else until federal agents arrived to take Potter into custody. By the tone and subject of their questions, clearly their minds were focused on the remaining explosives. But though Potter was still talking, he didn't seem to know anything about that theft.

As the group moved out into the parking lot, she could tell that Nick wanted to be part of the investigation. It was a no-brainer because she wanted in as well. But as she opened her mouth to protest being left out, something stopped her. She was too close. Emotion had clouded her contact with Dean Barton; she didn't want it to fog up the investigation into Correa.

"Nick, go. I know you want to. The house is under surveillance. Alex will give me a ride home."

He argued weakly but finally kissed her and followed the federal car out of the lot.

Carly yawned and looked at Alex. "Ready to chauffeur?"

"Did you believe Potter?"

"I don't think he shot those three gangsters, but the rest . . . Did *you* believe him? Is anyone that naive?"

"People see what they want to see." Alex shrugged. "Him as well as Masters. What do you think will happen to him?"

"I don't know enough about the evidence against him to speculate." She folded her arms. "Are you going to give me a ride or not?"

"Yeah, but I'm surprised you let Nick go and you weren't jumping to get in on things." He opened the passenger door.

"I think I'm too close to things to be an objective investigator." Her phone buzzed as she sat. She expected Nick's number, but the number she saw wasn't familiar.

"Hello?"

"Officer Edwards?"

Carly sat up straight. "Mary Ellen?"

"Yeah, sorry if I woke you, but something has happened I think you should know about. Here's Londy."

"Londy? I thought he was in the hospital."

"I was but they released me," Londy said. "I'm supposed to take it easy. But I'm not calling about me. It's about Victor."

"What about Victor? Does Jonah know the two of you are out at this hour?"

"He knows that we're looking for Victor

404

because he was upset. Crusher took a bad turn. He's coming out of it now, but Victor didn't know that. He left to find a gun. He wants to go shoot Correa. He's gone, Officer Edwards. I'm afraid he's going to do something stupid."

"Where would he get a gun?"

"I'm sure he'd find a Ninja to help him out."

Carly groaned, knowing that what Londy said was true enough. "Did you call 911?" She was aware of Trejo watching her. He had started the car but hadn't pulled out of the lot.

"They won't help because I didn't see him with the gun. And I can't say for sure where he went. He won't trust no other cops but you anyway. Please, Officer Edwards, you have to help us find him and stop him."

"I'm not sure what I can do, but everyone is looking for Correa, and they haven't been able to find him. What makes you think Victor will?"

"I guess I just don't like thinking about him running around with a gun."

That gave Carly pause. She didn't like thinking about a distraught ten-year-old running around with a gun either.

"He'll probably head down to where he saw Crusher meet Correa," Carly said, half to herself.

"If you send uniform cops, he'll just hide."

"Where are you now?"

"With Mary Ellen. We're at Half Baked. We were going to walk down to the transit mall."

Carly looked at the clock. Trains had stopped running almost an hour ago. "We'll meet you there. I'll be there in about fifteen minutes."

"Where do you want me to take you in such a hurry?" Trejo asked after she hung up.

"Uh, you don't —"

"None of that. I'm your chauffeur right now, so where to?"

She told him what Mary Ellen had said, and he began the drive to the transit mall.

Carly phoned Nick and got his voice mail. She left him a message with the details and promised him she'd be careful.

"Ha," Alex said when she was off the phone again.

"What's funny?"

"You. You probably have a plan in your head to be anything but careful."

She ignored him and leaned forward as they turned onto a dead-end street where the train track ended. She saw Londy and Mary Ellen right away.

Alex stopped in the red, and Carly got out to let Londy and Mary Ellen climb in the backseat.

"Londy, you look awful. Are you sure you shouldn't be in the hospital?" One of his eyes was still swollen almost completely shut, and there were scabs on one side of his face.

"They released me." Londy tipped his head. "My ribs are sore and I can't see so good out of my left eye, but I'm okay. It's Victor who needs my help now."

"Where do you think Victor is? Are you sure he even made it down this far? The train isn't running."

"He could have made it on the last train. Maybe he's at the Bluestone."

Carly shook her head, realizing that Londy didn't know that it was probably Walt's where Victor saw his brother meet with the three white dudes.

"Alex, let's take a drive down to the construction yard and Walt's. I have a feeling Victor is headed there."

Her phone vibrated, showing Nick's number. She signaled for Alex to wait a minute.

"What are you doing out looking for Victor?" Nick's tone wasn't angry as much as it was exasperated.

"Trejo is with me, and so are Londy and

Mary Ellen. Look, odds are Correa is long gone. Anyway, isn't ATF all over the dock?"

"They were, but there was a bomb threat in the harbor. It was called in about the same time we got Potter to the station. The bomb squad is mobilizing to head down there, and there's only a two-man team watching the old marina. I'd feel a lot better if I knew you were safe at home."

Carly bit her bottom lip, frowning. "I'll say that right back at you. Are you mobilizing with ATF?"

"I don't know what I'm going to do."

"What's happening with Ginny Masters?"

"We talked to her boss. Bottom line is there's no sign of foul play. And if she went to confront Correa, how could she find him? Everybody and their mother is looking for him and coming up empty. There are a lot of holes in Potter's story."

"Is he still talking?"

"Yeah, he hasn't lawyered up. Where are you looking for Victor?"

"Around the Bluestone, the construction yard, and Walt's. With luck, one of the federal agents down there will see Victor and grab him."

"Maybe I'll head down there. I doubt anything is going to happen with Masters because she's an adult and there's no proof that she's in danger. ATF will handle the harbor. Oh, you should also know that Harris plans to serve a search warrant on Jarvis."

"Now?"

"Soon. He was supposed to surrender himself at midnight. They filed criminal charges for his shooting. His boat is still there, so homicide is going to hit it at dawn if he doesn't show by then."

"Hopefully we'll have found Victor long before that and both of us will be home. We're starting at the Bluestone if you decide to join us."

"Be careful."

She disconnected and turned to find Alex watching her.

"Okay, boss, I take it that's where you want me to drive?"

"Mush," Carly said, pointing toward the coast. "We can start at the Bluestone. It's high ground. From there we'll walk down toward the old marina."

A few minutes later, Trejo pulled up to the fence that surrounded the Bluestone. He parked the car and all of them got out. Carly opened the gate, and they walked up to the hotel and around back. She was about to show them the path she'd discovered and ask Londy if Walt's could be the place Victor was talking about when a bright flash caught her eye. Then the boom of an explosion made her jump.

Something in Sandy Park exploded.

Carly stepped to the edge of the terrace and watched as flames shot into the air from an area densely filled with tents and tent trailers.

"What in the world . . . ?" Trejo voiced the astonishment she felt.

Carly gripped her phone to call Nick. As she waited for him to answer, she could see flames spreading.

"I was on my way to you," Nick said when he answered. Fire truck sirens sounded in the background. "But something happened in Sandy Park, and I've got to see if I can help. Fire and tents, plus all the trash that's been building up there . . . It'll be a mess."

Carly knew he was right and let him go, wanting with all she was worth to help as well, but knowing she had to see to Londy, Mary Ellen, and Victor.

"What do you think blew?" Trejo asked.

Carly paused and thought about the bomb threat in the harbor. Was this explosion accidental or on purpose? "Good question. It could have been a propane tank."

"The fire department confiscated them all as fire hazards." Alex's concentration was on the blaze.

"Well then, it could be anything. I know you want to get down there and cover that."

"I'm helping you right now."

She smiled grimly. "Okay, let's find the trail."

The sky was bright with fire in the park. Carly could see flames hopping from tent to tent. People were running, but the lights of the first fire trucks were already arriving on scene.

When they reached the hole in the fence, Carly saw that it had been repaired. No one was getting into the construction yard this way. They continued along the fence toward Walt's until she saw movement.

"Stop," she hissed, stepping in front of the other three. "Something moved down there." She squinted into the darkness.

"Let me call," Londy said. "It might be Victor."

Carly agreed, but she drew her gun as a precaution.

"Victor! It's Londy and Mary Ellen. Come out of there, man."

They waited a long moment. Carly silently counted the seconds. Finally the boy popped up.

"Londy? What happened? What was that noise?" Victor walked toward them, eyes big.

411

Carly figured the explosion had scared him.

"It's over in Sandy Park. You okay?"

Victor nodded but stopped when he saw Carly.

"It's okay, Victor. You're not in trouble. We're here to take you home."

He continued forward, weariness in his steps. "I didn't do nothing. Can't get through the fence. All the holes been fixed."

"You carrying?" Londy asked.

Victor looked them over, a sheepish expression on his face. He pulled a pocketknife out of his pocket. "This was all I could get."

Carly took it and put it in her pocket, then looked at Alex.

When he spoke, she felt as though he'd read her mind. "Let's get back to the car so I can get everyone home quick."

44

Alex sped to Victor's house. Carly didn't protest. She felt as much urgency as he did. When they arrived, Carly got out with Londy and Victor. Over Victor's complaints, Carly knocked on the door. It was opened quickly by a woman with a frown that turned to relief when she saw Victor.

After she hugged the boy, then admonished him to go inside and get cleaned up for bed, she thanked Londy and Carly and explained that Hector was doing well and would hopefully wake up soon.

"Victor is an interesting kid," Carly said to Londy as they walked back to the car.

"I was interesting too when I was his age. I just hope he grows out of it." Londy stopped short of the car. "I can walk from here; my house is only a couple of blocks away."

Carly peered into his bruised face. "You sure? It's late."

Londy nodded. "Yep, I'm good. Thanks for everything." He bent down and leaned into the car to say good night to Mary Ellen. They made arrangements to talk in the morning. When he straightened, he gave a half wave and turned to walk home. Carly climbed back into the car.

Alex continued the pace to Mary Ellen's on the far north side of the city. He had a scanner in his car, which Carly turned on. The city was still alive with sirens and emergency vehicles attending to the fire in Sandy Park. But it had already been nearly half an hour; soon all that would be left was mop-up.

Since Nick was a sergeant, Carly knew he'd be supervising. She strained to hear Nick's voice in the radio traffic but didn't.

"I know you want to get to Sandy Park," Carly said after they left Mary Ellen, seeing the light in Alex's eyes. "Just get me home."

"Why don't you come with me?"

"I want to get my equipment. By the time I get there, it will just be cleanup. If I go without the tools to help, I'll only be in the way."

"Fair enough." He made a U-turn and pressed the accelerator, traveling a little bit faster than he should. But again Carly didn't complain.

When he pulled onto her street, she noted the plain car was gone. It didn't matter. She didn't plan on being there long. As Trejo pulled into her driveway, her phone buzzed with a text from Nick.

Carly looked at the picture on her phone and the world stopped. Her breath caught in her throat; her heart began to pound. It was Nick — bound, blindfolded, and wearing a suicide vest.

How?

Where?

When?

The phone chirped with another text, but it took her a minute before she could move past the photo and read the new message.

HE DIES UNLESS YOU DO EXACTLY AS I SAY.

"What's the matter?" Trejo asked, car idling. "You look white as a sheet."

Carly couldn't speak. She held the photo up so he could see it.

"Is that a joke?"

Unable to speak, all Carly could do was shake her head as Alex put his car in park.

She waited an agonizing five minutes before the next text came through. SEASIDE POINT, COME ALONE. HURRY. YOU HAVE LESS THAN 30 MINUTES.

Carly tried to think, but fear clouded her mind.

"I've got to get to the point in less than thirty minutes." She spoke aloud to get her thought process moving.

"You're not going down there, are you?" Trejo gripped her arm.

"I have to. It's Nick. I need —"

"Call the storm troopers. For heaven's sake, Correa will kill the both of you."

"He'll kill Nick if I call the feds. Will you just listen? There's no time to argue. I need you to help me." She glared across the car at him, even as a plan formed in her mind. Her brain was sluggish, stuck in shock. It was the Oceans First protestors who gave her an idea.

Alex dragged a hand across his forehead and sighed. "In protest. But I'll do what you ask."

"I'm going to Seaside Point, but I'm not going to drive in with a big bull's-eye on my chest. Think: Correa wouldn't do that either. It's one way in. He must be docked there in one of the guest slips." She paused a beat and watched as the logic sank in with Alex.

"I'll swim in from the Seal Beach side. I can reach that side quicker and swim to Seaside Point. I can get the drop on Correa and save my husband. But I have to hurry. It'll take me at least fifteen minutes to dress and get there. I want you to find Fernando. Or call Jacobs and tell him. Just give me some time first."

"Carly, you're crazy."

"I'm going, Alex. Pray for me. Pray for us both." She opened the car door.

He stopped her with a hand on her arm. "Please reconsider."

She turned and pulled her arm from his grip. "I have to do this," she said and ran into the house.

Checking the clock, she had twenty-five minutes left. She grabbed her swimsuit and her summer wetsuit as she undressed, then hurriedly slipped them on. She picked up her weight belt and removed the weights before strapping it on.

The picture of Nick flashed in her mind. *Where is he?* Inside somewhere, but the only place he could be inside on the point was the bathrooms. They were all stone and gray stainless steel.

Next she pulled Nick's Koga kit from beneath the bed. She opened it and dumped it on the bed, sifting through the stuff he used for training. He'd gathered an assortment of illegal weapons — most easily concealable and dangerous — that he could use during search training. The belt knife, a small blade that was easily hidden, caught her eye. She grabbed it and hooked it on the inside of her belt.

Looking at the picture again, she saw that Nick was handcuffed. And she saw a bit of white. A small sink.

Not the point bathroom. But where?

Closing the phone, she found a pen that could be used as a handcuff key and jammed it up her sleeve. Nick also had a waterproof bag for a handgun and she put hers in it, along with her phone, and hooked it on her belt as well. Grabbing her keys, feeling time bleed away, she ran for her car.

When Carly reached the Seal Beach jetty, she had fifteen minutes to get to Seaside Point. The jetties formed the mouth of the flood control channel that carried water miles from the foothills to the Pacific Ocean. The south jetty wall was in Seal Beach. Across the flood control channel, the north jetty wall was the Las Playas border. The north side extended farther than the south wall because of the Las Playas marina. It curved around to Seaside Point and had a paved road while the Seal Beach jetty gave way to a sandy beach. In the daytime, fishermen on the south side and those at Seaside Point could holler back and forth. Swimming out to the point would be quick in the water calmed by jetties. She could see lights outside the bathroom, which was clearly visible to Seal Beach, but she couldn't see people.

Scurrying across the sand, she slid into the dark water and began her swim to the guest boat slips on the far side of Seaside Point, closer to the marina.

One thing gnawed. The guest slips were for small craft, dinghies. Correa couldn't tie his thirty-six-footer there.

Swimming freestyle as rapidly as she could, she slowed as she neared the slips. There was a Zodiac tied up but no one in it. From the water she couldn't see if anyone was on the point. For a minute she treaded water and prayed for Nick, that she was correct to choose a water approach and that Correa would be caught and brought to justice.

Pressing the light on her watch, she saw six minutes gone. She moved to the slip and put a hand up to steady herself in the gentle swells. Then she heard voices.

"She's not coming."

Jarvis! He was here, which meant the police hadn't taken him in yet. *He's working with Correa.* Carly almost felt defeat. She'd imagined confronting Correa alone. Now what?

"There's no way she could tell where that picture was taken. She'll come."

With a jolt, Carly recognized Mario Correa's voice. She remembered that voice toasting his crimes the night Jeff was murdered.

"Look, we're boxed in here. What if she calls the Coast Guard? We'll never get back to the *Tango.*"

Correa cursed. From the tone and their conversation, Carly realized Nick wasn't here. They wanted to lure her here, but where would he be?

She tuned them out and slipped away from the Zodiac, trying to see the picture of Nick again in her mind's eye. A small white sink in a boat bathroom.

The *Tango.*

Correa is here. His boat has to be here.

Without checking her watch because she knew she didn't have much time, Carly took off for the empty slip Alex had shown her. She prayed that the *Tango* was there now and that Nick was on it.

She swam hard, knowing that if Correa and Jarvis got in the Zodiac, she could never outswim them. Dock 15 was the last one and she had to hurry.

When she turned to find slip 22, she paused, breathing hard, straining to hear anything, afraid she'd hear the motor of the Zodiac bearing down on her.

All she heard was the beating of her own heart.

Then fear struck. What if he'd tied the *Tango* up somewhere else?

"Oh, Lord, please." She bent her head and allowed herself a couple of seconds to pray, now doubting the wisdom of her decision to swim here and doubting her instincts. Pulling herself together, she started toward slip 22, the water here smelling like diesel fuel and feeling oily.

Finally she was close enough to see that the slip wasn't empty.

Yes, she thought, *the boat's here.*

She made her way through the murky water and came up at the back of the boat. There on the stern was the name *Tango.* Correa's boat.

Placing her hands on the yacht's swim platform, she started to pull herself up.

Suddenly an explosion rent the air.

Looking over her shoulder at where she'd just been, she saw a ball of fire explode into the air above Seaside Point.

45

Carly felt as if she'd been kicked in the stomach, and the breath whooshed out of her lungs. She dropped against the hard fiberglass of the swim platform, half in the water and half out, and tried to breathe.

Had her husband just exploded with Seaside Point?

Oh, God, please, no, no. I pray I was right, that Nick wasn't out there.

She wasn't sure how long she sat there, unable to move or to think, terrified that her worst fear had materialized. *Like Elaine, I've lost my husband.* It was anger that brought her back to the here and now. Correa would be coming back to his boat to get away.

She pulled herself out of the water and all the way onto the platform, then looked down at her waterproof bag as if it were a venomous snake, thinking her phone had vibrated but not wanting to check. Wiping water from her face, she opened the bag, removed the gun, ignored the phone, and stood to get her bearings.

The deck of the cruiser was encased in a plastic and canvas enclosure. Carly didn't know much about boats, but this one was similar to the one she and Nick had chartered for the Maui swim.

Nick.

She made a fist and pounded her thigh as her legs threatened to give out under her, the thought of life without Nick sapping her strength. *Keep moving,* she told herself. *If I don't keep moving, I'll dissolve.*

She unsnapped the enclosure and stepped onto the deck. Straight ahead was the cockpit; off to the left, a seating area. Jaw set, resolute, she started to go below. *Correa isn't going to get away this time,* she thought.

The sound of a small boat motor floated in from a distance. Carly hurried below and quickly surveyed the galley and sleeping area. No one.

She reached for the door to the bathroom and slid it open, nearly howling with relief when her husband's blue eyes stared back at her. There was no sign of the suicide vest, and fear about explosives was tempered a bit by the joy that flooded Carly was like hot water after a tough swim.

But then the roar of a boat motor was on them. The *Tango* moved as something bumped into it. Voices. Then the boat shifted again as someone stepped aboard. The outboard motor went silent.

Nick sat on the commode, bound by handcuffs and duct tape, with a piece covering his mouth.

"Thank God you're okay," she whispered as she pulled the tape off.

"Ditto that. I'm not even going to ask what you're doing here," he hissed back. "I hope you have a cuff key."

The *Tango*'s motor roared to life and the floorboards vibrated.

Nodding, Carly pulled the pen key from her sleeve. She fell into Nick as the boat shifted sharply, moving backward. She undid his hands and then used the knife to cut the tape around his legs.

"You came prepared. What did he tell you?"

"No time. We have to get out of here. You had a vest on . . ."

"He took it with him, said he had a plan for it." He rolled his head as if his neck were stiff. "I heard an explosion."

"He blew up the bathrooms on the jetty." Their eyes held for a moment and Carly saw love, fear, and relief swirl in her husband's. He gripped her hand tight as if sensing she wanted to hold on to him and never let go, but they just didn't have the time right then.

"Did you find Masters?" he asked as the moment ended and they both moved out of the restroom.

"She's here?" Carly stopped, gun at the ready, watching the stairs.

The boat was moving slowly out of the marina.

"She was. He wanted hostages in case his escape was blocked." Nick gripped Carly's shoulders and moved her toward the sleeping area. He yanked up a mattress to reveal a large, open compartment. And Ginny Masters.

For a second Carly thought the reporter was dead. But then the woman moved. Carly handed Nick the knife so he could cut her free.

"We have to stop this boat," Carly said as they pulled a dazed Masters to her feet.

"I agree." Nick rubbed his wrists.

Carly heard footfalls coming their way. She held out the gun.

Nick shook his head. "Close quarters. You see to Masters." He pointed to the bathroom, and Carly pulled the wobbly woman that way.

"I got caught unaware once," Nick said. "It's not going to happen again."

Carly yanked Masters out of the way as feet appeared on the stairs.

Jarvis's heavy-lidded face, with eyes that always looked half-closed, registered shock as he saw Carly supporting Masters.

"Wha— ?"

Nick moved in behind him and executed a hair-pull takedown, jerking Jarvis's head back with one hand to encircle the neck with the other arm as he took the man down to his knees while simultaneously applying a carotid restraint.

The gun Jarvis was holding flew from his grasp as his hands scrabbled on Nick's arm around his neck. But it was too late to resist. Nick set the hold and his arm muscles squeezed the man's carotid arteries, cutting off the blood flow to the brain until Jarvis relaxed and then passed out.

Nick let him fall to the floor and quickly applied the handcuffs that had just been removed from him. Jarvis would come around in a few minutes.

While Nick was working with Jarvis, Carly grabbed the gun Jarvis dropped as Masters seemed to get her bearings. "He'll kill us all."

"Ms. Masters?" Carly looked at the woman.

"Correa. He's crazy. He's planned this for over a year," the woman said with a sob. Her face was a mess of smeared makeup and mascara, and she smelled as though she'd been without a shower for a while.

Carly saw angry red welts where the rough ropes binding the woman had been. "How long have you been here?"

"I don't know. I lost track of the days. We went out to sea and I thought he would kill me there." She leaned forward to rub her wrists and nearly fell on her face. "Please, some water."

Carly saw the sink a few feet away but no way to get the water to Masters. "Can you get to the sink and drink from the tap?"

"Help me, please."

Carly helped Masters to the sink and made certain she could support herself before turning to Nick, who was checking to be sure Jarvis was still breathing.

"We have to get out of here before he clears the harbor."

Nick nodded. "Ms. Masters, will you stay down here while we stop Correa?"

She shook her head. "Please don't leave me."

Carly looked at Nick. "No time to argue."

She handed him the gun she'd picked up while she kept the one she'd brought.

He took it and started up the stairs with Carly and Masters right behind him.

Nick moved quickly in the direction of the cockpit, wanting the element of surprise, Carly was sure. She worked to support a wobbly Masters, desperate to see what was happening.

She heard angry voices. Then the boat leaped forward, and the quick acceleration threw Carly and Masters onto the deck. Correa must have punched it. Carly struggled to get Masters and herself upright as her gun flew from her grasp and over the side into the water. There was no time to worry about the loss.

She looked toward the cockpit and saw Nick grappling with Correa. The boat swerved left, then right.

Carly grabbed the railing and put Masters's hand on it to help her up.

The boat slowed, throwing Carly forward, but she was able to stand and help get the reporter's legs under her. They both held on to the railing.

Under a brightening dawn sky, Carly saw that the boat was heading straight for the jetty.

Nick and Correa were still wrestling; she

didn't see the gun anywhere. She tried to leave Masters at the railing and go to the steering wheel.

But the boat's motor roared with acceleration and lurched forward abruptly, throwing her into Masters, who lost her grip.

Both of them went over the side, into the water, before Carly could do anything to stop it.

46

Carly came up for breath, calling for Nick, knowing he'd never hear her. She turned to see Masters flailing in the water a short distance away.

"I can't swim!"

Everything within her screamed to swim after the *Tango* and Nick, but Masters needed help. The woman was drowning.

Carly watched helplessly as the boat swung back and forth like a snake with its head cut off. A second later it slammed into the jetty with a sickening boom and a loud crack. The vessel had been traveling at such a high speed that it seemed to be cut in half on impact. Flames exploded as the fuel caught fire.

Carly felt punched in the face. If Nick had exploded in that ball of fire, her worst fear had just come true.

She wanted to cry out to God in anger. *Nick!*

Just then, arms slammed around her neck and tore her gaze from the flames. Masters had thrashed over to her in a panic to stay afloat.

Carly had no time to consider Nick's fate. Her lifesaving courses kicked in. She took a breath and went underwater, dragging Masters down with her until the woman let go. She swam a safe distance away before surfacing. Masters was flailing, choking on water, and cursing. But the only way to safely save a panicked drowning person was to wait until they were too weak to fight.

Masters needed to stop fighting and give up control in order to be saved.

Carly made herself look at the fireball that was Correa's yacht. She couldn't bear to think the worst. *God, why? We were so close . . .*

As clearly as if someone were speaking to her, Carly heard a line of Scripture: *"He answered their prayer because they trusted in him. . . ."*

I trust, she thought. *I trust.*

In a flash Carly saw herself thrashing like Masters — thrashing with fear for Nick, fighting to control that which was in God's control, and drowning. *I need to stop fighting and give up the need for control.*

Oh, God, I know you love Nick more than I

431

do. She choked on a sob that threatened to escape. *I trust him into your hands.*

A supernatural peace settled over Carly as she waited for the perfect time to approach the reporter. Over the struggling woman's curses and splashes, she heard the harbor patrol siren and knew someone was heading for the crash on the jetty. The sirens drowned out Masters's calls.

When the woman went under for what Carly thought would be the last time, she hurried forward and grabbed her. Making certain she was breathing and keeping her face out of the water, Carly positioned her arm across the woman's chest in order to swim with her to safety.

She looked over her shoulder at the now-dying fire on the jetty and kept praying.

With the sound of a boat approaching and a light probing the water, she recognized a Coast Guard vessel and slowed her progress, waving to be seen, needing help with Masters. In short order they were pulled safely into a boat.

From the deck, Carly kept her eyes on the smoldering jetty. A fireboat blocked her view, along with a couple of others she couldn't identify.

"I need to check you out." An officer handed her a towel as the vessel she was on turned toward the harbor patrol dock.

Carly started to protest, then stopped, suddenly feeling as though all the strength had left her body. She sat down heavily.

He handed her a bottle of water and continued with his assessment. Carly felt numb, but she knew she wasn't injured. Masters had been placed on a stretcher and covered with a blanket. The EMT seemed satisfied that the reporter would be okay, and he radioed that information to the paramedic team waiting on the dock.

Carly took a deep breath and repeated to herself that God was in control. Whatever had happened on the jetty with Nick, she clung to those words and felt a quiet peace replace the numbness. By the time the boat reached the dock, she was able to stand and felt steadier, strong even.

She again turned toward the jetty, where the smoke was now dissipating. Only the fireboat remained. The other two were chugging toward the dock.

When the radio crackled, she learned they had an emergency situation. The paramedics who'd boarded the Coast Guard vessel once it docked were tending to Masters. Carly heard the emergency tone on one of their radios. One of the incoming boats was broadcasting.

"Be advised — we have a neck injury. Need a backboard standing by."

Someone was seriously hurt.

Carly's heart began to pound and she made for the gangway, wanting to get to the dock to meet the incoming boat. She wrapped the towel tight around herself and hurried down the dock. Ignoring the rough wood on her bare feet, she jogged to the empty slip. Another paramedic team pushing a gurney with a backboard headed toward the same spot.

"What is it?" she asked.

"They pulled someone out of the water. Possible spinal injury."

Carly held her breath and prayed she'd see Nick as the boat docked. *Oh, Lord, please don't let the bad guys win this one.*

A gangway was extended, and the paramedics rushed aboard and secured their patient to the backboard. They carefully maneuvered the injured man down the gangway and placed him on a waiting gurney. Carly saw the man's face as his head passed by. She jumped back as if stung.

Mario Correa.

His face was bloodied and bruised, but he was breathing.

Where was Nick?

Carly took two steps back and ran into

someone. Turning, she saw Nick's blue eyes and the twinkle in them. The bruises and cuts she'd pay attention to later, but the light in those eyes made her shout with relief and throw herself into his arms.

47

"What happened?" Carly asked Nick when she regained her voice.

Nick was wrapped in a towel like she was. She could see now that he had taken a couple of good punches. One side of his face was puffy.

"I saw the jetty, knew he was going to ram it. I jumped first, and I guess he jumped a second later and hit the rocks."

"I heard possible spine injury."

Nick shrugged. "I don't know. I just kept his head out of the water. He was unconscious. I feel bad about Jarvis. I didn't mean for that to happen." He wrapped her in a tight embrace. "I hear you saved Masters."

"I just kept her head out of the water," she echoed, smiling at him, her heart about to burst with thankfulness. "Something occurred to me just now."

"Yeah? What?"

"Why I love my job, even though it can

aggravate me enough to think I want a change from time to time."

Nick arched an eyebrow. "Why?"

"Because we are the good guys. We catch bad guys like Correa and save the lives of innocent people like Ginny Masters. And even if there's never a thank-you or it's dangerous and scary, we'd do it again and again, because it's what we do."

Nick kissed the top of Carly's head. "Yep, that's true. And this call is over now; this nightmare is 10-7."

The sky brightened with morning sunshine. Seaside Point was still smoldering, but over at Sandy Park, it looked as though things were completely under control. Normally, working graveyard, Carly loved this time of the morning as the city woke up and people began their day. Right now, she felt enormous relief and profound thankfulness.

She leaned on Nick at the dock railing, watching the paramedics secure Masters to a gurney. Since Correa was more seriously hurt, he'd left first and now it was Masters's turn. Carly and Nick moved to the side so she could be taken to a waiting ambulance.

"She okay?" Carly asked.

"Looks fine," the EMT said. "Wet on the outside, dehydrated on the inside, and maybe a little hypothermic."

Masters was conscious, and when she saw Carly, she asked the medics to wait.

"You saved me." She tried to lean forward and rasped through the oxygen mask they'd put over her nose and mouth. "I hate you and you saved me."

"It's my job."

Masters's expression was unreadable as she lay back and was taken off the boat.

"Hey, my favorite crazy cop!" Alex came running up. "I was afraid I'd lost the both of you." He reached Carly first and gripped her in a hug. "Andrea would never have forgiven me if you'd blown up on Seaside Point." He pumped Nick's hand.

Jacobs, Harris, and Romo were right behind the reporter.

"I, for one, would like to know just what you were thinking, Trouble." Jacobs stood with his hands on his hips.

"Me too," Nick said, pulling her close to him as they both stood on the dock.

"I'd love to explain it all . . . over coffee."

The harbor guys opened their office and gave Nick and Carly some one-size-fits-all sweats to change into. Most important, there was a fresh pot of coffee brewing after they'd put on dry clothes.

Over the next hour, Carly learned that Jarvis had been waiting for Nick to leave the station when the explosion occurred in Sandy Park. Because of all the confusion, he wasn't missed until about the same time Carly was climbing onto Correa's boat.

"He rammed my car. I'm embarrassed to say that I was stunned, and Correa was there to drag me into the van," Nick explained. "It happened so fast and he was so prepared . . . He had the drop on me and then he told me that he had you and if I didn't comply, you'd die." Nick took a deep breath and a gulp of coffee. "Next thing I knew, he had the suicide vest on me and was snapping pictures."

"Were you ever at Seaside Point?" Carly asked.

"No. He dragged me straight to the boat. What made you look there?"

"The white sink. There's nothing white on the point except seagull poop."

"So that's why you went James Bond and swam in?" Jacobs asked.

"I had to act," she said, gripping Nick's hand. "I saw that picture and knew if I did what Correa demanded, we'd both die. I needed to surprise him."

"Which we did in the end." Nick brought her hand to his lips. Carly fervently wished they were alone and not in a room full of cops, reporters, and harbor authorities.

"Trouble —" Jacobs's phone jingled. He paused to read the text. "Ah, good news from Memorial Hospital. Correa is stable. He's not in very good shape, but alive."

"He'll survive for his day in court, then. I won't even mind trial preparation or testifying or anything." Carly closed her eyes and leaned into Nick, happy to be near him until they were released to go home, clean up, and get some rest.

On the way to the parking lot, Carly remembered that her car was at Seal Beach.

"You swam from there?" Nick asked.

"It seemed like the thing to do at the time."

Harris offered them a ride.

Agent Wiley was climbing out of his plain car when they reached the parking lot.

"Here's the man who should have information about the two explosions," Harris said.

Wiley nodded. "Yeah, while you two were out having a swim, I was working." His eyes twinkled and Carly realized this was the first time she'd ever heard Wiley crack a joke. "It's all preliminary, but it looks like the explosion in Sandy Park and the one at Seaside were both caused by the same type of device, and both employed C-4."

"I sincerely hope that's the end of the stuff," Carly said.

"Might be. We'll know more when the investigation is complete. I heard just now that Correa is alive. I hope he'll tell us why he set those devices."

Nick shook his head. "He was the angriest man I've ever seen. I can't imagine he'll cooperate on anything."

Wiley shrugged and turned to Carly. "You are always in the mix, in a good way," he said. "Have you made your decision about the task force?"

Carly folded her arms, looked at Wiley, and realized that she could tell him yes, she had made a decision. She wasn't certain when she'd decided, but she knew her answer.

"I'm going to stay here and not go running off with a multiagency task force."

Wiley looked surprised. "Is that your final answer?"

"Yeah, it is. I love Las Playas and the people in it. Serving this city is why I became a cop. This is where I want to stay."

"Fair enough." He held out his hand and she shook it. "If you ever think you need more of a challenge, you know where to find me." He gave her a mock salute as she and

Nick climbed into Harris's car for the ride to Seal Beach.

48

Carly sat between Nick and Alex in a packed courtroom. The trial of Galen Burke had taken two weeks, but the jury had only been out for a mere two hours of deliberation before they announced they had a verdict. The packed courtroom quieted as the jury filed back in. Carly tightened her grip on Nick's hand even as the DA turned and flashed a confident smile.

After legalese that seemed to last a lifetime, they got to the meat, and Carly breathed a thankful prayer as "guilty" followed each and every charge read. She leaned back and closed her eyes, body relaxing as if she'd just had a wonderful massage.

Nick leaned close, and she felt his warm breath on her ear. "You did it, babe," he whispered.

As soon as the judge accepted the verdict and set a date for sentencing, he banged the gavel, and the courtroom erupted in the noise of dozens of voices talking at once. Carly opened her eyes and accepted congratulations and thumbs-up from a lot of people. The DA stepped back, sat in the chair in front of her, and turned her way with a smile.

"We did it. And I bet now Correa will cop a plea."

Carly tilted her head, ambivalent about that. She didn't want him to get any kind of break, but she wasn't interested in going through another stressful trial either. Correa was paralyzed from the waist down as a result of running his boat into the jetty. That in itself was a type of justice. Jarvis had died; his body was recovered a couple days after the crash.

Correa wasn't talking but had said a lot to Ginny Masters when he took her captive. She'd been a wealth of information for the prosecutors. Even though Burke was in custody, Correa had told Masters that he'd been working closely with him. The money in the foundation accounts had been embezzled from the harbor business Correa oversaw. Correa was ready to use every last dollar to get revenge and free his friend Burke.

The pair's desire for revenge set everything

into motion. Correa admitted to arranging for the theft of the guns and explosives. He'd used contacts from high school — people both he and Barton knew — and since that had gone so well, when Barton was released, he brought him into the plan. He claimed shooting the gang members to start a gang war and keep the police busy was Barton's idea, but Masters didn't believe him.

Like Potter had said, Correa hadn't wanted to kill Carly right away. He and Burke wanted to discredit her first and make her testimony worthless. But Dean Barton made too many mistakes. He never did exactly what Correa asked; he always improvised. According to Masters, Correa thought Dean had ruined all his plans, and he told her himself that he was the one who killed Dean.

Carly knew that the FBI and the DA were working hard to find the evidence to charge Correa with everything they could. Besides the two dead gang members, two protestors had been killed in the explosion and fire in Sandy Park and dozens injured. He'd set that bomb in the hopes of attracting Nick. He had Potter's scanner and was listening carefully to police traffic, so he knew exactly where Nick was that night. And of course there was the murder of Barton, the death of Jarvis, and last but never least in Carly's mind, Jeff's murder. The best call Carly had made in a long time was the call to Elaine to tell her that Jeff's murderer was in custody.

All in all, Carly would be satisfied to see him get life in prison and never see the light of a free day again.

"Just make it the best deal in the interest of all his victims," Carly said.

"Will do," DA Martin said.

The courtroom had mostly cleared out. Carly and Nick stood.

"Can I buy you guys a victory lunch?" Alex asked.

"Not today. We have to get to the hospital."

Alex slapped his forehead. "That's right. I forgot. Hector gets out today."

"Yeah, there's going to be a little party for him before he leaves. Victor and his mother asked us to come."

"I hear he's a miracle."

Carly nodded. "He's walking and talking, and the hope is that his recovery will eventually be 100 percent. He doesn't remember anything about the night he was shot and he's still got a long road ahead of him, but he's doing good right now."

"You'll be at the dedication this afternoon?"

Carly groaned.

Nick put his hands on her shoulders. "Yes, she'll be there."

The nurses and doctors at the hospital had been so impressed with Hector, they'd gone all out for his send-off party. A section of the cafeteria was decorated with good-luck signs, and there was a large chocolate cake with his name spelled out in candles. He would still need physical therapy — his right side was weak and he had difficulty concentrating — but he was about 80 percent and able to function, and he wanted to go home.

Londy, Mary Ellen, and Victor were putting the finishing touches on balloon decorations when Carly and Nick stepped in. Along with the hospital personnel and all of Hector's brothers and sisters, Pastor Rawlings was there and a couple of Ninjas Carly had seen in church with Londy once or twice. Erika and Ned were there as well. Half Baked had donated the cake and the coffee. Ned understood traumatic brain injury and had gotten close to Hector.

Carly did a double take when she saw her supervisor, Sergeant Barrett, in attendance with his wife. Alicia Barrett was a physical therapist who'd been working with Hector. Carly had met her when Barrett brought her to church one Sunday. The couple was still separated but they were talking to each other — and seeing Pastor Rawlings.

While Carly and Nick were pouring coffee, Hector was wheeled in to applause. It was hard to decide who had the bigger smile, Hector or Victor. Londy had told her how the boy was so excited to have his brother home that he'd cleaned up the room they shared and sold his iPod to buy Hector a welcome-home present.

Hector was able to walk with a cane, so he got out of the wheelchair to take a seat at the table. The party went on, with hospital staff presenting various gifts to him that would assist in his rehabilitation. The last present he opened was the one from his brother Victor.

Carly murmured with surprise when she saw it was a Bible — a nice one with a leather cover engraved with Hector's nickname, Crusher.

"That's awesome," she said to Londy.

"It is. And you know what else is? Hector remembers one thing from the night he was shot."

"He remembers who shot him?"

"No, he remembers D. He was praying

and Hector asked D. to pray for him, too. D. said he would." Londy choked up and took a minute to compose himself. "Anyway, he knows D. prayed for him and that's why he's alive. That made a huge impression on Victor."

"Has Victor joined your youth group?"

"Not mine, but the one at his mother's church. He's learning. Now that Mr. Correa is in jail and the other guys are dead, and Crush is good, he figures prayer is cool. He wants his brother to help him learn to read the Bible, figures there's more good stuff in there."

"He's right about that," Nick said, gripping Carly's hand. "It's about time for us to go change for the dedication."

Carly looked into his sparkling blue eyes, thinking she would try to talk him out of making her go. Being honored and given an award for doing her job would just make her feel uncomfortable. But in truth, she couldn't say no to him. She'd follow him anywhere.

DISCUSSION QUESTIONS

1. At the beginning of *Avenged*, Carly feels unsatisfied in her role as a patrol officer but then is unexpectedly offered a job on a federal task force. Why does this offer appeal to her? What are the potential downsides? Were you surprised to see what she decided? What would you have done?

2. After a confrontation at a coffee shop, Carly faces some harsh, very public accusations from the media. Though her friends support her, she feels frustrated by the negative attention. Have you ever been in a similar position or had a friend in one? What would you do in her place?

3. As a former gang member, Londy is in a unique position to witness and minister to his peers. What did you think of his character transformation from *Accused*, the first book of the Pacific Coast Justice

series? What mission fields do you have in your life?

4. Coffee shop owners Ned and Erika are surprised to learn Ned's half brother has found them. But despite the threat Dean poses to his family, the couple is quick to forgive, though not endorse, his actions. What is admirable about this attitude? Is it appropriate? Why or why not?

5. Several characters in this story are driven to avenge someone in their lives, including Carly, who hopes to see justice for a fellow officer's death. What does Romans 12:19 say about revenge? What does that mean when it comes to modern justice systems?

6. In chapter 19, Sergeant Barrett asks Carly some personal questions about her marriage and forgiveness. What did you think of her answers? How would you respond in a similar situation? Would your answer change depending on whether you were talking to your boss or to your friend?

7. In chapter 30, Nick gets angry with Carly for not sharing her problems with him. Is he justified in his frustration? Why or why

not? What does a biblical marriage look like?

8. In *Accused,* Carly and Nick had been separated and were planning to get a divorce. How have they grown as individuals and as a couple throughout the series? Are you pleased to see where their relationship is now? How would you write their story going forward?

9. At a critical point in *Avenged,* Carly realizes she's been fighting God for control in her life. What does she do to "let go and let God"? How might something similar play out in your life?

10. What evidence did you see that Carly's faith had grown in this book and from the beginning of the series? What lessons can you take away from her spiritual journey?

AN EXICTING PREVIEW OF JANICE CANTORE'S NEXT BOOK, *CRITICAL PURSUIT*

SEVENTY-FOUR PERCENT of abducted children who are murdered are dead within three hours of the abduction.

The grim statistic rumbled around in K-9 Officer Brinna Caruso's brain like a hand grenade without the pin. There was no evidence that six-year-old Josh Daniels had been abducted, yet the statistic taunted her.

Brinna and her K-9, Hero, a four-year-old Labrador retriever, were part of a team of officers fanned out across El Dorado Park, the largest city park in Long Beach, California, searching for Josh. He'd disappeared from an afternoon family picnic two and a half hours ago.

The huge park successfully created the illusion of wilderness, dense in some places, open in others. There were a thousand places to hide — or be hidden. Brinna normally loved the park, the smell of pine trees and nature, the illusion of pristine innocence and safety. Today all she could think about was how quickly innocence could be lost or, worse, stolen.

Hero trotted ahead on a well-beaten path, panting in the summer heat. Brinna and Officer Maggie Sloan followed a few feet behind. Maggie had left her partner back at the picnic site with the boy's family.

"You are so intense it's scary," Maggie said.

"What?" Brinna glanced from Hero to Maggie, who regarded her with a bemused expression. She wasn't just another officer; she was Brinna's confidante and best friend on the force.

"I'm just keeping an eye on my dog," Brinna explained, wiping her forehead with the back of her hand. "He's definitely following a scent."

"That's good news, isn't it?" Maggie asked. "It means we should find the boy. Why the frown?"

Brinna shrugged. "I want to find a boy and not a body."

"Harrumph." Maggie waved a hand dismissively. "There's no indication Josh was snatched. The best guess is he got lost playing hide-and-seek. El Dorado is to parks what Disneyland is to carnivals. He could be anywhere. You always imagine the worst where kids are concerned."

Brinna gritted her teeth. "Because you know as well as I do, if a kid is abducted, the chances are overwhelming that they will be a victim of murder."

Jaw set, Brinna returned her full attention to the dog. She'd had this conversation before, with Maggie and others, almost every time a child went missing. The guys on her team liked to say that since Brinna didn't believe there was a God watching out for kids, she'd given herself the job.

"The operative word is *if*. You're such a glass-is-half-empty person." Maggie slapped Brinna's shoulder with the back of her hand. "What about the ones found alive? Elizabeth Smart, Shawn Hornbeck, Brinna Caruso?"

"For every three of us rescued, there're nine who die," Brinna shot back. "You know my goal is 100 percent saved."

Maggie snorted in exasperation. "All the time you spend riding rail on registered sex offenders and monitoring any missing kid case flagged suspicious." She shook her head and wagged an index finger. "You can't save them all."

Brinna said nothing, hating that truth. Hero came to a stop, and like dominoes, so did Brinna and then Maggie.

"Maybe I can't save them all," Brinna conceded. "But it certainly won't be for a lack of trying."

Maggie followed Brinna's gaze to Hero, then turned back to her friend and smiled. "You sure earn your nickname, Kid Crusader."

Brinna watched the dog. His nose up, testing the air, Hero trotted off in a more determined fashion than before. When he caught a scent, the hackles on the back of his neck rose ever so slightly. Brinna felt her own neck tingle as if there were a sympathetic connection between her and the dog.

"He's got something stronger." She stepped up her pace after Hero, Maggie on her heels.

They jogged to the left, into an area thick with tall pines and full oaks. After about a hundred feet, Hero barked and sat, turning toward Brinna. It was his practiced alert signal. Brinna's heart caught in her throat. If her dog had just found Josh, the boy wasn't moving; in fact, he wasn't even standing.

She followed the dog's gaze to a pile of leaves and held her breath.

When she heard muffled sniffling coming from the leaves, Brinna exhaled, rolling her eyes in relief. Then she saw the toe of a small tennis shoe sticking out. The boy was hiding. Turning to Maggie, she pointed at the shoe. Maggie smiled.

Brinna spoke to the quivering mass. "Josh, Josh Daniels. It's the police. Is that you?"

A half sob and an intake of breath emanated from the pile. The leaves moved, and a dirty-faced blond boy peered out at her.

"The po-police?" He cast an eye toward Hero. "That's not a coyote coming to eat me?"

Kneeling, Brinna bit back a chuckle. The boy's fear was plausible. He'd wandered into a particularly dense section of the park. The only things absent were dangerous animals. She understood a lost boy's imagination getting the best of him.

"Nope, it's my dog, Hero. Hero is a police dog. He doesn't eat little boys. He helped me find you."

Josh sat up and the leaves fell away, revealing a boy smudged with sweat, soil, and grime. He sniffed. "I was playing and I got lost. I called and called, but my mom didn't come. Then I heard noises. I was afraid of wild animals, so I hid."

"Well, your mom and dad sent us to find you," Maggie said. "Are you ready to go home?"

Josh nodded vigorously and stood, brushing off dirt and leaves as he did so. "Can I pet your dog?" he asked Brinna, the tears already drying.

"Sure," Brinna said as she stood, ignoring the triumphant smirk Maggie shot her. Brinna pulled out her handheld radio and notified the command post that the situation was code 4, all over and resolved. "We're on our way out."

Brinna smiled as she took the boy's hand. The statistic tumbling around in her mind disappeared in a poof, like a dud.

"Officer Caruso! Officer Caruso!"

Brinna groaned. Tracy Michaels, the local police beat reporter, was hailing her. Brinna had almost made it to her car avoiding all contact with the press. She wished Maggie were still with her. Maggie always knew how to talk to the press. But Maggie was with her own partner, seeing to the happy family reunion.

"Officer Caruso! I have the okay for an interview."

Brinna stopped at her K-9 unit, a black-and-white Ford Explorer, and turned, counting to ten so she wouldn't say anything she'd regret. Reporters only wanted bad news. They thrived on tragedy. She faced Michaels, a young, eager woman who approached with a pad and pen in her right hand.

"Tracy, we found the kid in a pile of leaves, alive and unmolested — not much excitement in that story."

The reporter shook her head. "I don't want to talk about Josh Daniels. I want to talk about your upcoming anniversary."

"My anniversary?" Brinna frowned.

"Don't tell me you don't mark the day in some special fashion," Tracy said, hands on her hips. "Next week, it will be twenty years to the day since you were rescued after being abducted."

At 4 a.m., Jack O'Reilly awoke from the dream as he normally did, screaming his wife's name and clutching his pillow as if he could somehow use it to drag her back from the dead.

The cries died in his throat as he opened his eyes to the dark living room, and the terror of the dream faded. Since Vicki's death, the couch had become his bed. The bedroom he left untouched, preserving it as it was on the last day his wife left it.

He sat up, breathing deep, heart pounding. For the briefest of moments he imagined he caught a whiff of his wife's scent, and he inhaled deeply, hoping to prolong the illusion, but it evaporated.

The dream was always the same. He and Vicki were walking and smiling. He held one hand while she rested her other on her expanding belly as if hanging on to the life growing there. The first feelings associated with the dream were those of profound happiness. The bleak reality of the last year disappeared in the pleasant subconscious illusion.

But it didn't last.

At some point Jack was aware of an approaching car. He wanted to tell Vicki to watch out, to move, but his voice was suffocated by dream-state paralysis. The car roared by and took Vicki with it. Her hand was wrenched from his as his screams wrenched him from sleep. He awakened to the empty life he'd lived for almost a year.

Tossing the pillow aside, Jack headed for the shower. To sleep again so soon after the dream would be like trying to put toothpaste back in the tube.

Standing in the shower with hot water pounding into his chest, Jack stared at his hands. He clenched and unclenched a fist, touched the cool tiles, and wondered how it was that he was still alive.

I don't feel alive, he thought. *Maybe I'm dead, and I just don't know it. If it weren't for the pain, I'd feel nothing.*

Toweling off, Jack grabbed a robe and padded barefoot into the kitchen to start coffee. He glanced at the calendar stuck to the refrigerator and saw what was keeping him alive. The date circled in red was a little more than two weeks away. It was the date of the sentencing.

Vicki had been driving to an afternoon doctor's appointment in her economical Honda. She'd called Jack before she left the house, bubbling with excitement about how active the child inside her was. "He'll be big and strong like his daddy," she'd gushed, though they didn't know what sex the baby was yet. Jack knew now. A little girl had died with his wife.

Fresh from a wet lunch, Gil Martin had started up his brand-new Hummer. Ignoring at least seven vehicles who'd honked a warning at him, Gil got on the 710 freeway going north in the southbound lanes. Investigators estimated his speed was close to sixty when he crested a small rise and hit Vicki head-on. She never had a chance.

Martin had already been found guilty of gross vehicular manslaughter. All that was left was the sentencing. Jack hated the man as much as anyone could hate.

The hate, he thought. *That's what's keep-*

ing me going, keeping me alive. I just need to be sure he gets what he deserves. If the court doesn't give it to him, I will.

Jack sipped coffee in the kitchen, staring at nothing, until it was time to get dressed and go to work. He put on his suit and tie, clipped his badge and duty weapon to his belt, and climbed into his car.

Hanging from the rearview mirror was the cross he'd given to Vicki on their second wedding anniversary. It had hung around her neck until the coroner removed it and placed it in an envelope for Jack. While Jack no longer believed in what the cross symbolized, he cherished the necklace because it had been near Vicki's heart when it had beat its last.

Half-listening to the radio, Jack would reach up from time to time and rub the cross between his thumb and forefinger as he drove. There'd been an officer-involved shooting last night. If he'd felt alive, he thought, the news would have given him a jolt. Homicide investigators handled all officer-involved shootings. But Jack felt no excitement, no drive to learn the details.

He'd asked six months ago to be taken off the normal homicide rotation. Now he filed paper and reviewed cold cases all day. But not the pictures. Jack couldn't stand the bodies anymore. In every female victim Jack saw Vicki's mangled body and in every dead child the little girl they'd never had a chance to name.

I'm a dead man working homicide, he thought. *But only for two and a half more weeks. I just need to hang on for two and a half more weeks.*

ABOUT THE AUTHOR

A former Long Beach, California, police officer of twenty-two years, **Janice Cantore** worked a variety of assignments, including patrol, administration, juvenile investigations, and training. She's always enjoyed writing and published two short articles on faith at work for *Cop and Christ* and *Today's Christian Woman* before tackling novels. A few years ago, she retired to a house in the mountains of Southern California, where she lives with three Labrador retrievers, Jake, Maggie, and Abbie.

Janice writes suspense novels designed to keep readers engrossed and leave them inspired. *Avenged,* the sequel to *Accused* and *Abducted,* is the third book in the Pacific Coast Justice series, featuring Carly Edwards.

Visit Janice's website at www.janicecantore .com and connect with her on Facebook at facebook.com/JaniceCantore.